Praise for *A Strand of Doubt*

Fast-paced action and a love triangle that will keep you guessing until the the very end. Top that off with a few good plot twists and a beautiful Oregon setting and you've got several hours of reading pleasure. I enjoyed the break from reality this book offered. Thank you, Donna! —Kelly Nelson

Good LDS-oriented fiction. The descriptions and character building was very good. Enjoyed the read! —jacek

I really did like this book and the fact that it kept you guessing and kept your interest. I sure would like to see a story on Trevor, though, and a follow-up to Jared. Amazing writer! I thoroughly enjoyed her book. Five stars for sure. —Karryon

Reading this was a wonderful way to spend a weekend! I am looking forward to [Donna's] next novel. —j.mac

Fun, relaxing read—romantic, funny, exciting. Well-built characters and an intriguing story line with lots of twists to keep you reading. A great read!! —Julia Wagner

Clean content, numerous plot twists. The Christian perspective was LDS and was quite refreshing. This was author Donna Gustainis Fuller's first novel. I really liked it! —S. J. Christensen

I loved the romance part of the book. Great storyline. The plot was exciting with some unexpected twists. Excellent good clean fun book. I would highly recommend it. —Jared M. Jones, Sr.

Really enjoyed it. Lots of unexpected twists and turns and a very satisfying ending. —JLW

Amazing writer! I thoroughly enjoyed [Donna's] book. Five stars for sure. —Amazon Customer

Great book. Enjoyed it all the way though. —Kelly Chisholm

A Strand of Doubt *weaves intrigue, romance, and soul searching into a cohesive story that keeps the reader guessing. The author revealed just the right amount of information at just the right time to lead the reader along through a plot full of twists and turns. . . . I wasn't sure which fella I wanted to win out in the love triangle until the very end when the main character and I picked the right one together. Nicely done, especially for a debut novel.* —T. Deighton

Great read! I will pass this on to my friends and family to read as well. You will enjoy each page. —Dallin R.

I couldn't put it down! A simultaneously fun, suspenseful, and heartwarming novel. I hope [Donna] writes another one! —BP

Reading this book was a great way to spend my day. It was a fun story with good character development and just the right amount of suspense for me. . . . I heard this was the author's first book and didn't expect to be so impressed. I liked the characters so much. Can't wait to see what Ms. Fuller comes up with next. —Cynthia Woods

I read the whole book in one sitting. A delightful story well told. —DW

I really enjoyed A Strand of Doubt *by Donna Gustainis Fuller. She made me interested on the first page and I was interested the whole way through and didn't want to put in down. Anxious to read her new one when it comes out.* —Heritha Davis

Code Name SCORPION

DONNA GUSTAINIS FULLER

WALNUT SPRINGS PRESS

To my mom, Evelyn Zemaitis, who always encouraged
me to seek out my dreams; and to my grandchildren,
Jenika, Kierra, Charly, Nash, and Ophelia.
May you always follow your dreams.

Text copyright © 2017 by Donna Gustainis Fuller
Cover design copyright © 2017 by Walnut Springs Press
Interior design copyright © 2017 by Walnut Springs Press

ISBN-13: 978-1-59992-166-2

Printed in the United States of America.

Acknowledgments

Just as it takes a village to raise a child, it takes a village to raise a book. I would like to thank my villagers.

For Linda and Walnut Springs Press: thanks for believing in me.

For my partners in crime—I mean, in writing: Julia for being there with me every step of the way, Jenn and Mandy for joining me in my writing habit, Christine for encouraging me, and for my husband Darrel, who listened to my rants, gave critiques, and made his own dinner when I was on a writing roll.

For all the women in OHPA Writers—Julia, Beth, Mandy, Teresa and Amanda—thank you.

None of this would have been possible without my loud cheering section: my husband Darrel and our children—Jenn and Kyle, Nate and Ashley, Nick and Kristy, Mandy and James and Jace. Finally, my brother and sister, Albert and Elaine.

One

Trevor Willis slunk through the streets of Portland. Clutching a plain brown bag, he entered a dark alley and plodded through putrid water and ankle-deep trash. Every few seconds, he glanced over his shoulder. He pushed the button on his Walmart watch, and a glow emanated from the dial to reveal the time: 11:57. An uncharacteristic week's worth of stubble, uncombed hair, and a coat from the Salvation Army hid his identity.

Clothed in an Armani suit, Alejandro Morales stepped out from the shadows and blocked Trevor's path. Trevor glanced back over his shoulder. Two heavily armed bodyguards closed off any chance of retreat.

He swallowed hard and faced Morales again. "M–Mr. Morales? I c–can't believe I get to meet you." Trevor held out a grimy hand sheathed in a fingerless glove. "The stuff you make is p–pure."

Morales looked at Trevor like he was a cockroach to be smashed. "You have the money?"

"I got it." Trevor raised the bag.

"Hand it over, now."

Trevor moved the bag out of reach. "W–where's the stuff?"

Morales's eyes narrowed. After a tense moment, he made a nearly imperceptible gesture with his head, signaling one of his thugs. Trevor flinched as something sailed above him and into the grasp of Morales.

"Here is the product." Morales held out a plain package. "Shall we conclude our transaction?"

"Yes, sir." With a shaky hand, Trevor yielded the paper bag and accepted the parcel in return. He turned to leave and met two guns leveled at his chest. "What's going on? Mr. Morales, t–tell them to back off, please. The money's all there."

"I've decided to use my own people for distribution," Morales declared.

Trevor backed away from the armed men and glanced at Morales, who repeated the gesture with his head. The thugs fired their weapons. Both bullets hit Trevor in the chest, sending him reeling into the dumpster at the same moment two sniper shots reverberated through the alley. Cursing, Morales's bodyguards dropped their weapons.

Gun-wielding men stormed the alley from both directions. A voice split the night air. "FBI! Don't move!"

The two thugs rolled like tanks through the line of law enforcement personnel, blocking the agents from reaching Morales, who ran toward his car. Another shot split the air. The fleeing man cried out in pain, grabbed his leg, and fell to his knees. One of his bodyguards attempted to reach him, but a bullet caught the guard in the arm. Within minutes, the three criminals were taken into custody and read their rights. EMTs provided first aid to the injured men before loading them into an ambulance.

Special Agent in Charge Don Townsend strolled over to his downed comrade and helped him to his feet. Trevor glanced into the open rear door of the ambulance. Daggers of hatred flew from Morales's gaze.

"You will regret this," he shouted. "My father will reach across the Rio Grande and choke the life from you."

Trevor shook off the words and addressed Don. "You sure took your time moving in." Without the stutter, irritation flowed through his words. "What if they had aimed for my head?"

"Our snipers were ready to shoot at any moment. Besides, we bribed someone to replace the bullets with rubber slugs, and they were aimed at your vest, not your head. You weren't in any real danger."

Trevor removed the ragged coat, about to toss it into the trash, but Don grabbed it. "Those holes in the jacket are evidence." He called to an agent who was making notes of the scene. "Zack, come take his coat."

"Sorry. I guess my close brush with death must have shaken protocol right out of my brain," Trevor muttered. He pulled off his shirt, revealing the Kevlar vest with two dents directly over his heart. "This was too close for comfort, Don." Trevor removed the vest and gingerly touched the bruises appearing in corresponding spots on his chest. "No more 'just one more time' jobs for me. I'm done."

"Yeah, yeah. You always say that."

Trevor moved closer and poked a finger into Don's chest. "The only reason I've helped you this long is to protect your rear. I can't stand the thought of my sister ending up a widow. Tomorrow is a start of a new life for me. I'm through."

Don rolled his eyes and shook his head.

"Hey, you will be there, won't you?" Trevor asked.

"Of course, brother. I wouldn't miss it." Don pounded him on the back. "Do you want Traci and the kids to pick you up?"

"No, Jared's sister will bring me. I think it's his way of making sure nothing else happens to postpone the event."

"Dani's picking you up?" Don raised his eyebrow.

"What?"

"Are you getting sweet on her?"

Trevor's cheeks burned. "Who says 'getting sweet' these days?"

"Your sister's husband does. Stop changing the subject. Are you?"

"Maybe. But she just thinks of me as her brother's friend."

"Whatever. We'll be there," Don said before turning to direct one of the agents collecting evidence.

§

Enrique Rios stood in front of the study's ornate double doors. He reached for the knob then dropped his hand. A sigh escaped before he squared his shoulders and knocked firmly.

A magnified voice issued a command through a small speaker next to Enrique's head. "Come in."

The door opened. Don Francisco Morales, whose charisma and genteel manners belied his reputation as one of the most ruthless men in Mexico, sat at a heavy mahogany desk from which he controlled most of the heroin traffic into the United States. He pushed aside the papers in front of him, then stood and embraced his trusted assistant.

"Hola, mi amigo. Sit down. What is on your mind?"

Enrique sat for only a few seconds, then arose and walked around the chair, clasping the back for support. "I have very bad news," he said, remembering the last man to bring bad news to Don Francisco. Enrique had been tasked with informing the man's family of his untimely end.

"Señor Stoddard has spoken to me about Alejandro." Enrique swallowed, his mouth as dry as the Sonoran Desert.

The only reaction came in the form of a twitch below Don Francisco's left eye. "Continue, Enrique. Why would our esteemed American lawyer contact you, my assistant, regarding my son?"

Enrique met the gaze of the man behind the desk. "Last night, Alejandro was arrested."

Don Francisco frowned. "How did the police get close enough to him? Where were his bodyguards?" The older man paused, then waved his hand in dismissal. "Have Señor Stoddard post bail and fly Alejandro home immediately."

Enrique cleared his throat. "One of the charges leveled against your son is the attempted murder of an FBI agent. The judge ordered Alejandro held without bail. It seems he is considered at risk for fleeing the country."

Don Francisco's face darkened. He pushed himself up from his leather chair and crossed the luxurious burgundy carpet to stop in front of a bookcase. One silver frame encased a picture of his five daughters, while an eight-by-ten of Don Francisco and his only son, Alejandro, occupied a place of honor. No one could miss the pride and adoration on Don Francisco's face in the image where he stood with his arm around his firstborn. The drug lord picked up that picture and stared at it. "Tell me more," he said, then reverently placed the photo back in its spot.

"Alejandro was deceived by an agent masquerading as a dealer in Oregon," Enrique replied. "Your son was set up in a sting operation."

Don Francisco turned sharply and slammed his fist against the dark paneling. "This is an outrage! Who is the agent?"

Enrique flinched. "I do not know. He is not regular FBI. Our informant has no intelligence about him."

A calm that spoke louder than rage enveloped Don Francisco. He seized a pen from his desk and grasped the writing instrument so hard his knuckles turned white. The quiet intensity of his voice could not hide his anger. "I want his name. He will learn what happens when he threatens my family."

With a slight movement, Don Francisco snapped the pen in half. Red ink splattered like blood on his hands and clothes.

Two

The padded turquoise chairs in the Relief Society room faced the accordion curtain concealing the baptismal font. Dressed in white clothing, Jared Carpenter paced the floor in his bare feet, looking toward the door every few seconds. His wife Jana played a walnut-stained piano in the corner of the room. The melody of "I Am a Child of God" mingled with the sound of running water. Jared cast an encouraging glance Jana's way, then opened the curtain to check the water level. Holding the curtain handle as an anchor, he reached across the font to turn off the faucet. He stood to his full height of five foot eight just as Zack Lasky entered the room in a whoosh.

"Well, Jared, do you think he'll make it this time?"

Jared extended his hand in greeting. "We filled the font, didn't we?" He recited the same mantra he'd been repeating all morning. "I have complete confidence that nothing will get in the way of Trevor getting baptized today." He looked heavenward and whispered, "I hope." He shook his head. "Anyway, I asked my sister Dani to pick him up, and she hasn't called in a panic—yet."

Zack flipped his hair out of his eyes. "What is this? The third time."

"No, if you include the first time when we were interrupted by Jana getting kidnapped, this is the fourth."

"You sure? Okay, let's figure this one out." Zack began counting on his fingers. "Number one, kidnapping. Two, car thieves in Florida."

Jared continued for him. "Three, the freak snowstorm in Houston. And finally, my personal favorite, all planes in Phoenix being grounded because of excessive heat."

"Townsend sure keeps Trevor busy, especially since he's no longer with the Bureau." Zack lifted a bag and motioned toward the door. "Come help me with these."

"Sure."

In the kitchen, they removed boxes of Dunkin' Donuts from the sacks and placed them on the counter.

Zack opened a container and popped a couple of donut holes into his mouth, then asked, "Why did the donut cross the street?" He paused. "Give up? It fell off the truck." Crumbs sprayed into the air as he laughed at his own joke.

Jared rolled his eyes. "Not funny." He walked out of the room, wiping at donut crumbs on his shoulder.

"Hey, if he's a no-show again, you can't blame the FBI," Zack called after Jared. "They rounded up the drug dealers last night, not too far from here. No grounded planes or freak snowstorms to stop him this time."

The outer door slammed, bringing Jared around. Trevor ran past, dressed in a pair of baggy, stained pants with a piece of clothesline cinched around his waist to keep them from falling in a puddle at his feet. His plain white undershirt obviously belonged to a larger man who needed a stronger antiperspirant.

"Made it!" Trevor turned back to shake Jared's hand, then checked the time on his black plastic watch. "And with a minute and a half to spare. I bet you were starting to worry."

"Not at all," Jared fibbed. "It was nice of you to dress for the occasion."

Trevor chuckled and continued toward the Relief Society room. The missionaries greeted him in the hallway.

Elder Watson started to hand him a white jumpsuit, but on further examination of Trevor's state of cleanliness, he pulled it back. "Um, maybe I should carry it for you. We kind of like it to be white when you enter the font."

Trevor followed the missionary toward the changing area.

Seconds later, Jared's sister burst through the door from the parking lot. "I'm sorry we're so late," she told him. "Trevor called just before I left, and I picked him up at the Bureau office downtown."

Jared took her arm. "He still has to change. Slow down and walk with me. Tell me what's happening in your life."

"Did I tell you he offered me a job when I graduate next month?"

Jared frowned a little. "No, you didn't. What job?"

"Do you remember the summer camp he talked about?"

"Sure. The one for kids who've lost a parent?"

Dani nodded. "He wants me to be the director."

"Wow. Tell me more about it after the baptism," Jared said just as they entered the Relief Society room.

The missionaries waited on the front row with two empty seats next to them. Jared chose a chair next to the piano, while Dani claimed one by the elders.

§

Several minutes ticked by before Trevor emerged from the dressing room, with wet hair and minus his beard. He smiled at Dani and took his seat next to her.

Still facing forward, she inclined her head toward him. "You clean up remarkably well, Mr. Willis. That must have been a very quick shower."

"It was. And after today, it's *Brother* Willis to you." He glanced around the room. "I'm a bit nervous."

"Don't worry. Jared won't keep you under too long. There are too many people around." Dani patted his hand.

The ward mission leader stood at the podium, ready to begin the service. Following the opening song and prayer, Zack stood up to talk about baptism. He looked around at the people in the room, fanning themselves with their programs.

"Obviously the AC is on the fritz. That reminds me of a story about President Gordon B. Hinckley. On a hot afternoon, the air conditioning went out in the Tabernacle during general conference. President Hinckley stood up to address the congregation and said, 'It's warm. We're sorry. But it's not as warm as it's going to get if you don't repent!'" Zack waited a moment while everyone laughed. "That brings me to the subject of my talk. One of the first principles of the gospel is repentance . . ."

When Zack finished speaking, Jared and Trevor entered the baptismal font. Trevor took a deep breath and said, "I'm ready."

Jared spoke the words of the ordinance and then immersed Trevor in the warm water. When he broke the surface on his way up, a grin split Trevor's face. The two men embraced with a customary slap on the back. "Thanks, Jared. I told you we'd be friends someday."

"I hate to say it, but you were right. Congratulations."

Trevor glanced at Jana and then at Jared again. "Yep. I got the gospel, and you got the girl. Almost an even trade."

Before he exited the font, Trevor's eyes found his sister Traci among the people in attendance. His heart lurched in his chest. *I'm almost afraid to blink for fear it will all disappear.*

Three

Following his baptism, the group met at Trevor's home on the Willamette River. After lunch, Trevor and Dani faced Jana and Jared in an intense game of volleyball. Zack was an unofficial referee, his animated voice announcing each serve, point, and infraction of the rules. Jana served the bright-pink ball over the net, while Trevor and Jared slammed it back and forth with more aggression than necessary for a recreational game. Team Trevor narrowly won the set.

As everyone retreated to the lawn chairs, Jared said, "We let you win that one, but next time, prepare to be whipped."

Trevor chuckled. "Jana, I do believe your husband's nose just grew a few inches."

She squeezed Jared's hand. "Definitely. He'd never let anyone win."

"I'll say," Dani interrupted. "He never let me win at anything when we were kids."

Zack jumped up from his chair when his wife Caitlyn walked down from the house with a fresh pitcher of lemonade and plastic cups on a tray. "Let me take that," he lifted the tray from her hands and set it down on the table. He bent over and gently rubbed her swollen belly. "How's Zack junior today?"

Caitlyn smiled. "Active, as usual."

He set the lemonade on the table. Once Caitlyn had poured several cups, Dani grabbed three, saying, "I'll bring these down to Traci and Don."

She walked over to the riverbank and sat on the grass next to Trevor's sister Traci. They watched the kids race stick boats in the fast current of spring runoff. Four-year-old Scott threw sticks, rocks, and leaves into the water. Don reached out to grab him as he tottered close to the edge of the bank. Eight-year-old Emy brought over a stick for Traci's inspection. "Mommy, look at this one. See how the moss makes a pretty pattern?"

Little Trevor, or Buddy, as his uncle called him, seemed to evaluate each projectile for aerodynamic properties before launching it. He pressed a stick into his father's hand. "Okay, Daddy. This one is the best." Buddy's six-year-old voice seemed incongruent with his serious tone. "See how I took off the bark to make it smooth? This little bump will be a rudder."

Don ran his hand over the stick. "Good job, Trevor."

"I'll climb up that tree and watch it." The boy hesitated a moment, ducking his head and kicked at a clump of grass. "Dani, you can come with me, if you want."

She grinned and jumped to her feet, then held out a hand to Buddy. "Of course. Let's go."

He dragged her to the climbing tree at the river's edge. "Remember, Daddy, you need to toss it gently in the water." Buddy stopped and told his dad, "Make sure the bump is at the bottom."

Don held the stick up. "Will do, Son."

Dani and Buddy climbed the tree until they reached the branch with the best view. They jerked around when Trevor yelled and ran toward them, waving and shouting.

"What's wrong?" Dani called out.

Before he could answer, a loud crack split the air. Suddenly Dani and Buddy's perch jerked toward the swift water below. She quickly lowered the boy to his dad. Then she leapt, reaching for the branch above her as the lower limb beneath gave way and crashed into the Willamette. Trevor scrambled up the trunk with the ease of a boy raised in the woods of New England. He splayed his length on the branch Dani clung to and captured her arms in an iron grip. With another thunderous clap, the branch snapped, dropping them both into the river. The limb landed on Trevor and knocked the breath out of him. Dani managed to keep hold of his arm and dragged him to the surface. Her lifeguard training kicking in, she used her arm to secure his head above the water and grasped the floating branch with the other arm. The current rushed them around the bend, where Jared stood, holding out a boat hook. Dani kicked toward him. With the hook, Jared pulled Trevor and Dani to the edge of the river, and Don and Jared dragged them ashore. Jana wrapped a quilt around Dani, while Jared worked to clear Trevor's lungs.

After a couple long minutes, Trevor coughed up water and looked around frantically. "Dani? Where's Dani?"

She walked over to share her quilt. "I'm right here."

"She rescued you," Traci said.

Trevor stood up and pulled Dani close. "I'm so sorry. I should have warned everyone." His voice shook with spasms from the cold. His attention shifted to her eyes, and he smoothed back her hair. "Someone's coming on Monday to take care of the trees. The spring storms really did a number on them."

Dani returned his gaze, her cheeks flaming. At a tug on the hem of her T-shirt, she took a step back. Little Buddy, with tears on his cheeks, raised his arms to her. She knelt and embraced him. "It's okay, Buddy. Everything's okay."

She got to her feet and turned to Trevor. "I'm glad you didn't drown."

A slow smile spread across his face. "Yeah, me too."

Four

Still wearing his gun holster across his back, Zack sat at his paper-strewn desk with his suit coat draped over the chair. He rocked his legs from side to side, the chair swaying with him. With the phone cradled between his neck and shoulder, he doodled on the paper in front of him. "I'm sorry, Cait. Don has me catching up on my paperwork. I'll be late tonight."

"Sounds like business as usual," she replied with a smile in her voice. "I'll keep your dinner warm, and I'll even wait till you're home to put the applesauce cookies in the oven."

"You're a doll. Hey, you know what the difference between prison and work is? In prison you get time off for good behavior. At the office, you get more work for good behavior! Love ya."

He hung up the phone and swiveled his chair around to face the file cabinet. He flinched at the sight of a man standing behind him. "How long have you been there?" Zack asked, his eyes flying to the phone.

The guy grinned. "Only since 'love ya.' I'm trying to get a feel for the way things run here, so I was reviewing some old cases. I wanted to ask you about this report."

Zack narrowed his eyes at the folder in Larry Preston's hand, then glanced up at him "The Alejandro Morales case?"

"Yeah. How did your operative get into that organization? He must have been one heck of an agent." Preston looked like a kid talking about his hero.

"He's good, Larry. Why do you ask?"

"I'd like to meet him. I bet he could give me a pointer or two."

Zack smiled. Trevor was the best. "Sorry, friend. That's a need-to-know."

"Hmm. That's too bad," Preston replied before he gave an abbreviated wave and exited Zack's cubicle.

Zack pushed away from the cabinet and rolled across the mat, focused on getting through the mound of papers. Then he stopped. *The new guy is staying awfully late for his first day on the job. And he's awfully interested in Trevor.* Zack got to his feet and headed down the hall.

Larry Preston hovered at the door marked *Special Agent in Charge, Don Townsend.* Zack moved quietly and didn't speak until he was directly behind the man. "Hello, Larry. Anything I can help you with?"

The man jumped at the greeting. "Uh, no. I was just deciding if I should bring up something with Don," Larry stammered. "It can wait." He scurried away.

Once Agent Preston had disappeared around the corner, Zack knocked on the door and opened it.

Don looked up from a case file. "Done with your reports already? Your wife must be cooking something really good for dinner."

Zack didn't smile. "That new agent, Larry, has been asking about the Morales operation—specifically about the man who infiltrated the organization. It strikes me as strange."

"You're not the first to mention it," Don replied. "It could be totally innocent, but then . . ."

Zack sat on the edge of the desk. "What are you going to do?"

Don tapped his pen on his computer keyboard. "First, I'm going to tell Trevor to lay low. Aside from me, you're the only one in this office who knows his real identity." Don dialed his phone, then looked up at Zack with his hand over the receiver. "Go find out what our new friend is doing right now. Then come back here. I have an assignment for you."

§

Don's attention turned to his call. "Hey there, Trevor. How are you doing?"

"The answer is no," Trevor growled.

"You don't even know what the question is."

"Why else would you be calling?"

"You're my favorite brother-in-law. Can't I call to just shoot the breeze?"

Trevor sighed. "I'm your *only* brother-in-law. I can hear you tapping your pen. Is that Morse code, or are you going to tell me what's going on?"

"All right." Don paused, then added in a sober tone, "I'm concerned about you. We have a new agent in the office. It's his first day, and he's asking a lot of questions about the Morales case. More specifically, about the undercover agent's identity."

"Have you done an in-depth check on him? Bank records, debts, etc.? Could he be on the take?"

Don stood and paced the floor. "It's a possibility. I'll have Lasky start on it first thing in the morning."

"Good."

"Trevor, I think you should make yourself scarce for the next little while."

"Sure thing. I was planning on taking a few weeks to work on the camp anyway. I'll just bump it up to Monday."

"Maybe you should leave sooner." Don glanced out into the large room full of cubicles and desks. Windows made up an entire wall of his corner office.

"Can't. You know I work with the Scouts at church. We have a campout this weekend, and I have to teach their class on Sunday. I promised the women's group I would teach a self-defense class too."

Don sighed. "Okay, okay. It's only been a month since you were baptized and they keep you busier than I ever did. I'll let you play Boy Scout, but then you need to leave. Morales's case comes to court in a few weeks—unless that slimeball Stoddard invents another reason for delay." Don shook his head in disgust. "You're our top witness."

"I know," Trevor said. "I'll be there."

§

Trevor hung up and moved to the window. He leaned on the sill, staring at the view of Portland without seeing its beauty.

His secretary peeked into the room and called tentatively, "Mr. Willis?" She walked up behind him and touched his shoulder. "Mr. Willis?"

In a quick, fluid motion, he whipped around and pinned her arms to her sides. Just as suddenly, he loosened his grip. "Brenda, I'm so sorry. I didn't hear you come in."

The middle-aged woman straightened her jacket. "That's obvious." She paused, then said dryly, "Note to self: 'don't sneak up on the boss when he's lost in space.'"

Trevor chuckled. "I'll be heading out of town on Monday. You're the only one I'll have contact with."

This wasn't the first time he had left without any explanation. Brenda, his assistant, always took everything in stride and never asked questions.

"All right, Mr. Willis."

"You know you can call me Trevor."

She smiled. "Oh, I know, but I'm pretty old school. It seems odd to call the boss by his first name."

"Whatever makes you comfortable. Thanks for everything. You are the best."

"Of course I am." The wrinkles around her eyes appeared with her smile. "That's why you pay me the big bucks." She headed toward the door.

"One more thing, Brenda. Could you send Dani Carpenter in here? She should still be in the building."

She nodded. "I'll tell her to wear protective gear."

Trevor retreated to the private bathroom adjoining his office and turned on the cold water. He splashed some onto his face. Don's call had unnerved him. *I can only imagine what's going through Brenda's head.* He combed back his black hair and leaned closer to the mirror. With his head turned to one side, then the other, he touched his temple, where a few gray hairs had sprung up. *I blame Don for each one of these.* Trevor opened the medicine cabinet and used the tweezers lying on a shelf to pluck the offending hairs.

A knock sounded at the office door. Trevor returned the tweezers, turned off the light, and stepped out of the bathroom. His long strides quickly covered the distance to the office door. Remembering Dani's daily visits while he was recovering, he smiled. He looked forward to seeing her again. He swung open the door. "Dani—"

He stopped in midsentence. The person who entered the room definitely was not Dani Carpenter.

"I wasn't expecting you," Trevor muttered.

Five

Recovering from his initial shock, Trevor reached out his hand to the man who could be the poster child for Geeky Science Dudes of America. "Bruce, come on in. How are you liking Portland? It's a pretty big change from Phoenix."

"Yes, sir." Bruce's eyes darted from side to side as he wiped his hands on his white lab coat.

Trevor sat at the edge of the desk. "How's the research coming?"

"Good, sir."

"Tell me about it."

Bruce's brow furrowed. "What's your clearance?"

Trevor chuckled. "I think you can tell the head of the company about your research."

"Regulations, sir. I don't want to get in trouble my first day on the job. This might be a test."

"Don't worry. I have top-secret clearance."

Bruce turned and shut the door. "We developed a pulse that disrupts all electronics in its path. Unfortunately, the disruption is permanent. We're trying to adjust the frequency to make the breach temporary. I am making headway."

"Great." Trevor nodded. "That's why we hired you. You're the top man in the country. Keep up the good work." He strode around to his chair. "Now, what can I do for you?"

Bruce shuffled his feet. "You know, my daughter and I just moved here. I still don't know anyone in town."

"Yes. And?"

"Can I . . . I mean, I was hoping . . . would it be okay if I use you as an emergency contact at my daughter's daycare?"

"Uh, wow. Are you sure someone else isn't more qualified?"

"She's a good girl," Bruce said. "Extremely intelligent for her age. She's never a problem."

"I'm sure she's a good kid. I just think a person with a family would be a better candidate."

"There's no one else here I trust more than you, Mr. Willis."

Trevor stood, and after a pause he smiled and reached his hand over the desk. "I'd be glad to help you out. Brenda can give you whatever information you need."

Bruce stood and vigorously shook Trevor's hand. "Thank you, sir." He stumbled over the chair in front of the desk. He caught himself from falling but knocked over a vase of flowers near the door. "I'm so sorry." He reached behind him, opened the door, and stepped back, almost colliding with Dani. "Excuse me, ma'am," he mumbled just before he made his escape.

Chuckling, Trevor righted the vase and replaced the flowers. Then he told Dani in a low voice, "Good thing he's brilliant."

She smiled. "Brenda said you wanted to see me."

"You know how we were supposed to go up to the camp at the end of the month?" Dani nodded, so Trevor continued, "Those plans have changed. We're leaving on Monday."

She turned and paced the floor, mumbling to herself, "I'm still in a hotel room. I was going to find a place to live in the next week." She faced Trevor and shook her head. "I can't do it."

Trevor raised his eyebrow. He wasn't used to employees telling him no. Then again, Dani wasn't just an employee. She was a friend. "Hey, if it's a place to live that's worrying you, don't. I have a solution. Check out of the hotel and stay at my place till you find an apartment."

She opened her mouth and closed it again, then crossed her arms and gave him an indignant glare.

"I . . . Oh, no, no, Dani. Not 'my place' as in where I live. I still have the apartment here in Portland. It's fully furnished, and no one's living there. You can stay as long as you need to."

Her shoulders relaxed. "For a second there, I thought I was going to have to talk to your bishop."

Trevor chuckled. "Don't worry, I would never ask you to compromise your standards. Since you are the camp director, I thought you would want to come and help make decisions, but if you prefer I make all the decisions about the camp, that's fine, I'll go up alone. The offer of the apartment still stands. I'll see you in a week or two." He sat and turned his attention to the papers on his desk.

"No!" Dani protested.

Trevor glanced up at her. "Is there something else?"

"I'll have to make it work. What time do we leave on Monday?"

"Early. About 5:30."

Dani gasped. "In the morning?"

"Of course. We'll beat rush-hour traffic. Don't eat breakfast. We'll stop at a café on the way."

"Sure thing," she said, her brown eyes sparking her displeasure. As she reached the door, she muttered, "Five thirty AM? Vengeance is mine."

"Oh, Dani?" Trevor said.

She turned back and raised her eyebrows.

"I'm teaching a class in self-defense at Relief Society this Thursday. Do you want to come?"

"I need that one," came Brenda's voice from the outer office.

Trevor threw back his head and laughed.

"Sure," Dani said. "You never know when I might have to defend myself." She hummed the song "Kung Fu Fighting" as she left the room.

§

In Beaverton, Bruce Miller and his four-year-old daughter Ady entered their apartment. "Sorry we took so long to get home. I had to get this paper signed."

"It's okay, Daddy." She opened her Happy Meal bag and pulled out the chicken nuggets and french fries. "I'm hungry."

He flattened the bag on the wooden table and squirted some ketchup on to it. "Did you want ranch dressing too?"

"Yep." She dipped her pinkie in the red circle and slurped it off her finger. "More ketchup, please."

He complied, then tousled her reddish-blond hair. "Ady, look at me."

She gazed at him with her mother's hazel eyes as he tipped her chin up. "I have the letter we got signed today, and I put it in this envelope." He held it in front of her, then showed her a photograph. "This is Mr. Willis. If for some reason I can't take care of you, he will."

Ady's solemn expression belied her young age. "Yes, Daddy. Are you going somewhere like Mommy did?"

"No, honey. Mommy went to heaven. I'm staying here. This is just in case I have to work late or go out of town. If Mr. Willis brings you home from daycare, I want you to give him this letter. I'm putting it in your *Froggy* book in the pocket of your backpack. Do you understand?"

Ady's pudgy hand wiped away a tear. "O–okay."

"I'll always be here for you. Don't worry." With a prayer in his heart to keep them both safe, Bruce hugged her close.

That man behind me yesterday was only a coincidence. It had to be.

Six

Trevor helped Dani move from her hotel to his unused apartment. As they entered the foyer, he pointed to a digital picture frame with the Honeywell logo prominently displayed at the bottom. Pictures of his sister's family alternated across the screen. "This is the alarm system. When you walk in, you have two minutes to disarm it. Do you remember the codes?"

"I think so." Dani punched a button on the side of the frame. A security screen appeared and she typed *H-A-1-7*.

"That's good. The alarm is disarmed, but you just activated the security cameras. I'll see everything you do in here."

She faced the screen, her hands hovering above the panel. She reached to press a number, but drew her hand back again. "Stop it. How do I stop it?"

He laughed. "Don't worry, it's easy to fix." Trevor reached over her shoulder. "Did you see which commands I used?"

She nodded, heat rushing to her cheeks at his nearness.

"Good. Now put in the other code I gave you."

She took a deep breath and tried again: *H-A-2-2*.

"Excellent. Now, where do you want your suitcases?"

After moving everything into the apartment, Trevor showed Dani how to rearm the security system. "You can put your own pictures into the frame, if you like," he told her. "Now, are you ready to go to the self-defense class?"

She grinned impishly. "Yes. I'm looking forward to this."

"Why does it feel like I'm walking right into trouble?" he mumbled.

As they headed toward the elevator, she glanced over her shoulder at him and hummed "Kung Fu Fighting" again.

$$\S$$

"We are pleased to have Brother Trevor Willis here to teach our self-defense class."

Twenty pairs of hands applauded.

Trevor strode to the front of the room and cleared his throat. "Good evening, ladies. In the next hour and a half, I'll be instructing you in some basic self-defense strategies. The first is to be aware of your surroundings."

On the board, he wrote *Be and Act Aware*. "Most attackers choose easy victims. If your shoulders are back, your keys are in your hand, and your walk is purposeful, you are less likely to be targeted than someone digging in her purse for her keys."

Underneath, he scribbled *Take Charge* and then *Get Help*.

A woman in bright pink sweats raised her hand and spoke without waiting to be called on. "What do you do if someone is in your car and threatens you with a gun or knife?"

"Hopefully you would have been aware enough to realize he was there, and you wouldn't have gotten into the car. If you do find yourself in that situation, use step two. Take charge. He may have a gun to your head, but you're still in control of the vehicle. You can do one of several things. You can drive someplace with a lot of people such as a mall or nearby police station. Don't ever head to a secluded location. Zigzag the car or run into something—a bush, a tree, a mailbox, a police car. Chances are, the attacker will be thrown off balance, and you'll be able to escape. Finally, step 3 is to get help.

A petite woman with light-brown hair raised her hand. "My husband would be pretty upset if I crashed the car."

"I think he'd prefer to look for a new car instead of a new wife," Trevor replied.

The class chuckled and the woman blushed.

Sister Pink Sweats interrupted once again. "Brother Willis! Brother Willis!"

He pointed to her. "Yes?"

"No one would dare come at me where I can see them." The women laughed. "I'm worried about someone coming at me from behind. What should I do?"

"That's a very good question. Let me demonstrate. Dani, can you help?"

She looked around, then pointed to herself in an exaggerated manner. "Me?"

"It seems as if she's a little shy. Let's encourage her." Trevor started clapping. The noise grew until Dani blushed and gave him a look he hoped wouldn't kill him.

He reached out his hand to help her up. "Come on." He positioned her in front of him and said, "Act like you're waiting for a bus."

Dani crossed her arms and tapped her right foot, then checked her watch.

Standing behind her, Trevor reached around her neck. "Remember number 2, take charge. The first thing to do is lock your chin down."

She followed his directions.

"This will make it so your attacker cannot cut off your air supply." Still holding onto Dani, Trevor continued. "One move won't be enough, so think in multiples—a heel to his instep and an elbow to the solar plexus."

Dani acted quickly, stomping on the inside of his foot. He grunted and let go of her neck. She finished with an elbow to his stomach.

Trevor groaned and grasped his abdomen. "Excellent demonstration. Did everyone get that?"

Dani smiled innocently. "Should I do it again—in case someone missed it?"

"No. no. That's good. You can sit down."

Seven

They headed toward Portland in silence. Finally, Dani spoke up. "I'm sorry, Trevor. Sometimes I get a little carried away. Jared says it will get me in trouble someday."

"He just might be right. Or it might *save* you from trouble." Trevor winked at her. "In my case, at least you were wearing sneakers instead of heels."

"I thought about wearing heels."

He turned into a parking lot and stopped the vehicle. "You did? Seriously?"

With a sideways glance, Dani said, "At least the sneakers won out."

Trevor chuckled. "I guess I owe you an apology, too. We can leave as late as 8:00 if you like, though we'll still stop for breakfast." He paused. "How'd you learn those defense moves, anyway?"

"I've got an overprotective big brother who happens to have a black belt in karate. Are you okay? I really am sorry."

"I imagine my muscles and my ego will be pretty sore in the morning, but I'll survive."

Trevor escorted her to the apartment, and after she successfully disarmed the security system, he said, "Well, good-night. I'll see you at the office." He tucked a piece of Dani's hair behind her ear.

She smiled. "Okay. Good-night."

He held his stomach and exaggerated a limp as he headed for the elevator.

"Thank you," she called just before the doors shut.

Dani closed the door, armed the security system, and looked around. The keypad returned to the slideshow. She laughed at a picture of Trevor and his nephews. The boys had Trevor pinned to the ground and held their arms up in a victory pose. Her hand rose without permission and touched Trevor's face. *Stop that!*

She ran her finger across the modern table in the foyer, which featured a tall, sleek black vase with an arrangement of silk flowers. The pristine white couch with red and black pillows faced a flat screen TV hanging on the wall. The glass coffee table held an assortment of remotes. A computer had sat on the corner desk the last time she was here, but not even a layer of dust showed where the monitor had rested. With amazing attention to detail, the kitchen was a chef's dream. *Too bad I hate cooking,* Dani mused. She opened the fridge. Fresh fruits and vegetables, milk, butter, eggs, bacon, and lunch meat. The freezer contained juice concentrate, an assortment of frozen dinners, and peanut-butter-cup ice cream. Dani made a fist, pulled it down quickly, and exclaimed, "Yes!"

In the bathroom, all the drawers were empty. The medicine cabinet held only an electric razor and a small shaving kit. She moved those onto the top shelf of the linen closet and touched the plush towels folded neatly there.

Moving into the bedroom, she jumped onto the king-size bed. "I could really get used to this." The walk-in closet held two suits, a few shirts, and a tie hanger. Dani moved these to the front hall closet and hung up her clothes in their stead. Then she closed the suitcase and placed it in the corner of the closet.

"I think I hear some ice cream calling my name." She reached the fridge at the same time her cell phone rang. "I guess the ice cream will wait a few minutes," she sighed.

Dani followed the ringtone and finally found her phone under a cushion on the couch. "Hello?"

"Hi, Sis. How're you doing?"

"Hi Jared. I'm fine."

"I thought my call was going to go to voicemail."

"Sorry. I had to search for my phone." She plopped down on the couch.

"Trevor must be paying for the hotel room if it's big enough to lose your phone in."

"I'm not at the hotel anymore. I moved into his place."

Silence sounded on the line for several seconds before Jared growled, "I'm counting to ten before I get in my car and drive up to Portland to bring you back here. I might sock Trevor in the jaw again—if he's within striking distance."

"What are you talking about?"

"I'm talking about you moving in with Trevor."

"I didn't move in with him. I moved into his place. He still has the apartment in Portland, remember?"

"The apartment?" A whoosh of air escaped Jared's lungs. "I'm so sorry, Dani. I should have known better."

She laughed. "Don't worry about it. I thought the same thing when he mentioned it to me."

"Speaking of Trevor—"

Dani rolled her eyes. "Ah, so now we get down to the real reason for this call."

"Hey, chill out. I was just wondering how things are going with you two."

"There isn't any 'you two' when it comes to Trevor and me. We're friends. That's it."

"After the tree incident last month, it sure didn't seem that way."

"Okay, Jared. If you want to know the truth, I might be attracted to him—a little. But he's my boss, for goodness sake."

"Just tread lightly. Even though he's my friend, I'm still not entirely convinced that he's changed."

"Well, thanks for the warning, brother dearest, but I am old enough to make my own decisions. And I never rush into anything."

"Of course. I'm sorry for treating you like a kid. I better go. Love you."

"Love you too. Oh, I forgot to tell you, we'll be heading up to the camp on Monday instead of the end of the month."

"Thanks for letting me know. Remember to take it slow with Trevor."

"Uh, did you just hear what I said?"

"I did. You said you were attracted to him. I'll talk to you later." Jared disconnected the call.

Dani stared at the home screen of her cell phone. "Chicken!" she grumbled. *Jared's selective hearing is worse than Dad's.*

She dropped the phone on the couch and headed for the kitchen.

Eight

Trevor Willis turned left onto Highway 99 from College Avenue. Knowing his turn was coming up soon, he pulled into the far right lane of the one-way street.

"My dad got a ticket for doing that last week, Brother Willis," Sean said.

Lost in thought, Trevor had almost forgotten the boy was in the car with him. "Oh really? I didn't realize it was illegal."

As if on cue, red and blue lights flashed in the rear view mirror of Trevor's red Toyota Tacoma pickup. His heart sank and he groaned. "Of all the luck." He looked at Sean. "I guess I should never have given that speech about being on time for the campout."

"Yeah, they'll never let you forget it."

"Maybe this'll be quick." He turned into a parking lot on the right and rolled down the window. "Sean, can you grab the registration out of the glove box?"

Taking his time, the officer walked over to the truck and said, "Good morning, sir. Are you in a hurry?"

"I'm trying to get to a Scout campout."

"May I see your license and registration, please?"

Trevor read the name badge. "Of course, Officer Mills."

"Do you know what you did wrong?"

"I didn't know until this fine young man informed me that I wasn't supposed to turn into the far lane."

Officer Mills nodded. "That's correct. I'll be right back."

A minivan slowed with the window down. Luke stuck his head out and laughed, pointing his finger until they disappeared around the corner.

Sean followed the vehicle with his eyes. "I thought about suggesting a bribe, but Luke will never let it go."

Trevor drummed his fingers on the steering wheel and glanced in the rearview mirror. "This isn't going to be quick."

Several minutes later, the officer returned to Trevor's vehicle. "Sir, could you verify your Social Security number?"

"I'm sorry, Officer. I don't give that out freely."

Officer Mills let out a breath. "Mr. Willis, I'd appreciate your cooperation. I don't want to have to take you in."

"No, no. That won't be necessary. Could you tell me why you need my Social?"

"Yes, sir. There is a warrant out on a man whose name is very similar to yours. I've got to verify your identity."

"Let me write it down for you."

The officer turned his notepad to a clean sheet of paper and handed it to Trevor, who wrote down the number.

"This sure is freaky," Sean said once the officer walked away with the notepad.

"You can say that again."

"Do things like this happen to you all the time?"

Trevor's baritone laugh filled the cab of the truck. "I guess I do have more than my share of freaky incidents."

The policeman's voice startled both of them. "Mr. Willis, please step out of the car." The officer rested his hand on his holstered service weapon.

"Of course." Trevor slowly got out of the truck.

"The man we're looking for has a tattoo that runs across his shoulder and down his left arm. Could you please remove your jacket?"

Trevor complied, baring his tattoo-free arms.

Officer Mills nodded. "Thank you for your cooperation, Mr. Willis. It'd be very embarrassing to have one of America's most wanted slip through my fingers. You lucked out this time. No ticket, just a warning."

Trevor threw the jacket into the truck and then got behind the wheel.

"Wait a minute." The officer reached into his pocket and handed a card through the window. "Call me if your Scouts would like a tour of the station."

"Thank you."

Trevor and Sean continued on their way. When they arrived at the parking lot, Brother Markham and the rest of the Scouts were waiting impatiently. Before Trevor could put the truck in park, Sean jumped from his seat and called out, "You guys will never guess what happened to us on the way!"

Luke guffawed. "We already know."

"You missed the best part. Brother Willis had to take his jacket off to prove he didn't have any tattoos." Sean crossed his arms. "It was awesome."

"Well, does he?" Luke punched the younger Scout on the arm.

"No." Trevor ruffled the boy's hair. "I don't have any tattoos. Let's get going."

Nine

Evergreen trees lined the narrow road leading to the secluded campsite. Two minutes of driving on the gravel, and all the vehicle windows were closed against the dust. Trevor pulled to a stop in the circle at the end of the lane, then waited for the air to clear before opening his door.

The tent sites formed a semicircle around the fire pit. Beyond the campsite, the breeze whispered through the pine needles. The lake was only a short distance away.

The Scoutmaster, Brother Markham, stood by the fire pit directing the placement of coolers, chairs, and camp stoves. Standing in the back of his truck, Trevor called out, "Sean and Jeff, you think you can handle putting up a tent?"

Sean held out his arms. "Sure, Brother Willis."

Trevor tossed him a brand-new tent, still in its box. The boys carried it to the campsite, ripped off the tape, and dumped the contents in the dirt. "Uh, Brother Willis?" Sean said.

"Yeah?" Trevor threw a sleeping bag on the growing pile.

"How do you put this thing together?" The boy held up two mismatched poles.

"I'm almost done unpacking. Read the instructions, and I'll be there in a minute."

More Scouts joined Sean and tried to figure out the tent.

"I think we need to put these together," said Sam, holding some poles.

"No way. You have to start with the short ones," Jeff replied.

Sean sat on top of the tent with the directions in front of him. His shoulders sagged and he crumpled the instructions into a ball. "You'd have to be Einstein to figure this out."

Jeff's eyes darted around to each of the boys, and he lowered his voice. "Hey, I heard Brother Willis works for the CIA."

"Don't be a dweeb. He owns a company or something." Sam attempted to fit poles into loops on the tent.

Sean threw the wadded-up instructions at Jeff. "Yeah, and Martians are landing on the other side of the lake."

Trevor vaulted over the side of the truck and slipped behind the adventurers. "So, have you figured it out, yet?"

They all jerked around to see their leader. Jeff recovered first. "Whoa, Brother Willis. Where'd you learn to do that?"

"No trick. You guys were so engrossed in the tent set-up, you didn't hear me."

Jeff mouthed "CIA" to the other boys, who gaped at Trevor.

Trevor and Brother Markham shouted instructions. Within fifteen minutes, two tents stood immovable in the campsite, a new camp kitchen gleamed near the fire pit, and Hormel chili simmered in a large pot on the stove. The table held a two-gallon cooler of lemonade, individually sized bags of Fritos, shredded Tillamook cheese, and a bag of Red Delicious apples.

Two Scouts stood watch over the pot. Sam stirred while Luke called out to the boys, "Food's done. Come and get it!" He ripped open a package of plastic forks and secured the first place in line.

The other Scouts approached with the grace of a herd of elephants, jostling each other to get closer to the food. After the prayer, each boy carefully opened a Fritos bag and ladled chili into it. A handful or two of cheese completed the meal. For the first time since leaving Newberg, the troop was silent.

A short time later, with dinner cleared and dishes washed, Luke ran up to the leaders and asked, "Can we go throw rocks in the lake?"

Unsheathing a camp chair from its sack, Brother Markham nodded. "Remember the buddy system. Stay together—and don't go in the water. Be back in about an hour."

He lowered his body into the chair. "These are great. Thanks for the donation. I can't wait to try out the new cot."

"No problem," Trevor replied. "We might as well camp in style." He relaxed in his own chair with a built-in footrest.

Bursts of laughter interrupted the silence.

Trevor inclined his head toward the lake and addressed the Scoutmaster. "Hey, Marsh, does that sound suspicious to you?"

"Yeah, seems fishy."

"You want me to check it out?" Trevor rose from the folding chair.

"Might be a good idea," replied Brother Markham "Whenever Luke's involved, it's always good to keep our eyes wide open. I'll go with you."

At six feet tall, Luke towered over the other Scouts. His intimidating size persuaded even the most reluctant boys to follow him, and most of his adventures included some element of danger.

Trevor and Brother Markham followed the short path to the lake, ducking under low-hanging branches. When they got close enough to observe the boys, they knelt down but stayed out of sight.

"Come on. It's your turn," Luke said just before he soaked Jeff's pant leg with insect repellant.

"I . . . I guess so," Jeff replied in a shaky voice.

Luke clicked his lighter and set the damp cloth on fire. The flame burned off the bug spray and extinguished itself.

Trevor rushed toward the boys. "Ahhhhhh! Fire!" He lifted all 160 pounds of Luke and dumped him into the lake. Then Trevor brushed off his hands and turned toward the boys. "Anyone else want me to make sure they're not on fire?"

The boys stared at Trevor and then at Luke as he emerged from the water.

"Good," Trevor continued. "Now, I'll be confiscating all incendiary devices, including matches, lighters, flint and steel wool, etc. I'll hang onto them for safekeeping." He passed in front of each boy with his palm up. "I'll turn these over to your parents when we get back to the church."

"Go on, Jeff," one of the Scouts urged the boy.

"Yeah, ask him."

Jeff was pushed forward. "Why me?"

"'Cause it's your idea," said one of the boys.

Trevor stood in front of Jeff, who seemed to grow smaller by the second. "You have something to ask me?"

"Uh, no, I don't." Jeff tried to blend into the crowd, but they stepped back, leaving him alone.

"Go ahead. Ask him," whispered another boy.

"All right, all right." Jeff looked up at Trevor and swallowed hard, then stuffed his hands in his pockets and kicked a pebble in the dirt. "Uh, Brother Willis?"

"Yes?"

"Are you with the CIA?"

The boys relaxed as Trevor's laughter boomed over the water. "I am not, nor have I ever been, in the CIA," he replied once he could speak again.

"Well, then, the FBI or Secret Service or something?" Jeff pressed, braver now.

Trevor rumpled his hair and patted him on the back. "Let's get going, guys. We have just enough time to tell a few ghost stories around the campfire before we hit the sack."

Ten

Early on Saturday morning, Dr. Bruce Miller searched his briefcase as he walked from the parking garage to the office building. Suddenly, two large men grabbed him and dragged him toward a black car with darkened windows.

"What—what are you doing? Let go of me!" Papers from the briefcase scattered over the asphalt. Bruce threw back his head and smacked one of his attackers on the bridge of his nose.

The man, whose head was closely shaven, clutched his face and growled, "I'm bleeding! He broke my nose."

"Shut up." The other assailant, who wore a trimmed beard but no moustache, punched Bruce in the jaw, then pushed him inside the car. He called out to the man with the bloody nose, "Grab those papers. Hurry."

Bruce looked toward the parking exit. The security guard emerged from his station and ran toward the black car. Bruce tried to leave the car from the other side, but he couldn't find the door handle.

"Hey, what's going on here?" shouted the security guard, drawing his gun.

The bearded assailant whirled at the voice and reached into his jacket. Bruce slid across the seat and knocked the assailant off balance as the man popped off a shot at the guard. The bullet missed the target, but shattered the window of a parked car. The guard ducked down behind a concrete pillar and returned fire. Bruce attempted to slip by the gunman and found the barrel of a weapon pointed at his chest. Baldy ignored the rest of the papers on the ground and pushed Bruce back into the vehicle, then jumped into the back seat and closed the door behind him. Bullets pinged off the side of the car as it sped away from the scene.

§

Trevor drove toward Newberg, his truck packed with Scouting equipment. Sean sat next to him, while Luke took the seat near the window. After the bug-spray incident, he gave Trevor a wide berth and actually seemed to listen when he spoke. *I wonder how long that will last.*

They followed Brother Markham's vehicle as he turned into the far lane on the 99. Sean pointed at the SUV. "Uh-oh, he's gonna get a ticket."

Trevor smiled. "Just in case, I think I'll turn into the closest lane. Nobody has to tell me twice."

As Brother Markham passed a police car, the vehicle's red and blue lights flashed and the siren began to blare. The Scoutmaster pulled his van into a Domino's Pizza parking lot.

Sean leaned over Luke and yelled, "Serves you right!"

"I do believe that is Officer Mills, Sean," Trevor replied. "What do you think?"

"Ha. You're right."

Trevor's cell rang. He tapped his earpiece. "Trevor Willis."

"It's terrible. They took Dr. Miller from the parking garage!" Trevor's secretary shouted into the phone.

"Calm down, Brenda. What about Bruce Miller?"

"He . . . ki . . . apped."

"He what?" Trevor cupped his hand over the earpiece as they entered a treeless area.

Brenda enunciated each word. "He was kidnapped."

Trevor's foot pressed the gas pedal harder, bringing a gasp from the boys. "We have got to increase the security in the parking garage."

Brenda's next words were lost in static.

"Can you repeat that? What about his daughter?"

"The daycare is waiting for you to pick her up."

"But why? Oh yeah, he put me down as an emergency contact." Trevor ran his fingers through his day-after-campout hair. "I have to drop these boys off at the church. Text me the daycare address and I'll be there as soon as possible."

As soon as Trevor ended the call, the boys peppered him with questions.

"What's wrong?"

"Was someone hurt?"

He forced a smile. "No, everything's okay. One of the scientists at my work just needs some help. I'm going to watch his daughter for a little while."

Sean nudged Luke with his elbow and whispered. "Maybe Jeff was right. Maybe he really is with the CIA."

Trevor laughed. "Like I said, I'm not with the CIA. Camping in the woods always brings out spooky stories and conspiracy theories." He turned into the church parking lot. "I'll need your help unloading everything, and then I need to get going."

The boys jumped out of the truck. Between the three of them, it was unloaded by the time Brother Markham pulled his van into the parking lot, looking sheepish.

"Thanks for your help, guys," Trevor said to Sean and Luke. "I'll see you in the morning."

Trevor handed the incendiary devices to the Scoutmaster before climbing back into his truck. He waved goodbye and turned left onto Deborah Street.

Eleven

At Smart Cookies Day Care, Trevor was greeted by a woman in her mid-thirties, holding a baby on her left hip. After Trevor introduced himself, she said, "It's nice to meet you, Mr. Willis. I'm Carolyn Jackson."

He attempted to wipe the camping grime off his hand, then decided against a handshake. "I received a call to pick up Bruce Miller's daughter, Ady. I hope you'll excuse my condition. I just returned from a Boy Scout outing."

"Can I please see your ID so I can verify the information we have on file?" A minute later, Carolyn returned Trevor's driver's license and said, "Everything checks out. Ady is in the back room playing with my daughter. They're making dinner. I think it's chicken nuggets and French fries. Ady's specialty." Carolyn smiled.

The look on Ady's face when she glanced up at Trevor nearly broke his heart. Her bottom lip quivered as tears gathered in her eyes.

What have I gotten myself into? he thought. *I don't know a thing about little girls.*

"Ady, Mr. Willis is here to pick you up," Carolyn explained.

Without a word, the child went to the cubby wall and removed her backpack from a pink bin. She took Trevor's hand and waved goodbye to her teacher and her friend.

"Hi, Ady, I'm Trevor."

"I know. Daddy showed me your picture."

"He did, did he?"

"He said if he couldn't pick me up, you would." Ady stopped as they reached Trevor's truck. "Is he in heaven with Mommy now?" One by one, large tears dripped down the girl's face.

Trevor took a deep breath. "No, Ady. He just had to go away for a little while."

She wiped her tears and sniffled. "Good. I would miss him so much."

Trevor opened the door and lifted her into the front seat, then handed her his clean handkerchief.

She blew her nose and said, "I need a car seat."

"A car seat?"

"Uh-huh. I need a car seat until I'm forty pounds or four foot nine. I'm not either one."

"Well, I seem to be fresh out of car seats."

Ady smiled. "Daddy has an extra one in the garage."

"I need to take you home to get your things anyway. You'll be staying at my house for a little while."

"It's not too far, and I'll duck if we see a policeman." She demonstrated her expert ducking skills.

Trevor grinned. "Okay, Ady, you do that."

When they pulled into the driveway, Ady removed a house key from her backpack. "Daddy gave me this. Just in case."

"Your daddy's a very smart man."

"Uh-huh. Mommy always said he was the smartest man in the whole world."

They entered the Miller home and switched on the lights. Ady opened her backpack and pulled out a book, from which she removed an envelope. "Daddy said to give you this, just in case you ever brought me home."

Trevor accepted the envelope. "Thank you. Now can you get the clothes and things you'll need for the next few days?"

"Okay."

He opened the envelope and read the first document.

Temporary guardianship of Ady Miller given to Trevor Willis. If Bruce Miller is unable to care for his daughter, this arrangement will be made permanent.

Trevor sat down on a hard kitchen chair. *Custody? What is going on?*

Underneath the guardianship document was a letter.

Mr. Willis,

I want to thank you for watching Ady. She's such a good girl and will do whatever you ask her to do. If you're reading this letter, the feeling that I've been followed since Phoenix was not paranoia. Please keep my precious little girl safe until I return. If I don't, tell her I love her and that we'll be together in heaven someday.

Sincerely,
Bruce Miller

There were several dry water spots on the letter. Trevor placed the page on the bottom of the pile of papers from the envelope and started on the next sheet. The top line read, "Important Instructions Regarding Ady Miller."

Ady entered the room with a blue *Frozen* suitcase. "I'm ready to go."

He looked up from the letter, blinking back tears. "That was fast."

"Daddy packed for me. Just in case." She looked at the floor. "Mr. Willis, can I bring some dolls?"

"Of course you can. Bring whatever you want." He looked back at the papers until the noise of drawers and doors slamming caught his attention.

A few minutes later, Ady reappeared in the doorway, dragging two bulging pillowcases. "I'm ready."

"That looks like a lot of toys," Trevor replied, trying to estimate the amount of space he had in the guest room.

"All my dolls and stuffed animals miss Daddy too. I couldn't tell them no."

Trevor's heartstrings pulled hard enough to hurt. He picked up Ady's blue bag and filled pillowcases and escorted her out the door. "Never let it be said that I left a man—or stuffed animal—behind," he muttered. Then he knelt down to look her in the eyes. "Don't worry, Ady. I'm going to bring your daddy back home."

She wiped a tear from her cheek and nodded.

Twelve

Dani met Trevor at his home in Newberg. He led her to a guest bedroom and inched the door open. In the glow of a pony night light, Ady slept, clinging to her white unicorn. Her breath was still ragged from crying.

"Who is she?" Dani asked as they headed back to the living room.

"Her name is Ady. She's Bruce Miller's daughter."

"Where's Bruce?"

"He was kidnapped from the parking garage today. He asked me to be her emergency contact, but now it looks like he has arranged for me to be her temporary guardian."

Dani sighed. "Poor little thing. Where's her mother?"

"Cancer took her about a year ago."

"What can I do?"

"If you wouldn't mind staying here a while, I'd appreciate it. I need to clean up and then do some shopping for our trip. I don't want to leave Ady alone, not even to shower, in case she wakes up."

"Sure," Dani said. "I'll stay as late as you need me."

Trevor squeezed her shoulder. "Thanks. You're amazing."

A faint blush appeared on her cheeks. "Thanks, boss."

"I thought we'd take her up to the camp with us. She might be safer there—the sooner, the better."

"You're probably right," Dani said. "Should we leave after church tomorrow or wait until Monday morning?"

"I don't know. I need to teach the deacons, and my ward doesn't start until 11:30."

"Sounds like Monday would be best. I'll come by tomorrow after church and we can make a picnic for dinner. Then you can pick me up Monday morning—even at 5:30, if you want."

"It sounds like a plan. Let's do it." He headed down the hall to wash away the grime of the campout.

§

Ady woke up screaming around two o'clock in the morning. "Daddy! Daddy! No!"

Trevor struggled to extricate himself from the sleeping bag he had spread out in the hallway in front of her bedroom door. He rushed into her room. The little girl put her arms around his neck and clung to him, her shoulders shaking.

"I dreamed Daddy went to live with Mommy in heaven."

"It's okay, it's okay," Trevor soothed, stroking her hair. "Would you like me to sing for you?"

Ady sniffled and nodded.

"Here's one my mother used to sing for me:

Daisy, Daisy, give me your answer do
I'm half crazy all for the love of you.
It won't be a stylish marriage,
I can't afford a carriage,
But you'll look sweet, upon the seat
Of a bicycle built for two."

Ady finally drifted back to sleep. Trevor watched her for a while before he climbed back into his sleeping bag.

§

Dani was waiting on the front porch when Trevor and Ady returned from church. Soon, Ady sat on the stool in the kitchen, watching Dani prepare a picnic lunch.

"I make the best peanut butter and jelly sandwich. The secret is to spread a layer of peanut butter on each slice of bread, and then swirl the jelly into the peanut butter."

Ady used her pinky to swirl the peanut butter and jelly. "This is fun." She slurped the extra jelly off her finger.

Dani hugged her close. "You might not want to tell Mr. Willis you used your finger on his sandwich instead of a knife."

"I'm sorry."

"Hey there, it's okay. What Mr. Willis doesn't know won't hurt him." Dani winked.

Ady closed one eye while the other wavered between open and closed.

§

On Monday morning, Dani turned over in bed and hid her head under the pillow. At the muffled sound of the doorbell, she gave up on going back to sleep. Wrapped in a fleece blanket, she stumbled through the living room and opened the front door.

"What are you doing here so early? You said we could leave as late as 8:00." Dani finger-combed her hair.

Trevor looked at his watch. "It's 8:03 and 43 seconds. We were here on time, but it took you a while to answer the door."

She grabbed his wrist and bent it to read the time. "Oh, no. I must not have set my alarm."

"You're funny," said a young voice.

For the first time, Dani noticed the little girl standing next to Trevor. "Good morning, Ady."

Ady ran to her side and gave her a giant hug. "I missed you last night, Dani."

"I missed you too, sweetie. You and Mr. Willis can go in the kitchen and get some juice, and I'll take a quick shower and then we can leave."

"Do you have Lucky Charms?" Ady asked.

"I might just have a small box in the cupboard."

Ady clapped her hands together. "I'm hungry."

Trevor put his hands on Ady's shoulders to lead her into the kitchen. "Dani, run before she asks any more questions."

Twenty minutes later, Dani pulled two suitcases behind her and exited the bedroom. Her damp hair clung to her face. "I'm ready to go."

"It's about time." Trevor reached up and pushed her hair away from her eyes. Then he grabbed her luggage and wheeled the suitcases to the door.

"Wait, I have my computer case, too." Dani picked it up from its resting place by the side of the couch and put it over his shoulder. "Are you ready, Ady?"

The girl's shoulders sank. "Aw, I've only eaten two bowls of cereal."

"You can take the box with you."

"Yay!" She grabbed it off the table.

Trevor reached for the doorknob. "Wait!" Dani called out.

He sat on one of the suitcases. "What now?"

"I have to grab my pillow and blanket." She ran back to the bedroom. Half a minute later, she wrapped the blanket around his neck and stuck the pillow under his arm, then took Ady's hand. Dani set the alarm code, and they left for the camp.

In the parking garage, a shadowy figure bent near the right front bumper of Dani's Subaru Outback. Seconds later, he stood and exited the parking structure, whistling an Irish folk song.

Thirteen

The sun hung low on the horizon by the time they reached Trevor's cabin across the pond from the new camp. They had stopped at restaurants, a couple of playgrounds, a grocery store, and a toy store.

When they checked in at the front-gate guard station, the guard leaned out the window. "You're here later than we expected, Mr. Willis."

"Yeah, Tony. Ady is staying with me. We thought she might like the great outdoors. We wanted a nice, quiet place."

Tony nodded. "Understood, sir. All's quiet."

"Check in with me before you leave."

"Yes, sir."

Trevor's Mustang followed the driveway to the main cabin. He unloaded the car while Ady explored the house. He found Dani lost in thought on the deck and walked up behind her and blew in her ear. She whirled around with her hand ready to strike. "You scared me. I almost used some of those defensive moves Jared taught me."

Trevor chuckled. "I'll make more noise next time." He pointed to the cabin. "Ady's wanting to claim a bedroom."

She stepped inside the cabin but looked at the white rug and then at her shoes. "Should I take them off?"

"No, you're fine," he said, then called out, "Ady, can you come over here."

While waiting for Ady, Dani looked up and spun around. The entire back wall consisted of floor-to-ceiling windows with a majestic view of the pond. A balcony with several doors overlooked the great room. "Wow, Jana wasn't kidding. This place is no more a cabin than I am an Olympic gymnast. There's so much room we could go for weeks and never see each other."

"Yeah. You and Ady will be upstairs. Tony and I will stay in the bunk room off the kitchen."

Ady ran into the living room. "I'm here."

Trevor knelt down. "Let's figure out where you'll sleep. Would you like your own room, or would you like to share with Dani?"

She grabbed Dani's hand as an answer.

Trevor swept Ady up onto his shoulders. "Okay, let's go up to the really big room."

He galloped into the master bedroom and gently tossed the little girl onto the soft, quilt-covered bed. Her giggles warmed his heart. *Little girls should be laughing and playing, not crying because their father just disappeared.* He glanced at Dani. *I wouldn't mind hearing* her *laughter the rest of my life, either.* He briefly entertained the idea of the three of them as a family, but forcefully thrust it away. *Ady needs her daddy, and I will move heaven and earth to bring him home.*

"Oooh. These blankets are so soft!" Ady rubbed a fuzzy red throw against her cheek.

Trevor picked her up, blanket and all. "Ready to eat?"

"Yes!" She nodded emphatically.

"What do you want to eat?"

Her grin exploded. "Chicken nuggets and french fries."

Trevor laughed. "Chicken nuggets and fries it is. I'm sure glad I thought ahead to buy some."

Ady spread her arms wide. "With lots and lots of ketchup."

"Did you hear that, Dani? Heavy on the ketchup."

Dani saluted. "Got it."

§

After washing and putting away the dishes, Trevor hoisted Ady onto his shoulders and raced Dani into the living room.

Ady threw her arms in the air. "We won! We won!"

Trevor set her on the floor. "Want to help me build a fire?"

Dani knelt in front of her. "Or do you want to help *me* build a fire?"

Looking between the two adults, Ady placed her index finger on her chin and swayed back and forth. "I. Choose. Uhhh . . . Dani."

Dani threw her arms in the air and yelled, "I won! I won!"

Trevor gave a deep bow and sat in the chair to watch.

"Okay, let's start by putting these logs right next to each other on the bottom." Dani held out a split log.

With the greatest of care, Ady pushed the larger logs together until there was no space between them.

"Perfect," Dani said. "Now put these smaller logs across the other way."

Trevor rose and looked over Dani's shoulder. "Uh, I think you might have this a little backward."

"Excuse me." Dani crossed her arms and glared. "Who's making this fire?"

Ady crossed her arms too. "Excuse me?"

"All right. All right." He raised his hands in surrender. "Since I'm not needed here, I'll go to the kitchen and drown my sorrows by eating something yummy."

Ady erupted in contagious giggles.

Trevor reached down and captured her. He threw her up in the air, and she laughed even harder. When he caught her, he gave her a hug. "I'm so glad you came up here with us." His voice lowered to a whisper. "I've got a surprise in the kitchen and I'll bring it out after you're done with the fire." He put his finger to his mouth. "Shh. Don't tell Dani."

Ady mirrored his gesture. "Shh."

Trevor put Ady down and said, "Dani, make sure the fire is going strong by the time I get back."

She huffed. "Would you like to try that again?"

"What I meant to say was, 'I would appreciate it if you would build up the fire by the time I come back from the kitchen."

"Apology accepted. What do you think, Ady? Should we do what he says, or should we put the fire out?"

"Make it big!" She spread her arms wide and jumped around the room.

"Now that we're alone"—Dani's voice rose at the last word, assuring Trevor could hear her from the kitchen—"we'll continue. Take these small logs and put them across the top."

After trying unsuccessfully to arrange the crooked logs, Ady moaned, "Daddy never built a fire like this."

"Apparently, Mr. Willis hasn't, either. Now use these shingles and let's tear up this newspaper."

"Should I crush it?"

"Just a little, Ady. Then we'll put it on top."

Ady layered the newspaper on top. "Now do we light it?"

"Almost, sweetie. Let's put these small pieces of wood right there."

"Okay, is it ready now?" Ady raised her shoulders and let them fall with a huff.

"Not quite. Do you see that metal handle in there?"

"Uh-huh."

"Pull it down."

Ady reached into the fireplace and pulled as hard as she could. "I can't do it."

"Here, let me help." With both of them pulling, the damper finally moved. "Now we're ready." Dani looked around the room. "Can you take that newspaper and roll it up like a log?"

Ady folded the newspaper in half and rolled it into a stick as crooked as the natural logs. "I'm not good at this."

"It's perfect for the fire," Dani assured her. "Now let me light this match."

"Wow, that's big."

"Yes, Mr. Willis doesn't do anything small." Dani struck the match and lit the newspaper roll on fire. "Now, hold my hand and stick it up the chimney. Let's count to ten."

They both started the count. "One, two, three, four, five, six, seven, eight, nine, ten."

"Now, let's light the fire."

The flames devoured the paper, and the kindling caught fire. "Do you want to throw some newspaper balls on top to make it a little hotter?"

"Uh-huh." Concentration showed in Ady's features and she crumpled each sheet of newspaper into a sphere. Then she and Dani tossed them onto the fledgling flames. Ady squealed when the logs started to burn.

"Is that fire ready?" Trevor called from the kitchen.

"Ready for what?" Dani turned to Ady. "Do you know what he's up to?"

Ady clapped her hands over her mouth and snickered.

"Look what I brought," Trevor announced as he entered the room.

Ady clapped her hand. "I love s'mores."

"Dani, can you get those sticks?" He pointed. "Over there. On the side of the fireplace."

She grabbed the marshmallow forks and gave them to him.

His hand lingered on hers for a moment. Her breath caught and she lowered her eyes.

"Great job on the fire. I was worried since fire-building wasn't on your résumé, and when I saw the way you started . . ."

"Oh, I have a lot of talents that aren't on my résumé." Dani wiggled her eyebrows.

Trevor met her gaze. "I can't wait to find out what they are."

"Can I do two marshmallows at the same time?" Ady's voice broke in.

Trevor coughed. "I'll bet we could even do four."

"No. Two's just right."

"Let's put it over the fire." He guided her hand. "If you keep it there just above the fire and turn it carefully, you'll end up with the perfect golden brown toasted marshmallow."

"Oooh. Yummy."

Dani took her spot in front of the hearth and plunged her marshmallow directly into the fire. It erupted into flames, and she pulled it out and blew on it. "Mine's done." She slid the blackened blob off the fork and onto her Reese's Peanut Butter Cup–topped graham cracker and covered it with the other square.

Ady and Trevor stared at her with open mouths.

Trevor broke the silence. "I can't believe you just did that."

"Did what?" Dani took a bite of her treat and tried to speak with her mouth full. "Used a peanut butter cup instead of a Hershey bar?"

"No. You burned the marshmallow to a crisp."

Ady looked at her own toasted marshmallow. "Daddy says you never, never, ever, ever set a marshmallow on fire."

"Well, that way takes too long," Dani replied. "I don't want to wait."

Trevor shook his head. Ady mimicked him. "Shall we show her the error of her ways?" he said.

Ady's head bobbed up and down. "Yes."

"Let's put yours together first, then I'll make a special one for Dani. What kind of chocolate do you want?"

She grabbed a blue-wrapped one. "Crunch bar."

Ady munched on her treat while Trevor demonstrated the fine art of marshmallow roasting. He handed Dani the perfect s'more and watched as she took a bite. A marshmallow string stuck on her chin. "Oh, this is so good," she said. "I never knew the center was supposed to melt like this. Now, let me make you one."

Dani attempted to gently toast the marshmallow, but finally gave up and caught it on fire. After she blew it out the flame, she squished the marshmallow between the chocolate and graham crackers. "Sorry. Perfect takes too long."

"In more things than marshmallows," Trevor muttered.

Dani wiped the chocolate off Ady's face and declared, "I think it just might be bath time."

"Do I have to?" Ady whined.

Trevor smiled. "Yes, you do."

When he reached for her, she threw herself on the ground, squirming and screaming. "I don't want to go to bed!"

Trevor gave Dani a pleading look. "That's okay, Ady," she said. "Maybe I'll go ahead and use that bubble bath upstairs." She stood and walked toward the stairs.

Ady's fit stopped.

"It has Anna and Elsa on the bottle. I can't figure out why he'd use girl bubble bath." Dani lifted her eyebrows in a question to Trevor.

"Hey." He held up his hands. "I'd do anything for my niece—including keeping bubble bath on hand."

"Ady, who do you think the bubble bath is for?"

Giggles exploded from Ady. "Mr. Willis."

Trevor's mock anger brought more spasms of laughter from Ady, and he reached out to tickle the little girl who had wormed her way into his heart.

Fourteen

Dani padded down the stairs in her bare feet with her frog-patterned fleece blanket wrapped around her shoulders. "Ady's asleep on the sofa in the bedroom."

Trevor watched the flames in the fireplace. "Good. I want to talk to you about something. When we were first coming up here, I was going to have you stay here, and I would stay at the lodge, but Ady's changed that."

"Go on," Dani said.

"I don't know what's happened to Bruce, and I don't know if someone is searching for Ady."

"I've wondered the same thing."

"I can't be a quarter of a mile away at the lodge. I have to stay here to protect her." Trevor got up and stood in front of the fireplace. "Are you okay staying upstairs with Ady while I stay down here? Like I said, Tony will bunk in there with me."

Dani nodded. "Of course. I'm fine with that."

Trevor let out the breath he'd been holding. "Thank you. Let's sit down and enjoy this fire you built."

"What happens if Ady's dad doesn't make it back?"

Trevor leaned his elbows on his knees and cradled his head in this hands. "I don't know. I can't bear the thought of her losing another parent."

Dani stared into the fire. "Do you know what she said when I asked her who her favorite sister in *Frozen* was?"

"No. My niece likes Elsa."

"Ady likes Anna."

"There's nothing wrong with that," Trevor said quietly.

Dani wiped a tear from the corner of her eye. "She likes her because she found a way to be happy after her mommy and daddy died."

Trevor stood up and faced away from Dani. "She's lost so much already."

"Have you noticed she doesn't talk about her dad much?"

"Now that you mention it, you're right."

Dani frowned. "She thinks he's dead."

"You don't know that."

"Actually, I do. Ady told me."

Trevor paced the rug in front of the couch. "I'll get in touch with Don and see what they've found out. We'll move on from there."

Dani got up and reached out to touch Trevor's arm. "What if Bruce doesn't come back?"

Trevor sat the couch again. "Apparently, he thought he might not. He filed paperwork with an attorney to make me Ady's legal guardian if anything happened to him."

Dani sat next to him. "Oh no, Trevor."

He put his arm around her and she leaned into his shoulder. They watched the fire die down to a soft glow.

§

The next morning, Trevor stood in the living room with a cell phone to his ear. "Have you got any more information about Bruce's abduction?"

"There are no clues and no ransom demands," Don replied, his frustration evident. "It's like he disappeared into thin air. I'm perplexed."

"Could it have anything to do with the Morales case? Could this be an attempt to flush me out?"

"I've checked, but there doesn't seem to be any connection. We're out of leads."

Trevor leaned against the fireplace. "We've got to figure out what's going on. This little girl has already lost her mom, Don. Imagine if it were Emy."

"I imagine that every day," Don said quietly. "I worry about what would happen if I weren't around to take care of Traci and the kids."

"I'm sorry, Don. It's just . . . well, Ady has wiggled her way into my heart."

"I understand. Speaking of business, I'll need you back in three weeks. Remember the new agent Zack was worried about?"

"Yes. Did you manage to get any info on him?"

"I found out the left hand over here doesn't know what the right hand is doing."

Trevor let out a dry chuckle. "You just realized that? You're talking in riddles, Don. Just say it."

"Larry Preston was sent to prepare the case against Morales and make sure nothing went wrong. He's an attorney. He wanted to find out information before anyone knew who he was. The brass didn't bother telling me that. Instead, they let me think he was a new agent."

"Okay," Trevor said, drawing out the word. "Do you trust your information?"

"It came directly from Lee Evans. I've also managed to slip someone in as a double agent. He—"

Trevor interrupted. "Don, I've got to go. Dani and Ady are coming. Bye." He turned and watched them hop down the stairs. This time, the frog blanket was around Ady's shoulders.

"How are my two girls this morning?" Trevor twirled Ady around, then picked up Dani and spun her.

She laughed as he let her down. "What are you doing?"

"Just wishing the two most beautiful women in the room a good morning."

Ady was grinning. "Do it again, Mr. Willis."

He picked her up and said in a grave voice, "Ady, I think we have a problem."

The little girls eyes opened wide and filled with tears. "Wh–what?"

"Don't cry, sweetheart." He bopped her nose with his finger. "We just need to figure out what you're going to call me. I feel so old when you call me Mr. Willis."

"Uh-huh."

"What do you think?"

"How about Trouble?" Dani suggested.

Ady giggled. "That's silly. No one is called Trouble."

"Thanks, Ady. It's nice to have someone on my side. What do you think you should call me?"

"What do other kids call you?"

"My nieces and nephews call me Uncle Trevor."

"No." Ady shook her head. "Did your mommy call you something when you were little?"

"Hmm, let me think." Trevor cradled his chin between his thumb and forefinger, tapping the index finger as he thought. "I know. When I was around your age, my mom called me Crash."

Ady put her hands out to the side. "That's silly—just like Trouble."

"Wow, talk about ammunition if I ever need to bribe you." Dani laughed. "How in the world did you get a nickname like that?"

He pointed at her. "No more teasing or you'll never find out why."

Ady and Dani clamped their hands over their mouths. "We're sworn to secrecy." Dani answered through her hand in a smothered whisper.

Ady unclamped her hand. "I'll never tell anyone. Not even if they tickle me till I cry."

Trevor glanced around the room, making sure the door was closed and the corners contained no lurkers.

"What are you looking for, Trevor?" Dani asked. "We're alone."

"Okay, but this doesn't leave the room. *Capiche?*"

Ady's face scrunched up. "Huh?"

Trevor bent to her level. "It means 'understand?'"

"Will you just tell us?" Dani blurted.

"Okay, okay. When I was little, I would run straight ahead while looking backward. I ran into a few walls."

Dani tried to stifle a laugh, but it burst from her lips.

"It was kind of reinforced when I took up juggling," Trevor explained. "Things didn't always land in my hands—especially my mom's good china."

Ady's eyes went wide. "Your mommy must've been mad."

"Fortunately, she could never stay too angry when I smiled." Trevor winked at the little girl.

Tony's vehicle pulled into the driveway. When he got to the front door, Trevor opened it. "Tony. Come on in."

Instead of his guard uniform, today Tony wore a casual shirt and faded jeans with holes at the knees. "I'm ready to get to work on the camp today, boss."

Trevor closed the front door behind Tony. "Thanks for helping out. Do you want to join us for breakfast?"

"I ate, but that was an hour or two ago. Maybe I'll have something. I got my stuff to move into the bunk room today." Tony looked down when Ady tugged on his shirt.

She gazed up at him. "Mr. Tony?"

"Just Tony."

"Mr. Willis says I can call him Crash now. He used to crash into walls and drop his mommy's plates."

"Ady!" Trevor said sternly.

She looked at him with wide eyes. "We're still in the room."

Dani laughed. "You did say it stayed in this room."

"Mr. Willis, I'm sorry." Ady's lower lip trembled.

He picked her up and hugged her. "It's okay. Don't cry." He wiped away her tears. "It'll be fine. Tony won't tell anyone, 'cause he knows who pays his salary." Trevor sent a stern look to his chief of security.

"No problem, boss." Tony put up his hands. "At least until I see the rest of the guys," he mumbled under his breath.

Everyone walked out onto the back deck. Trevor carried a tray of assorted pastries, Tony brought juice and milk, and Dani held paper plates and a bag of plastic cups. Ady skipped ahead with her own little box of donut holes.

Dani rubbed her arms and shivered. "Brrr. It's sure a lot colder than it looks. I'm getting my jacket."

"It'll warm up in an hour or two." Trevor swung Ady and her donut holes onto his shoulder. "You couldn't ask for a more beautiful morning."

Tony grabbed a couple of cushions and placed them on Ady's chair. "Thanks, Tony, and thanks for the donut holes," she said. She stepped next to him and motioned for him to come down to her level. "You can have one if you want."

He picked a chocolate glazed bite and threw it in the air and caught it his mouth. "Thank you. It was delicious."

"You forgot the prayer," Ady chided him.

Tony bent down. "I'll open my mouth while you say it."

"Okay." She waited for Dani to sit down and said a simple prayer, blessing the food and asking for her daddy to be safe.

Trevor took a bite of buttered croissant. "Tony, can you check the perimeter of the camp and make sure no animals broke down any fences last winter?"

"Sure, boss."

He reached out and touched her hand. "Dani, I'd like to take you around the camp so you can get the lay of the land."

She pulled her hand away, yet still cradled the spot he touched. "Okay. Will Ady come with us?"

"Uh-huh." Ady sidled up to Dani.

Trevor stood behind the girls with a hand on Dani's shoulder. He pointed with his other arm. "See the dock out there?"

Ady nodded. "Uh-huh."

"Would you like to take the boat across to the camp?"

She jumped up and down. "Yes! Yes! Can we?"

Dani chuckled. "Of course."

Fifteen

The trees surrounding the cabin almost made it look like a treehouse. The sun filtered through the leaves, creating a world of swaying shadows. A person could almost believe in fairies. But Trevor searched the landscape for something much more menacing.

Tony headed out in front of them, pointing out birds and flowers. When they reached the dock on the pond, Trevor, Dani, and Ady got into the boat.

"I'm gonna check the trail and make sure there are no obstructions," Tony said after he pushed the boat off. "See you on the other side, Crash."

"You better watch out, Tony," Trevor called out.

Tony's laughter faded into the woods. Trevor pulled the oars through the water with strong, steady strokes. "We could have canoes on the pond for the kids at the camp."

"I like that idea," Dani agreed.

Once they arrived at the dock, he secured the boat to the post and lifted Ady out. He turned to help Dani. She had one foot on the dock on the other in the boat.

"Dani!" He grabbed for her hand just as her momentum pushed the craft farther out into the water.

With a shriek, she fell into the muddy pond. Trevor fished her out and pulled her onto the deck. He embraced her and whispered, "You're fine. Everything's fine."

She pushed away and made a feeble attempt to brush off the water and mud. "Are you trying to drown me?"

"What? You're the one who pushed the boat away with your foot."

"I d–did n–not," Dani stuttered as spasms of cold shook her body.

"Look at you, you're freezing." Trevor pulled off his sweatshirt and wrapped it around her. "Tony!"

The security chief barreled through the trees, reaching them quickly. "What's wrong?" He turned in every direction as if assessing a threat.

"Everything's okay. Just a little accident. I'm taking Dani back to the cabin to get warmed up. Can you take Ady to the camp and show her around?"

"Sure thing, boss."

"I'll get in first, then you help her, Tony." Trevor stepped into the rowboat.

With her teeth chattering, all Dani managed was a shaky nod. Once Trevor was situated in the boat, Tony attempted to pick up Dani. "No, I just need a hand," she told him. He held her arm and steadied her with one hand on her back while she stepped with wobbly legs into the boat.

By the time they reached the other side of the pond, Dani's lips were blue and she shivered uncontrollably. Trevor secured the boat and picked her up, but she wiggled and kicked. "I'm not an invalid. I can w–walk."

"Well, at least all that kicking will warm you up a little," he mumbled under his breath.

"W–what did y–you say?"

"Nothing. Let me help you." He put his arm around her waist. Halfway to the cabin, Dani's legs gave out, so he lifted her and carried her inside. He climbed the stairs and set her down in the master bathroom. He flicked the switch for the ceiling heat lamp and helped her out of his sweatshirt and her jacket.

"Get out of your wet clothes and wrap yourself in this," Trevor urged, handing her a clean white blanket before he started running warm water into the jetted tub. He turned around and she hadn't moved. "Dani, come on. Do you need help?"

"N–no!"

He wrapped the blanket around her and rubbed her arms. "Come on, Dani, we need to get you warmed up. I don't want to leave you alone." He grabbed the *Frozen* bubble bath from the cupboard and poured some into the tub, then turned on the jets. Desperate, he removed the blanket and threw it in the shower, then placed Dani, fully clothed, into the filling tub. "I'll wait here until you're warm."

"I think the shivering has stopped," she said a few minutes later.

"Let me get you a towel." He opened the cabinet. "It looks like I need to grab some from the laundry room. How many did you use last night?"

"Just enough to dry off, turban our hair, and wipe the floor."

"I get it. This is a spa now, not the men's locker room it used to be." Trevor chuckled. When Dani didn't respond, he said, "Okay, so wait right here and I'll grab some towels and your clothes."

"Trevor?"

He paused at the door.

"I'm sorry for yelling at you," Dani said softly.

Trevor grinned. "It's okay. I'm sure I'll do something in the near future to deserve it."

Several minutes later, he returned with two warm-from-the-dryer towels. "Will two be enough?"

"Plenty."

"Let me know if you need any help." Trevor winked.

Dani threw a wet mesh scrubber at him. "I can do it myself." Trevor dodged the projectile and said, "I'll be downstairs."

A minute later, he adjusted the frequency on the radio and called into the microphone, "Tony. Are you there?"

"Sure thing, boss."

"Just letting you know Dani has thawed out and is fine."

"Ady's been worried."

"What's she doing?"

"Swinging on the hammock I put up in front of the lodge."

"Is everything quiet?"

"Not a creature is stirring, except the mouse that took up residency in Cabin 4."

Laughter carried across the connection. "I thought I saw a receipt for a mouse trap in your expense report."

"Well, I came face to face with Squeaky when I went to set the trap."

"Squeaky?"

"Did I say Squeaky? I meant Fang. He threatened to haunt my dreams, so I let him live to save future campers from a ghost mouse."

"Wow, I'm impressed. You took one for the team."

"Yes, sir."

"I'm about to start lunch so please bring Ady back over to the cabin."

"Sure thing. Be there in a few minutes."

"See you then. Thanks for watching out for her."

"Glad to do it," Tony said before Trevor replaced the microphone on its stand.

Trevor heard Dani's weak voice calling his name. He walked into the living room, where she sat on the couch. "I'm right here. How are you feeling?"

"Drained, but not drowned," she replied. "That's good."

"You scared me." He joined her, then brushed her lips with his and held her in his arms. "I've gotten used to having you around."

After a minute, Dani pulled back and leaned up to kiss him. "I've grown pretty attached to you too, Trevor. Now we'd better get back to Ady."

"She's coming in for lunch right now." He kissed Dani's cheek. "You sit here and rest a bit."

Dani leaned back on the sofa and stretched her arms over her head. "You know, this is what I've always wished for—a man to draw my bath and cook for me. Do you do foot rubs? Back rubs?"

"I do give foot and back rubs." He knelt down in front of the couch and started working on her foot. "I'm better at calling for take-out than I am at cooking, and I'd love to draw your bath anytime. Pencil or watercolors?"

Dani chortled. "You make me laugh."

He stood up and brushed her cheek. "I hope you'll always feel that way." He paused a moment before turning toward the kitchen. "I better go get lunch ready for the troops."

Before Trevor could leave the room, the big, tough, muscled security chief galloped onto the deck with a giggling little girl perched on his shoulders.

"Giddy-up!" Ady shouted.

"Neigh, neigh." Tony slid the door open and bucked Ady off onto the soft couch.

"You're a good pony, Tony," Ady crowed. "You might be even better than Crash."

Trevor straightened his shoulders and put his hands on his hips. "Hey, you told me I was the best pony."

Ady snickered and peeked around Tony. "You can try to be the best pony again."

With a quick movement, Trevor snatched Ady into his arms and placed her on his shoulders. He cantered around the house and into the kitchen. "Now, who do you think is the best pony?"

"You!"

He lifted her off his shoulders and plopped her down on the kitchen stool.

Ady swirled back and forth on the stool and offered Trevor an impish grin. "And Mr. Tony, too!"

He tickled her. "You are so silly."

"Uh-huh!"

§

Dani watched Trevor gallop into the kitchen. Warmth radiated outward from the pit of her stomach, and she held onto the back of the couch to steady her wobbly legs.

"Feeling lightheaded?" Tony interrupted her thoughts.

Dani shook her head. "I must have tripped on the rug."

"He's crazy about you too."

"I . . . I don't know what you're talking about." She started up the stairs. "I need to clean up the bathroom."

Sixteen

Dani watched through the lodge window as Ady swung back and forth on one of the tire swings Tony had hung in the camp. This wasn't your run-of-the-mill, donut-shaped model. Precise cuts had been made in the original tire until it resembled a horse.

Tony pushed the swing higher and higher before slipping under the pony and rider. He walked the few paces to the lodge.

Ady laughed and shouted, "Giddy up!"

"What a great idea," Dani said to Trevor, who stood next to her. "I wonder where Tony found them."

"A guy at church makes them. I thought they'd be great over here.

"What he didn't tell you"—Tony clomped his feet on the mat before he entered the lodge—"is now that man has an offer from a major playground supplier."

"Tony," Trevor warned.

"And it happened just after he got laid off from his job."

Trevor glared at his security chief. "Why don't you check on the mouse in Cabin 4?"

"Okay, boss." Tony winked at Dani, then stepped out the door and called to Ady, "You wanna go see Fang?"

She jumped off her mount and followed him.

Trevor directed Dani's attention to the storage system for the tables. "See, they all push back into the wall. That clears the floor for other activities. Good design, isn't it?"

"Yes, it is," she replied. "But what was Tony trying to say?"

"He likes to point out what he feels are coincidences, but I don't think there are a lot of those in this life. Most of the time, there's probably more of a divine influence than we realize."

"Hmm. So a person who helps someone else is divine?"

"Well, we all have divinity within us. But what I'm saying is that if a person can help someone, whether it be giving a hug, mothering a little girl when her dad is missing, or even having the connections or financial means to help someone, it's not a coincidence that he or she is in the right place at the right time. I believe a loving God uses people to answer prayers."

"How many times have you been in the right place at the right time?" Dani asked.

Trevor shrugged and looked away. "Once or twice."

§

The sun took the chill from the morning air. Dragonflies danced through the reeds surrounding the pond, occasionally flitting across the water's surface. Dani and Trevor swung their feet off the edge of the dock while Ady ran through the grass chasing a monarch butterfly.

"Let's play Twenty Questions." Dani suggested.

Trevor clasped her hand in his. "Okay, I'll go first. What's your favorite food?"

"Cinnamon rolls are my downfall. What about you?"

"Lasagna. I need to have Jana teach me how to make it."

"Maybe I'll learn with you. We can both be domesticated."

Trevor grinned. "Ha! I doubt I'll ever be domestic. I have another question for you."

"Wait a minute. Isn't it my turn?"

"No. You asked about my favorite food. Now I get to ask you." He squeezed her hand. "Are you starting to fall in love with me?"

Dani's jaw dropped and her face and ears turned crimson. "I . . . I . . ."

Ady interrupted with a quiet, but urgent summons. "Crash, Dani, come see."

Dani jumped up immediately and Trevor followed close behind. Ady held her hand up to reveal a monarch butterfly resting on her index finger. Trevor eased his phone from his pocket and took a picture. Seconds later, the butterfly flew off over the meadow.

"He must have felt safe," Dani said.

"So, what's the answer to my question?" Trevor probed. "Are you falling in love with me?"

"Uh, well, I. . . " Dani looked around for an escape.

Just then, Trevor's phone rang. He looked at the screen, mouthed "Sorry" to Dani, then turned away and held his hand over his free ear. "Willis."

Ady tugged on Dani's shirt. "I know the answer. Can I tell him?"

"No!"

"But you love him." Ady scrunched her shoulders. "Right?"

Dani knelt down to her level and put her finger to her lips. "This can be our secret."

Ady mimicked the gesture. "Our secret."

Trevor held out his cell, his features grave. "It's Jared."

Dani took the phone and spoke into it. "What's wrong?"

"We tried to call your cell," Jared said tightly.

"There's no reception up here. What's wrong?"

Her brother drew in a breath. "Dad's had a heart attack."

Dani's heart plummeted. "How is he?"

"He's stable. Mom wants us there."

"Yes, of course. I'll get there as soon as possible."

"I can take you right away," Trevor whispered in Dani's ear.

The tremor in her hands reached her voice as she told Jared, "Trevor can bring me."

"Good, you'll get there faster. Drive safe."

"We will." She almost disconnected the call but heard her brother's voice.

"And, Sis? Everything will be fine."

As soon as she handed the phone back to Trevor, he knelt down to Ady's level. "Ady, Dani's daddy is sick and we need to take her to see him. When we get back to the cabin, can you run upstairs and grab what you'll need for a few days?"

"Can I bring toys?"

He tousled her hair. "Of course, sweetie. Let's be out of here in twenty minutes."

Ady grabbed Dani's hand. Trevor was making arrangements on the phone as they headed up the hill.

§

Ady fell asleep while coloring. Her head rested against the door, and a crayon dangled from her relaxed right hand. Dani leaned her elbow on the armrest and chewed on her pinkie nail. Trevor reached behind her and massaged her neck.

"Tell me about your dad," he said softly.

She leaned forward and rubbed her knees with her palms. "I can't remember a time when he wasn't there. He was at every gymnastics meet, softball game, and all of Jared's football games. He attended every school function we performed in." A sigh escaped. "One of the things I remember about my childhood was my dad's love for the stars. We had an observation deck above our garage. He would wake us up at all hours of the night to show us meteor showers or lunar eclipses."

"He sounds like a great father."

"Oh, you need to take the next exit. I didn't realize we were so close." She sat up and began directing Trevor to the hospital. "I forgot to tell you. Jared texted. He wants your help to give Dad a blessing."

Trevor stared at Dani. "Are you serious? I don't know how."

"Look out! Keep your eyes on the road."

He steered the car back into the correct lane. "I've only had the priesthood for a couple of weeks."

Ady woke up and asked if everything was okay.

"Everything's fine," Trevor told her. "I just had to change lanes quickly. We're almost there."

"Don't worry, Jared will help you with the blessing," Dani said, then continued navigating.

Soon they pulled into the hospital parking garage. A minute later, a nurse at the information desk directed them to the ICU. Trevor picked up Ady and held Dani's hand. The closer they got to her father's room, the slower she moved.

"I'm afraid." She tightened her grip on his hand.

"Hey, I'm right here with you."

Dani's mother caught sight of her in the hallway and hurried out to embrace her. "I'm so glad you're here, Dani."

"How is he?" Dani's words came out a whisper.

"He's doing surprisingly well. The doctors are talking about releasing him in a few days."

"Thank heavens." Dani hugged her mom again.

"Only one or two people are allowed to visit him at a time," her mom explained. "Do you want to go in and see him after you introduce me to your friends?"

"Sorry! Ady and Trevor, this is my mom, Angela Carpenter."

Angela said hello to Ady, then shook Trevor's hand. "I haven't heard anything about you from Dani, but I sure have from Jared and Jana. It's nice to finally meet you."

Dani blushed. "Mom, please."

"Oh, honey. You go in and see your father while I get to know these two a little better." Angela urged Dani toward the room.

Dani pushed the door open and peeked anxiously behind the curtain. The tubes leading from her father to the beeping machines made the big man look so small and pale. She wiped the moisture from her eyes and spoke. "Dad?"

"Dani girl? Come over here. I'm so glad you came." He raised the bed so she could give him a kiss. "Is Jared coming?"

"Yes, he'll be here soon. How are you feeling?"

"Like I was run over by a Mack truck. They found a blockage and put in a couple of stents. I'm grateful to be alive."

"Me too, Dad. Me too." Dani pulled his hand to her face and kissed it.

"Now, I've been hearing rumors about someone who might be interested in my little girl. Tell me about this man who makes you blush like that."

Dani put her hands up to feel the heat in her cheeks. "I seem to be doing that a lot lately. I plan on exacting some sisterly revenge on Jared." She pulled the straight-backed chair closer to the bed. "Trevor is my boss."

"Oh, one of those thoroughly modern girls from the twenties who marry their bosses."

"Dad! I've been fighting it."

He reached for her hand. "Just because the last guy turned out to be a jerk doesn't mean they all will. Is he a good man?"

"Yes, he is. He does a lot for other people." She stood and paced the small floor space before sitting again. "He dropped everything and drove me all the way up here."

"Hmm. How does he treat you?"

"Like gold. He is a gentleman and he's funny. He laughs at my jokes."

Ben laughed. "I've heard your jokes. If he laughs at them, he must be crazy about you—or just plain crazy."

"Thanks a lot, Dad," Dani said, but she couldn't help smiling. He stroked her hair. "I can see you're falling for him."

She sighed. "I am. And it scares me."

"Just follow your heart. It'll lead you where you need to go." Ben's eyelids began to droop. "I think I'll just rest a bit."

"I'll be right here." Dani kissed his forehead and watched him sleep.

When Jared arrived, she walked out and slugged him on the arm. "You've been spreading rumors."

"Ouch. I'm not spreading rumors, just telling the truth. How is Dad?"

"He's resting."

Jared pulled Trevor aside and said, "Are you good with helping me give him a priesthood blessing."

"I've never done that before. What if I mess up? Will that negate the effects of the blessing? Is there someone else?"

"Just you and me. And don't worry, I'll walk you through it."

"You've got this, Trevor." Dani looked in her father's room. Ady was kneeling on the chair by the bed.

"Hello, who are you?" Ben asked.

"I'm Ady. I know who you are. You're Dani's daddy."

"Yes, I am."

"No one can find my daddy. Crash and Dani take care of me. Crash says he's going to find my daddy." Ady lowered her voice to a whisper. "Dani loves Crash, but shh." She put her fingers to her lips. "He's not supposed to know."

At that, Dani sneaked up behind her and grabbed her shoulders. "Who is telling all my secrets?"

"I didn't tell Crash." Ady's bottom lip trembled.

Dani kissed the top of her head and hugged her shoulders. "It's okay. I'll tell him someday."

"What are you going to tell me?" Trevor asked Dani.

"Oh, nothing. Just that there's a hole in your shirt. Are you guys ready to give him a blessing?"

Trevor looked down at his shirt. "Where?"

"Right there, where you head goes through," Dani said, laughing.

The men stood on either side of the bed as Jared coached Trevor in the mechanics of giving a priesthood blessing. Then Jared finished his part.

When Trevor moved into the hallway, Dani squeezed his hand. "Good job, Crash."

She pulled everyone together in the ICU waiting room. A nurse joined them and said, "With all his medications, he'll be sleeping through the night. You might all want to go home and get some rest."

Angela shook her head. "I don't want to leave him."

Trevor stepped up. "I have a suggestion. Why don't you all get some rest and I'll stay here with Angela. That way, you'll be fresh in the morning."

"Are you okay with that, Mom?" Jared put his arm around Angela.

She looked at her son and daughter, then at Trevor before nodding her head. "That would be good. You go and get a good night's rest. I'd like to get to know this young man better anyway.

The next morning, the doctors pronounced Ben out of trouble. Trevor brought Angela home to get some rest while he slept soundly on the couch. He and Ady left for the cabin, and Jared promised to bring Dani back there when their father was settled at home. Before Trevor left, he gave Dani a quick kiss. She didn't object.

Seventeen

Trevor and Ady sat in the lounge chairs on the deck off the master bedroom. With every noise, she jumped up and ran to look over the railing to see if Dani was home yet.

"She's home. She's home." Ady jumped up and down with excitement.

"It's only been a couple of days," Trevor said, but inside he was just as excited as Ady.

She grabbed a picture she had drawn for Dani, and the two ran downstairs and waited. When the door opened, Ady ran with her picture and jumped into Dani's arms, nearly knocking her over. Dani whirled her around, then let Ady down and met Trevor's gaze.

"I drew this for you. Do you like it?"

Dani looked at the picture. "I love it, sweetie. Thank you. Can you hang it on the fridge?" Her gaze drifted back to Trevor.

"Welcome back," he said, then gathered her in his arms and kissed the top of her head.

"It feels like I'm coming home."

"Hello?" Jared interrupted. He was pulling a couple of suitcases behind him. "Last time I checked, Sis, this wasn't your house."

Trevor released Dani and said, "Jana and Jared, come on in."

Jana gave Trevor a quick hug. "Ben is doing really well. He's not going to be down long."

"I have soup in a slow cooker for dinner," Trevor said. "I assume you'll be spending the night."

Jana and Jared exchanged a look before he answered, "Yes, that would be nice."

Trevor smiled. "Ady, can you take Jared and Jana to their room? It's the one across from the bathroom."

"Uh-huh." She ran to the stairs. "Come on."

Jana and Jared headed up with their luggage, and Trevor embraced Dani again. "I missed you," he said before he kissed her. "I missed you too. Thanks for all you did for my family. I appreciate it. Dad is doing great."

"I'm glad. I have a surprise for you." Trevor wiggled his eyebrows.

"What is it?"

"If I told you, it wouldn't be a surprise. And besides, you can't see it until dark."

Dani shook her head. "You are such a mysterious man." She headed upstairs to make sure Jana and Jared got settled.

After sunset, the group made their way down to the lodge. As they entered the building Trevor whistled, and the lights turned out. Dani glanced up and gasped. He had painted the entire ceiling. The light from the stars shimmered from a navy-blue sky.

"I can't believe you did this." She turned around and admired the painted night sky.

Trevor stuffed his hands in his pockets. "It was nothing. Just a little paint."

"There's Orion, and the Big Dipper and North Star," Dani exclaimed, pointing at the constellations.

"It points true north." Trevor stood behind her and placed his hands on her shoulders.

She leaned back. "Wow, you have my favorite, Cassiopeia."

Jana pulled up some music on her phone. Frank Sinatra's voice filled the room, singing "Fly Me to the Moon."

Trevor held his hand out to Dani. "Would you like to dance?" He spun her into a foxtrot. Ady giggled as Tony appeared and twirled around the room with her. Jared and Jana joined in. After dancing for a while, they headed for the cabin. Ady fell asleep in Trevor's arms on the way, so he carried her up to bed. Then he and Dani walked down the hall, holding hands.

At the door he faced her. "I better leave."

"Just a minute. I wanted to thank you for everything," she said softly. "I have an answer to the question you asked several days ago." She paused. "The answer is no. I'm not falling in love with you."

Trevor's smile fell and he started to turn away, but Dani's quiet voice pulled him back around. "I'm already there, Trevor."

His smile returned. He picked her up and spun her around. "Woo—"

She put a finger to his lips. "Shh. Ady's sleeping."

He put Dani down and clamped his hand over his mouth. "Sorry." He leaned down to kiss her. Just before his lips met hers, he whispered, "I love you."

Eighteen

Dani and Ady followed Trevor as he brought the last suitcase downstairs. Ady turned back and sighed. "I don't want to go."

"Me neither," Dani said. "Even though we've only been here for three weeks, it feels like home and I'll miss it."

Ady looked up at her. "Are you going to miss Crash?"

Dani blushed. "I . . . I . . ."

"I saw him kiss you." She little girl swayed from side to side, giggling.

"Were you spying when you should've been in bed?"

"Uh-huh." Ady stood on her tiptoes, and Dani knelt down. "I don't mind. I like him lots," Ady whispered in her ear.

Trevor swooped up Ady and threw her in the air. "What's this I hear about you spying on us? I may have to recommend you for a job with the FBI." He set her on the floor again.

"Do you have to leave, Crash?"

"Yeah, I have to go. Hopefully, the trial will be quick and I'll be back soon."

"I'll pray for you right after I pray for Daddy."

Warmth filled Trevor's chest. "Thank you. I'll need it."

Ady jumped into his arms. "Come back safe—pleeease?"

"I will, sweetie. I will. Tony will take you and Dani to Portland to get her car. Then he'll follow you to Jared's house by the ocean. Tony will stick around to make sure you have enough Lucky Charms." Trevor lowered his voice. "Make sure you push him in the water."

Tony's reply floated through the open door. "I heard that!"

Trevor and Ady dragged the suitcases to the car while Dani ran back to grab the cooler. He unlocked his Mustang, pressed the button to open the trunk, and put his keys in his shirt pocket. Ady hopped into the driver's seat to be a race car driver. "Vrroooom, vrrooom. Ady is leading." She swayed and screeched with every turn.

Trevor placed his suitcases in the trunk and felt his keys slip from his pocket. He turned to see if Dani had emerged from the house, when Tony reached up and closed the trunk.

"Hey, wait!"

"What's wrong, boss? I thought everything was in there."

"Yeah, everything's in there—including my keys."

"I'm sorry. Do you have a spare?"

Trevor ran his hand through his hair. "In my suitcase, in the trunk."

"Maybe I can pick the lock?" Tony offered.

"I paid extra to upgrade to one that can't be picked."

Dani stepped out of the house with a cooler in her hand as Ady's car noises continued.

"What are you two doing?" Dani said as she approached.

Trevor tapped the trunk of his car with his knuckles. "Keys are locked inside."

Dani glanced at the trunk. "Too bad I don't have a hairpin. Jared taught me how to pick a lock."

"I wonder." Trevor looked in the window at the back seat. "I wonder if Ady could get the seat down and crawl into the trunk?" He nodded his head. "Let's do it."

They all walked around the car. "Ady, sweetie, my keys are locked inside the trunk. Do you think you could go into the back and find the latch on top of the seat so you can crawl inside?"

Ady looked into the back and then at Trevor. "Uh-huh, but why don't you just press the button?" She pointed to the trunk release.

All three adults stared in silence until Trevor started chuckling. Everyone joined him until they were all laughing hysterically.

Dani finally caught her breath. "'And a little child shall lead them.' Ady, you're smarter than the rest of us."

"I am? I haven't even started school yet."

The laughter started again.

Trevor retrieved his keys, and he and Tony loaded the vehicles. Dani and Ady piled into Tony's SUV. Trevor leaned through the back window and kissed Ady on the forehead. Then he stuck his head through the front passenger window and kissed Dani. He stroked her cheek. "Be careful." She nodded and wiped away a tear.

He walked over to Tony's window. "You're not kissing me," Tony said.

Trevor rolled his eyes. "Take care of my girls, okay?"

"Sure thing, boss." As the window started rolling up, Tony called out, "See ya later, Crash!" He pressed hard on the gas pedal and left his boss in the dust.

Trevor made the two-hour drive to Portland. At the FBI building on Cascade Parkway, he presented his credentials and was ushered to a small, windowless interrogation room. Three chairs surrounded a wooden table. A bright industrial light hung from a cord in the middle of the room. Trevor paced back and forth, checked his watch, and paced again. He sat on the chair and tapped his foot. *It's been fifteen minutes, and I was right on time. This isn't inspiring confidence.*

The door handle jiggled, then stopped. Trevor heard murmured voices in the hall, but couldn't identify the words. He checked his watch again.

Finally, the door opened. Don and another man entered the room. Trevor stood up and growled at his brother-in-law. "I've been in here 26 minutes and 37.9 seconds. What took you so long?"

"I'm glad to see you're in such a good mood this afternoon." Don paused. "The documents faxed over from Seattle were delayed. Trevor, I'd like you to meet Larry Preston. He's making sure the case goes according to plan."

"If you can put Alejandro Morales behind bars, I'm pleased to meet you," Trevor said.

Larry Preston shook Trevor's extended hand. "As the man who got enough evidence to put him there, I'm more than glad to meet you. Let's get down to business. Would you like some coffee or something to eat? It's going to be a long day."

"I'll take some water and maybe a ham sandwich."

"I'll take care of that," Don offered, then exited the room.

"Mr. Willis, we'll start by developing a plan to keep your identity secret," said Larry Preston. "There are several precedents. In a Portland case, the judge agreed to have a partition erected in the courtroom. In Florida, the agent was able to dress in disguise and use the alias he assumed during the undercover operation. From what I understand, Judge Rasmussen is pretty open to the protection of agents."

"That's good to hear. I'd hate to see what Francisco Morales would do if he found out who imprisoned his only son."

"How did you infiltrate their organization?" asked Preston. "How did you gain Morales's trust?"

"I never completely gained his complete trust. The attempt on my life proves that. I was just a tool to move product until they worked out the kinks in their distribution network. Alejandro has a sick fascination with personally witnessing the executions. I knew when he agreed to meet with me that he didn't plan for me to leave the alley alive."

Don entered the room with lunch. "Time for a break."

The conversation continued late into the night.

§

Trevor entered the secure hotel room he'd be calling home for the duration of the trial. He took out a burner phone, complete with encryption, and called Dani.

"Hi. Did you guys arrive safely?" "We're fine. I think Jared is glad you and I are a few hours apart."

"He's just looking out for you."

Dani sighed. "I wish he'd remember I'm not the little girl he spent his life protecting."

"That's hard to forget. Anyway, how is Ady doing?"

"She's been worried she'd never see you again. You want me to see if she's asleep yet?"

"Yeah, I'd like that, but don't wake her up."

Trevor heard Dani walk down the hallway, then the creak of the door and her muffled question. "Honey, are you awake?" There was a pause. "Crash would like to talk to you."

Ady squealed with delight and spoke into the phone. "Crash! You're okay. You didn't forget me."

"I could never forget you. I just wanted to say good-night. Sleep well, sweetie."

"Like a bug in a rug."

He continued their game. "See ya later, alligator."

"After a while crocodile. I love you, Crash."

Soon, Dani came back on the line. "You made her day."

"Good. Now you can make my night and say you miss me."

"I miss you, Trevor."

"How much do you miss me?" he teased.

"More than I'd let my brother know." Dani's smile came through in her voice. "He's always warning me about you."

"Can't say I blame him. I'll have to win him over somehow. My infamous charm hasn't worked, so maybe I just need to show him that you'll be safe with me."

"I like that idea. How did it go with the legal counsel?"

"The storm is only beginning. It'll get worse until Morales is behind bars. I'm glad you're safe with Jared and Jana."

"I wish I were with you. But the most important thing to do right now is keep Ady safe."

"You're right, Dani. Let's see how well we can get to know each other over the phone. If you could take a vacation anywhere in the world, where would you go?"

"Well," she hedged. "You're going to laugh at me."

"I promise not to."

"Okay, you promised." She took a deep breath. "I'd like to go to Disneyland."

As Trevor broke out in robust laughter, Dani scolded, "You promised!"

"I know. But, in my defense"—a few more chuckles escaped—"I'm not laughing at you. I'm happy you chose Disneyland. It's one of my favorite places. I'd love to take you and Ady to the park."

"Really?"

"Really." Trevor's voice took on an announcer's timbre. "Now, Dani Carpenter, your boyfriend has just put a notorious drug dealer behind bars. What are you going to do?"

She played along. "I'm going to Disneyland!"

"Yay! Applause! Applause!" Trevor let out a whistle or two. "Now, who's coming to Disneyland with you?"

"Oh, Ady. Maybe Jared and Jana."

"And . . . " He stretched the word out while rolling his hand. "Is there anyone else?"

"Maybe . . . my parents." She teased.

He cleared his throat. "Isn't there anyone else you would like to take along?"

"Oh, yes," Dani exclaimed. "Of course. I almost forgot. I bet Tony would like to come."

Trevor gave an exaggerated sigh. "If I'm not wanted or appreciated, I'll just hang up."

"No—don't hang up. I guess you can come too."

"If this trial goes quickly, I'll take you anywhere you want to go," Trevor said in his normal tone. "Heck, I'll even rent out Disneyland. No crowds—just people you know and love."

"You're crazy."

"I am for you, Dani. Well, I better get some rest. Be careful and make sure you stay with Tony. He'll keep you safe."

"I'll do everything he says if it means you and I will be together again. I love you."

"Love you back."

Nineteen

Larry Preston stood in front of the Honorable Judge Clive Rasmussen. Behind him, at the defendant's table, defense attorney Quentin Stoddard shuffled some papers and whispered to his co-counsel.

Preston cleared his throat. "Your Honor, we are here today to petition a special request regarding the *State versus Alejandro Morales*. The court has received the proper documentation. The prosecution's key witness performs contract work for the FBI. He's frequently used for undercover operations. We have reason to believe if his true identity were made public, his usefulness to the agency, and also his life, would be in jeopardy."

With slow, deliberate steps, Preston walked to the prosecution's desk and opened a file. "Judge Rasmussen, I would like to present these photographs of the remains of agents who were prepared to testify against the Morales family."

Before Stoddard had a chance to object, Preston placed the photos in front of the judge. The revulsion written upon Rasmussen's face shot Stoddard out of his chair like a catapult.

"I object, Your honor. There have never been any convictions in those cases."

The judge struck his gavel. "Overruled. This has a definite bearing on this subject."

"But Your Honor—"

"Mr. Stoddard, since you have not seen the pictures, how do you know which cases they pertain to?"

"There have—"

"Take your seat, Mr. Stoddard. Bailiff, please give Mr. Stoddard his copies of the photos. Mr. Preston, you may continue."

"Thank you, Your Honor." Preston paced the floor before the judge. "We would like to request that our witness, Mr. X, be allowed to testify in disguise. We also request that he be secured in a witness booth not visible to the court."

"I object," Stoddard barked. "That violates my client's Sixth Amendment right to face his accusers."

"Overruled, Mr. Stoddard. The purpose of this hearing is to ascertain whether or not any rights are being denied." He turned to Preston. "Will you continue your petition, Mr. Preston?"

"I'd be glad to, Your Honor." Larry Preston pulled another folder from his briefcase. "These are the precedents that support our request. I assume your clerk already presented them to Your Honor."

"Yes, I've read them."

"It is proposed that the identity of Mr. X remain confidential."

"Thank you, Mr. Preston. Now, Mr. Stoddard, would you like respond to this request?"

"Yes, Your Honor, I would."

§

At the front desk of the Portland FBI headquarters, Larry Preston presented his ID and cleared security. When he reached the correct door, he took on a dejected expression. Stepping into the room, he hung his head and drooped his shoulders. "I just got back," he said with a sigh, then looked at Trevor and Don before collapsing into a chair. "I'm afraid things went . . ." He grinned. "Just the way we hoped. Stoddard tried to convince Rasmussen it would interfere with his client's right, but the judge didn't buy it." Larry gave Trevor a high five. "You're granted anonymity. We won our first battle."

"Fantastic!" Trevor grabbed Larry's hand and pumped it.

After a few seconds, the lawyer managed to extricate his hand. "But there's bad news."

The smile disappeared from Trevor's face. "Yeah?"

"No witness box. You can disguise your appearance, but Morales will be allowed to face you."

"At least I'm not testifying under my own identity."

Zack's phone rang. He drew a sharp breath at the number on the screen but accepted the call. "I told you not to call me during the day," he growled. "I'm at the office."

"I will call you whenever I desire, Señor Lasky," said the heavily accented voice.

"Just make it quick."

"Have you discovered the true identity of the man giving false testimony against the son of Don Francisco?"

Zack narrowed his eyes. "You haven't paid me enough to pretend I believe Alejandro was framed. They're keeping the agent under tight security. No one knows who he is."

"I need the information!"

"I know he'll arrive at the courthouse about forty-five minutes before he's scheduled to testify. I'll see if I can find out which entrance he will use."

"You better do more than just try, Señor Lasky. By the way, how is your wife? I've heard that sometimes women get a little clumsy in the final months of pregnancy."

Zack understood the threat. He disconnected the call, fuming. He paced the floor and then stared at the phone in his hand. He dialed home. "Hey, Cait. How are you feeling?"

"What's wrong?"

"Nothing's wrong." He tried to sound calm. "I thought you and your mom might want to go out of town for a few weeks."

"Zack, you know I'm due in a few weeks. I can't be far from the hospital."

"I think you should go anyway, just in case."

"O . . . okay. I'll call Mom now."

Zack's chest tightened at the fear in her voice. "No, I'll take care of the arrangements," he said. "I think we'll get you a new cell phone, too. I love you, Caitlyn."

"I love you too, Zack."

"Wait! What do cows wear in Hawaii?"

"I don't know, what do cows wear in Hawaii?" There was a smile in her voice.

"Moo-moos. Get it? Mooooo."

"Yes, I get it. See you in a little while."

Zack ended the call and placed the phone on the desk, then drummed his fingers on his desk, one by one.

Twenty

The wind blew off the ocean, whipping Dani's hair into her eyes. She wished she'd French braided my hair when she did Ady's. Dani pulled another strand out of her mouth and laughed as Tony and Ady worked on their sand castle. Tony showed Ady how to drizzle wet sand to shape droopy pine trees to surround their castle.

Dani waved at them. "I got the rest of the sand toys, and I brought some cold water."

"I'm thirsty," Ady said, barely glancing away from her growing tree.

Tony took a water bottle from Dani and opened it for Ady.

"Thanks." The little girl took a long drink.

"Let me show you what to do." Tony dug a small hole and set the drink inside. "You have a whole beach worth of sand to make cup holders."

"You're smart, Tony."

Dani sat down in the sand. "Jared and Jana should be here soon with the fixings for a hot dog roast. I think they mentioned s'mores, too."

A tear escaped Ady's eye as she gazed out to the ocean. "I miss Mr. Willis. When will we see him again?"

"Oh, sweetie." Dani hugged the little girl. "He'll be here as soon as he can. What happened to calling him Crash?"

Ady's shoulders fell. "It's not the same when he's far away. I miss Daddy, too."

"I understand. Hey, I almost forgot. Jana said a package from Trevor arrived today. There's something in it for you."

"He hasn't forgotten me?"

"Of course not. He misses you like crazy."

"What is it? I can't wait."

"You'll see when they get here. It shouldn't be long."

"Tony, hurry. We have to finish the castle." Ady shoveled sand into the castle-turret mold as quickly as she could.

By the time Jared and Jana stepped onto the beach, Ady and Tony finished their castle and dug a moat. They'd even made numerous trips to fill the moat with water and seaweed.

Ady rushed over to Jared and Jana. "What did Crash send? What did he send?"

Jana took her hand. "You'll find out when we get over to your castle."

"Well, come on." Ady pulled her across the sand.

Jana laughed. "Ady, you're pulling the wrong person. Jared has the surprise."

Ady dropped Jana's hand and dashed over to Jared. "Hurry, hurry. I can't wait." She couldn't grab his hand because he was carrying everything for the hot dog roast, so she pushed him from behind instead.

When he unloaded everything, he turned to Ady and said, "Okay. Close your eyes."

She closed her eyes, then clasped her hands and held them under her chin. She wiggled back and forth. "I'm ready."

"Open your eyes." Jared knelt in front of her with a butterfly kite. Sun rays shone through the vinyl's vibrant blues, purples, pinks, and whites. Streamers flowed from the points of the wings.

"I love it! Crash didn't forget me."

"Nope," Dani said, her arm around Ady's shoulder. "Now you just need to get it up in the air."

Jared and Tony both volunteered to help, and soon they rushed down the beach with Ady between them. Dani knelt by the fire pit and built the beginnings of a roasting fire.

"Should we start it now?" she asked Jana, who sat on one of the camp chairs around the pit.

"Sure. The fire will be ready when they're tired from all that running."

Dani set a match to the kindling. The newspaper caught hold of the flame, and soon the fire warmed the chill of their little part of the Oregon Coast.

With an eye on the kite-flying adventurers, Jana and Dani made preparations for the dinner.

"So, Dani, how are things going?" Jana asked.

"Good. We were up at the camp and got a lot of things done. We selected the rest of the cabin sites and met with a designer for the pool." Dani laughed at the three running down the beach.

"So you spent a few weeks with Trevor?"

"Yes." Dani drew out the word. "Are you wondering if I chose to go up there, or did Trevor use other means?"

Jana laughed. "I would never ask that. I just wanted to know how you two were getting along."

"I know Jared isn't very excited about my interest in Trevor." Dani sighed.

"Trevor's changed. Jared knows that."

"But, he's not going to make it easy on Trevor, is he?"

"No, he's not. Jared still has some unresolved feelings about him. Although when you baptize someone, it's hard to hold a grudge against him." Jana tucked a strand of hair behind her ear. "Are things between you and Trevor getting serious?"

A blush appeared on Dani's cheeks. "I was determined not to like him. You know, keep everything business."

"Yeah, I know. Trevor doesn't make that easy, I'm sure."

"No. At the cabin, he rowed Ady and me across the pond to the camp. When I was getting out of the boat, I fell in. He rushed me over to the cabin and got me into the bathtub."

Jana's eyes widened. "He what?"

"No, no. It wasn't like that. He plopped me in the water—fully clothed—until I stopped shivering. He was a total gentleman. When I came down the stairs, he kissed me."

"How did you feel about that?" Jana asked.

Dani averted her eyes. "I kissed him back. I know Jared won't be happy to hear about it. He's warns me every time I talk to him."

"Deep down, he admires Trevor. Did you know Jared considers him to be his best friend?"

"No way. I thought he considered him more of a frenemy."

Ady came running over. "I flied the kite. Did you see?"

"Yes, we did.," Dani said. "And I took some pictures to send to Crash."

"Yay!" The little girl jumped up and down.

"Are you ready to eat?" Jana reached over for the roasting forks. "Let's get you started."

Dani helped Ady put a hot dog on her stick. She then set up a child-size camp chair close enough to the fire for Ady to roast her hot dog. True to Trevor's tutelage, the little girl carefully placed her dinner above the flames and roasted it to a golden brown.

Dani prepared her own frankfurter for the fire. "Well, Ady, do you think I can learn the patience to get things golden brown instead of charcoal black?"

"Uh-huh. Crash will be happy." Ady turned her stick to brown the underside of her hot dog.

With a deep breath, Dani attempted to delicately brown her own hot dog. "How am I doing?"

"Really good. I'll tell Crash when he calls tonight."

"Thanks, Ady. He'll never believe it if I tell him." Dani gave Ady a one-armed hug and watched her hot dog sizzle.

§

Trevor's beard, which he had begun growing at the camp, covered his jaw. His hair dipped below his ears. The FBI makeup artists practiced his final look: dark circles under his eyes, a bit more weight on his cheeks, a missing tooth. With his hair dyed gray, and brown contact lenses, Marco Rossi, a sixty-two-year-old Italian-American man who relies on a cane, would be brought to life in the courtroom tomorrow. As far as Alejandro Morales was concerned, Trevor Willis had never existed.

Trevor spent the morning with Larry, who grilled him from a defense attorney's perspective. He volleyed every argument at Trevor that Stoddard could possibly pitch.

"Willis, I've never had a witness as unflappable as you. I'm confident we'll pound the final nail into Morales's coffin."

"I just hope you don't end up nailing the lid on MY coffin after this is over."

Larry's posture straightened. "What do you mean?"

"I've seen the pictures of people who have testified against Morales's men. What do you think he'd do to someone testifying against his own son?"

"Hey, we're taking every precaution. No one will ever find out it's you."

"Yeah, Larry," Trevor grunted. "I hope those aren't famous last words."

§

"Hello?" Dani answered the phone with Ady on her heels. "Is it him? Is it Crash?"

Dani put her hand over the receiver and whispered, "Yes."

"Let me talk. Let me talk."

"Okay, okay. Trevor, someone is anxious to speak to you." Dani pushed the speaker button.

"Crash. Thank you for the kite. It's so pretty! I like it a lot. Tony and me builded a castle and he showed me how to make trees with sand. Dani didn't burn her hot dog or her marshmallow. Jared was a horsey for me. You're better."

Trevor's laughter carried through the speaker. "Whoa there, Ady. Take a breath. Do you miss me?"

"Oh, yes, Crash. Tony is fun, but you're funner. I miss your stories, and Jared doesn't have Anna and Elsa bubble bath."

"No Anna and Elsa bubble bath?" Trevor exclaimed in mock horror. "We are going to have to right this injustice."

"What? You talk funny, Crash."

"It just means we'll have to do something about that."

"We can go back to the camp?" Ady asked excitedly.

"No, sweetie, we can't do that yet."

Ady's shoulders fell. "Aww."

"The trial should be over soon, and then I will come get you," Trevor promised.

"Okay."

"Why don't you let me talk to Dani now?"

"He wants to talk to you." Ady surrendered the phone and plodded her way to the back of the house.

Dani grasped the phone with both hands. "Hi, Trevor."

"It's so good to hear your voice. It's been a rough day." Trevor sounded exhausted.

"What happened?"

"Larry put me through the ringer. He wants me to be ready."

"If you were here, I'd rub all that tension out of your shoulders." Dani walked onto the porch and sat on the swing.

Trevor chuckled. "How do you know my shoulders are tense?"

"I can hear it in your voice."

"You're right. Hey, according to Ady, I'm a better horsey than Jared."

Dani's laughter floated on the ocean breeze. "I can see you blowing on your fingernails and rubbing them on your shirt."

"You know me so well."

"I know you well enough to know that you and Jared will be competing with each other for the rest of your lives."

"Hey, at least I'm winning one of the battles," Trevor said.

"Will we make it through the trial?" Dani asked after a long pause. "I'm scared. I mean, with Morales's reputation . . ."

"If I were there with you, I'd hold your shoulders and tell you—no I wouldn't be able to resist kissing you first. Then, I'd tell you everything is going to be okay. Good will always triumph over evil. I mean it."

"Oh, Trevor . . ."

"And then I'd kiss you again," he added softly.

"I miss you."

"I miss you too, Dani. Keep that little girl safe, okay?"

"Love you."

The phone went silent, and Dani's heart grew heavy. A sigh escaped her. *What if he doesn't come back?*

The scent of salt hovered in the breeze, and soon the rhythmic cadence of the waves breaking on the shore brought peace to her soul. She barely registered the screen door closing until she felt a child's touch on her knee. She pulled Ady into her embrace and rocked her back and forth.

"I'm scared about Crash."

"Me too." A tear trickled down Dani's cheek. The wisdom in Ady's eyes mirrored a soul much older than four.

"Don't worry. He'll come back." Dani stroked Ady's hair.

A sob escaped from Ady. "But . . . but Daddy might not."

Dani squeezed her. "Shh, shh. It's okay. It's okay."

Twenty-One

Window washers made their way up the outer wall of the Mark O. Hatfield Courthouse. *Those guys are crazy,* thought Trevor. Leaning on the carved cane, he exited a black SUV as Marco Rossi. He was flanked by agents wearing black suits and sunglasses. Trevor followed the lead agent under a canopy of riot shields and entered the courthouse through a private rear door.

The clock in the foyer ticked away the seconds. Seven thirty-two and sixteen seconds, seventeen seconds, eighteen seconds. Trevor moved through the hall to a security checkpoint. While his cane passed through on the conveyor, he leaned heavily on the arm of the FBI agent until he reached the body scanner. Trevor shuffled through the machine and retrieved his walking stick on the other side.

A uniformed man approached and said, "Please follow me." He led Trevor and his detail toward the rear of the building to a seldom-used elevator. "Right in here, sir."

Trevor entered through the sliding doors. The uniformed man inserted a key and pushed a button for the eleventh floor. He nodded to Trevor and stepped back. A lurch signaled the start of the upward ride. Ten seconds later there was another jolt and the door opened.

Larry Preston greeted Trevor with a handshake. "So far, so good."

"No one seemed to pay attention to me."

"Let's head to the holding room. We'll go over your responses again." Larry took Trevor by the arm and led him to a door down the hall from the courtroom. The security detail followed close behind.

"Larry, I'll go crazy if you go over one more potential argument. Tell me about the security precautions."

"Agents are screening people downstairs. There is another security station as they exit the elevator. All stairway entrances to this floor are blocked. Lasky is stationed at the exit closest to the courtroom."

"Good."

Larry glanced around. "You've been in the open too long. Let's hurry to that waiting room. Oh, by the way, Morales will be in the room down the hall." He pointed several doors down. "That's the holding cell."

A shiver ran the length of Trevor's spine. "Is he here?"

"No. Court starts at 9:30. He won't be brought in until around 9:00."

The wait seemed endless as Larry Preston paced the length of the witness holding room.

"Will you calm down?" Trevor said finally. "I'm the one with my life on the line for testifying against Morales." Trevor took a long sip of water and then reclined on the sofa again.

"We can't let anything go wrong. We've never been this close to Francisco Morales. We have his son in custody." Larry stopped long enough to slap the wall before making his return journey across the room. "I have a bad feeling about today."

"What could go wrong? There's practically an entire platoon on guard." Trevor pushed himself up. "With this disguise, no one will ever know it's me. I testify, Alejandro is found guilty, he goes to prison, and we all live happily ever after." Trevor rested a pair of thick glasses on his nose to finish his disguise.

"Willis, when was the last time you had an uncomplicated happily ever after?"

Trevor opened his mouth to speak, but closed it before any words escaped. His casual attitude evaporated. "Never. So, do you think they will try to kill me?"

"Yes. And no doubt Stoddard is up to his shifty eyeballs in planning it. His nerves are tighter than the seal on a Tupperware bowl."

"Are the other agents aware of your suspicions?"

Larry answered with a nod. "They're concerned too."

"What's the plan?"

Larry reached into a duffel bag on the floor and pulled out a Kevlar vest. "For starters, put this on."

"Alejandro Morales's employees approached me to set up a territory to deal high-grade heroin. We had several deals behind us, and I was finally allowed to meet with Morales himself," Trevor testified, using a shaky voice as part of his disguise.

"When we exchanged money for the drugs, Morales gave the order to kill me. At that point, the FBI closed in."

Larry turned to the judge. "We have exhibits 54, 55, and 56, the witness's coat, shirt, and Kevlar vest, each bearing a two bullet holes directly above his heart."

"Please turn the evidence over to Officer Jamison." The judge motioned to the bailiff.

"I have no further questions for this witness, Your Honor," Larry said before returning to his seat.

Judge Rasmussen nodded at the prosecutor. "Thank you, Mr. Preston. Now, Mr. Stoddard, would you like to cross-examine this witness?"

"Yes, Your Honor." Quentin Stoddard approached the witness stand. "Mr. . . . . oh, I'm afraid I don't know your name. Will you please state it for the court?"

Trevor leaned toward the microphone. "No, sir. With the judge's ruling last week, I am not required to state my name or be identified in any manner."

"Okay, Mr. X, as we shall call you, are you currently employed by any government agency?"

"No, sir."

Stoddard moved closer. "Are you in the Witness Protection Program?"

Trevor shook his head. "No, sir. I am not."

"Then what gives you the right to rob my client of his constitutional right to face his accuser?" boomed Stoddard.

Larry jumped up from his seat. "I object, Your Honor. This matter has already been ruled upon."

Judge Rasmussen banged his gavel. "Sustained. Move on, Mr. Stoddard."

"I'm sorry, Your Honor. I'll rephrase the question." The defense attorney stared at Trevor. "Can you tell me how you are associated with the FBI?"

"I am a retired agent. I consult for the FBI on occasion, when they need my expertise."

Before Stoddard could reply, Trevor's voice resonated through the courtroom. "My identity is concealed because most people who agree to testify against your client end up—"

"I object, Your Honor," Stoddard said, clearly attempting to speak louder than the witness.

"—having accidents or disappearing into thin air," Trevor finished.

The gavel sounded and the judge sighed. "Mr. X, you will answer the questions and not offer your opinions."

"Yes, Your Honor," Trevor said in Marco Rossi's shaky voice.

Stoddard stepped forward. "Judge, I move that the previous statement be stricken from the record."

"Agreed." The judge turned toward the jury box. "I will ask that you disregard the previous statement of Mr. X. You must not consider it when making your decision."

Stoddard nodded toward the judge. "Thank you, Your Honor. Now, as to this man's identity—"

"Mr. Stoddard," interrupted the judge, "as you well know, the issue of this witness's identity was resolved before trial. Do not waste the court's time with this line of questioning or you will be found in contempt of court. Is that clear?"

"Yes, sir." Stoddard took a deep breath and returned his attention to Trevor. "Now, Mr. X, you said my client gave the order to kill you?"

"Yes, he did."

"Did you hear him give the order?"

"No, I did not. He—"

"Well, Mr. X," Stoddard continued in a condescending tone, "why would you claim my client gave the order if you didn't hear it?"

"It was a nonverbal order."

Stoddard chuckled. "And you are an expert in nonverbal communication?"

"As a matter of fact, I am."

The grin vanished from the defense attorney's face. Before Trevor had a chance to rub it in, he glanced toward the window. A red beam of light caught his attention as it reflected off the sun-lit dust particles floating through the air. He dropped to the ground. "Gunman at the window!" he shouted.

The glass shattered, leaving a bullet hole where Trevor's head had been several seconds before. Officer Jamison shielded Judge Rasmussen, and Stoddard ducked under the defense table as U.S. Marshals rushed Alejandro Morales out of the courtroom. The bailiff pushed Judge Rasmussen toward his chambers.

Larry picked himself up from the floor and ran to the witness stand. "Willis, are you okay?"

"What? It's just me here. Marco Rossi. Where's Morales?" Trevor spoke through clenched teeth.

"Sorry, Mr. Rossi. Bullets always addle my senses. Morales is in the custody of the U.S. Marshals."

Automatic weapons fire sounded just outside the courtroom. Trevor and Larry bolted through the door. Five U.S. Marshals lay wounded on the floor. Morales escaped through the stairwell door. Trevor led a growing number of law enforcement personnel who sprinted toward the exit. Trevor stopped to check the downed officer by the door. Special Agent Lasky wasn't shot, but an ugly welt was raising on his forehead where the butt of a gun must have connected with it.

Trevor cradled his friend's head in his lap as the rest of the security force ran past them and down the stairwell. "Zack." Trevor gently patted the fallen agent's cheek. "C'mon, Zack. Open your eyes." Trevor called to a shell-shocked agent, "I need medical help. Now!"

The man seemed to break out of his trance and lifted his walkie-talkie to call for assistance.

"Are there any survivors?" Trevor jerked his head toward the escort guard of U.S. Marshals.

"I'm not sure, sir." The young agent scanned the room. His posture showed his indecision and his inexperience.

"Son, look at me." Trevor caught his attention. "What's your name?"

The man stood at attention and saluted. "Special Agent Gregory Austin. Former Marine Corporal."

"Okay, Corporal Austin, those men need your help," Trevor said. "I want you to check to see if any are still alive."

"Yes, sir." A minute later, the corporal reported "Three of the five are still breathing. The other two have no pulse."

"Good job, Corporal. See what you can do for the survivors. Then get someone into the courtroom to check on the jury and any other civilians still in there."

"Yes, sir."

Trevor tried to wake Zack, but to no avail. Sirens sounded and the loud whirring of a helicopter carried through the stairwell. "Corporal Austin, did law enforcement chase the shooters down the stairs or up the stairs?" Trevor asked.

"I think they all headed downstairs."

"Try to reach them on the radio. A helicopter is landing on the roof. That has to be their escape route." Trevor took off his jacket and rolled it into a pillow for Zack's head. "Gotta go, friend." He stood up, armed himself with Zack's gun and headed up the stairs.

Soon Trevor opened the door to the roof and saw Morales crouching in the middle of several men, waiting for the chopper to land. When the rails hit the roof, Morales was swept toward the open door. Trevor raised his weapon and shot at the waiting helicopter and the advancing men. Morales's body guards returned fire. Trevor dove back into the stairwell. He continued to fire at the hovering copter, but his bullets only ricocheted back toward the rooftop. The rest of the security squad reached the exit onto the roof. Each man bumped Trevor on their way through the door. He finally leaned against the stairwell housing and slid to a seated position on the pebbled texture of the roof. The chopper took off with Morales inside.

Don Townsend reached down to his brother-in-law and pulled him up. "This is becoming a little too common. Let's get you away from here and to a safehouse."

"How's Zack?"

"He'll have one heck of a headache, but he'll live," Trevor replied. "He was lucky."

Exhaustion overcame Trevor, and his knees buckled. Don propped him up and helped him to the elevators. Trevor's head popped up at the sound of the arriving elevator. Adrenaline surged through him at the image of Quentin Stoddard on his cell phone.

"No, Mr. Rios. I don't know who the witness is, but his lawyer slipped up and called him Willis. It shouldn't be too hard to figure—"

Mr. Stoddard's call ended when Trevor punched him in the jaw.

Don called to one of his agents, "Murray, get this scumbag to headquarters where we'll keep him in custody.

"Yes, sir."

His adrenaline rush over, Trevor collapsed into a chair.

Don snapped his fingers and motioned to an EMT. "You! Get over here and take care of this man."

§

Dani and Tony returned from the park with Ady.

"Hi there . . ." Dani's greeting faded away when she stepped into the tension-filled room.

Jared stood behind Jana's chair, his face like stone. Jana quickly paused the television and shared a look with her husband who nodded. Jana reached out her hand. "Ady, would you like to help me make dinner?"

"Yes! Can we have chicken nuggets and french fries?"

Jana laughed. "You're going to turn into a chicken nugget if you don't stop eating them so much."

"That is so silly. I'm a people, not a nugget." Ady clasped Jana's hand.

"Maybe we can go to McDonalds and get chicken nuggets for everyone."

"Yay!" Ady pulled Jana along with her. "Hurry."

After the back door closed, Dani approached her brother. "What's going on? What happened?" Her heart dropped to the floor and her hands began to tremble.

Jared put his arm around his sister and guided her to the couch. "Dani, I . . . we . . ." He patted her hand and reached for the remote control. He rewound the news report and let the TV tell the story.

"This is Miranda Rios from KATU News with breaking news. Earlier today, a prisoner escaped from the Mark O. Hatfield Federal Courthouse. Armed gunmen posing as window washers opened fire through a courtroom window. While news reports remain unconfirmed, it appears the prosecution's main witness was the intended target."

Dani drew in a deep breath and squeezed Jared's hand so hard that he too drew in his breath.

"The gunmen proceeded to remove the defendant from federal custody. Two U.S. Marshals were killed. An unknown number of victims were rushed to local hospitals with injuries. The identity of the defendant has not yet been released. KATU News will continue to follow this story."

Tears overflowed Dani's eyes as she looked Jared in the eye. "What have you heard? How is Trevor?"

"I've heard exactly the same thing you have. I'm going to try to reach Don. He should know something." Jared picked up his phone. "C'mon, Don. Answer."

"Townsend here."

"It's Jared Carpenter. What's happening? Is Trevor safe?"

The Special Agent in Charge lowered his voice to a whisper. "I can't say anything right now, but tell Dani she can breathe again. He's exhausted, but safe."

"Keep us informed." Jared disconnected the call and turned to his sister. "They can't say anything except that he's safe."

More tears fell as Dani hugged Jared. "Thank you."

Jared texted his wife. *Trevor's okay. It's safe to bring Ady home.*

I hope everyone is ready for McNuggets and fries, she texted back.

Twenty-Two

Enrique Rios stood tall in front of his employer. "Don Francisco, I bring good news."

"Bueno. What is this news?" Don Francisco rose from his desk and faced the window.

"Alejandro has been rescued. He should be here later this evening."

"That is good." Don Francisco turned to look Enrique in the eye. "Now, what of this witness? Do we know his identity?"

Enrique shook his head. "The Americans allowed him to testify in disguise, but Señor Stoddard has discovered a partial name." Enrique paused.

"Do not keep me waiting, my friend."

"The name is Willis. We do not know if it is the witness's first name or his last name."

Don Francisco returned to his desk chair. "Put our best men on this. Death is too good for this jackal." His hand formed a tight fist. "We will destroy him."

"Yes, Don Francisco." Enrique turned to leave the room.

"One more thing," the drug lord called after him, stopping him in his tracks. "When Alejandro arrives, please send him directly to me."

Enrique nodded and left Don Francisco alone.

§

After Dani finished reading *The True Story of the Three Little Pigs* to Ady, she tucked the child in bed and kissed her good-night. Then Dani went down to the living room and sat on the couch. A car drove by and she glanced out the front bay window. It wasn't Trevor. She got up to pace the floor.

A few minutes later, Jared stopped her with a hand on her shoulder. "Will you quit pacing? You're going to wear a hole in the floor and end up in the basement."

She gave a weak chuckle. "I'm so worried. What if Don was wrong? What if Trevor was . . ."

"Dani, stop it. You're driving me crazy." Jared pointed up the stairs. "You've got a little girl up there who needs you to be strong."

"You're right. I'm sorry for driving you crazy, although isn't that part of my job as your little sister?"

Jared hugged her and said, "Jana's making some cocoa. Why don't you see if she needs help."

"Thanks." Dani kissed him on the cheek. "You've always watched out for me." She headed toward the kitchen until Tony's voice stopped her.

"I'm going out for a short walk, Dani. Care to join me?"

She turned around. He put his hand to his ear and gave a slight nod. Dani got the hint. "Yeah, I'm ready to get out of the house. Let's go."

She grabbed some flip-flops and rushed out the door. Together, she and Tony walked down the street toward the ocean. Finally, Dani stopped. "What's happening, Tony? Have you heard from Trevor?"

"I can't say, ma'am."

She took a deep breath. "Where are we going?"

"To an undisclosed location."

"You're full of information. So, what will I find at this location?"

"Answers to your questions."

"You *have* talked to him. Is he there?" Dani grabbed Tony's arm and pulled him along. "C'mon."

He halted. "Dani, you're going the wrong way."

"Well, then, you lead the way, but do it quickly."

They left the sidewalk bordering the beach and walked toward an older gentleman leaning on his cane watching the waves.

Dani frowned in confusion. "Does this guy know where Trevor is?"

"Go ask him," replied Tony.

"Okay." She hesitated before approaching the man. When she touched his arm, he faced her. Trevor! Tears sprung from her eyes and she flung her arms around his neck. They clung to each for several seconds before he pushed her away and looked into her eyes. Their lips found each other's, and everything else faded away for a minute. Then he led Dani to a bench and sat next to her with his arm around her.

"Oh Trevor, I was so afraid you . . . you were dead."

He wiped away her tears. "I know, Dani. I know. That's why I sneaked out of the safehouse and over here. I had to make sure you were okay, to let you know I'm fine."

"Wow, Trevor." She touched his gray hair and stroked his beard. "I had no idea who you were until I saw your eyes."

He laughed. "Must be a good disguise if I fooled you."

"Thank heavens it is." She kissed his prickly cheek.

"How's Ady doing?"

"She misses you, Crash. She's afraid that her dad isn't coming back."

Trevor's brow furrowed through wisps of gray hair. "Why would she be afraid of that? I'm assuming they wanted him for his knowledge about EP's. He'd be worth more alive than dead." He paused a moment. "Apparently, the papers from the crime scene disappeared from the evidence locker."

"What?" Dani gasped. "Does that mean someone in the Bureau is working for Morales?"

"It's a possibility—one I don't like to think about. Did Don tell you Zack was hurt this morning?"

"Oh, no! How is he?"

"He'll live. He only got a bruise on the head from the butt of a rifle. He was lucky. Two U.S. Marshals are dead." Trevor's eyes held a faraway look. "It was like being in the middle of a war zone."

Dani held his face in her hands and kissed away the ghosts. "I'm so sorry, Trevor."

They sat on a park bench, with only the sound of the ocean and an occasional call of a seagull breaking the silence of the night. Someone cleared his throat.

"What is it, Tony? You playing chaperone tonight?" Trevor called out without looking at him.

"No, sir. I just dodged a call from Agent Don Townsend. I think he knows you're not at the safehouse."

"Okay, okay. Just give us a few minutes to say goodbye."

"Of course, sir."

Trevor and Dani stood facing each other, holding hands. "I hate to leave you," Trevor said softly, "but it's too dangerous for you if I stay. Oh, I almost forgot." He reached for a gift bag on the bench. "I got this for Ady. Tell her I miss her. Now, please close your eyes." A few seconds later he said, "You can open them."

The moonlight reflected off the diamonds on a ring with intertwined hearts. "Oh, Trevor, it's beautiful, but . . ."

He took her left hand in his and slipped on the ring. "I'm not asking for a commitment, Dani. This is a promise ring. I promise I will always come back to you—for as long you want me."

"I'll be waiting."

"Goodbye." He brushed her lips with his and disappeared into the fog creeping in from the ocean.

Tony escorted Dani back to the house and opened the door for her. "I'm just going to take a walk around the perimeter before I turn in."

"Okay, Tony." She squeezed his arm. "Thanks so much for everything tonight."

His blush could be seen even in the evening's shadows. "It was nothing."

Dani practically floated through the living room. She jumped at the sound of her brother's voice.

"Obviously that walk was just what you needed. Find anything interesting out there?"

She stared at the floor. "I . . . uh . . . I . . . the coast always brings me peace."

"Jared, why don't you go and get a snack or something while I talk with Dani." Jana urged her husband toward the kitchen. "So, Dani, it looks like you're feeling better."

"Much better."

"I take it Trevor was there?" Jana guessed.

"Why, why would you say that?"

Jana took Dani's arm. "Let's go sit on the porch, and you can tell me about that new ring on your finger."

Jared rushed in from the kitchen. "What ring? He isn't pushing you into something, is he?"

"Calm down, big brother. It's none of your business. I'm not being pushed anywhere I don't want to go."

"Jared, go back to what you were doing, Dani and I will be visiting on the front porch."

"But I—" he started.

Jana pushed Jared back toward the kitchen. "Okay, okay. I can take a hint."

Outside, Dani glanced at the intertwined hearts on the ring. "You're right," she admitted to Jana. "Trevor was there. How did you know?"

"You might say I know him pretty well."

"Sometimes I forget that you dated him. Is it hard for Jared to see him with me?"

"He's getting used to it. So, tell me what happened."

"We walked to the beach and . . . well, you wouldn't believe how different Trevor looks. He disguised himself as an old man for the trial. He had gray hair and a beard. I almost didn't recognize him."

"I would have liked to see that. Are you two engaged?"

Dani held her hand out and admired the ring. "No. It's just a promise ring. A promise that he'll always come back to me."

"That's very romantic. I think Trevor is sincere. I just hope he can keep that promise."

"Me too." Dani looked heavenward. *Please let him keep his promise.*

Twenty-Three

The next morning, Ady padded into Dani's room. Dani closed her eyes and pretended to be asleep. Ady tapped her on the shoulder, but Dani didn't budge. The tap turned into shaking.

"Dani." Ady shook a little harder. "Dani, wake up."

"I am awake, but I want to go back to sleep." She rolled over on her side and tussled Ady's hair. "Are you okay?"

Ady climbed onto Dani's bed. "I had a bad dream."

"Come over here. Want to tell me about it?"

"Uh-huh." She snuggled into Dani's arms. "I dreamed Crash was hurt. I tried to help him, but bad men took him away. The same bad men who took my daddy." A tear escaped Ady's eye. "Why didn't he call last night?"

"Oh, sweetie, he's fine. And he sent something for you."

Ady's face lit up. "He did? Where is it?"

Dani sat up and indicated a bag on the dresser. "Right over there."

The little girl slipped off the bed and rushed over to the gift bag. "Can I open it now?"

"Of course."

She dug through the tissue paper and brought out a wrapped item. "My mommy put tissue in presents." Ady carefully unwrapped a bottle of Anna and Elsa bubble bath. "I love it!" she squealed. She reached back into the bag and pulled out a box. Her mouth formed an O. "What is it?"

Dani laughed. "Open it and see, silly."

Ady opened the box and pulled out a silver snowflake necklace. "It's so pretty! Can you help me put it on?"

Ten seconds later, with the necklace on, Ady ran down the stairs shouting, "Tony, Jana, Jared—see what I got!"

They all gathered around her.

"The boss has good taste in jewelry," Tony commented.

Jana held the pendant in her hand. "This is so delicate and looks so pretty."

Jared knelt down to Ady's level. "That looks good on you."

"Can I call Crash and thank him?" Ady asked Dani.

"Let's go in the kitchen and get some breakfast. I can't call Crash, but Tony can get him to call us."

"Will you, Tony? Please, please, pretty please with cookies on top?"

He chuckled. "Sure. You eat your breakfast and by the time you're done, he should call."

Ady wrapped her arms around his legs. "Thank you, thank you!" She ran to the table. "I want Lucky Charms."

Dani pinged Ady's nose. "You want Lucky Charms, what?"

"I want Lucky Charms, pleeease!"

§

Trevor paced the floor of the safehouse. "What do you mean they're getting close to figuring out who I am? All Larry said was 'Willis.' There must be hundreds of Willises in Oregon."

"There are 1833 people in Oregon with the last name Willis. There are over four thousand with Willis anywhere in their name." Don rubbed his temples.

"So, how can Morales be closing in on me?"

Don let out a slow breath. "There might be a mole in the office."

"A mole? C'mon, Don, aren't there only three people who know my real identity? You, Larry Preston, and Zack . . ." Trevor stopped as it hit him. "Lasky. Zack is the mole?" He shook his head. "I don't believe it."

"There's no else it could be."

"Well, before you point fingers at Zack, you might want to look at Larry Preston. He's the new guy—no one here knows him. He's the one who called me by name at the trial. I think it's time to get some answers."

"We're working on that."

"Don, I have Ady to keep safe—and Dani, too." Trevor's tone was quiet but urgent. "I can't have someone on my tail. It's too important."

"I know, brother. I know." Don left the safehouse through the front door and passed the skeleton of a piano on the porch.

Trevor returned to the kitchen table. He chose a phone from the assortment piled haphazardly inside his briefcase and dialed Dani's number.

"Hey there," he said after her tentative hello.

"Trevor. It's so good to hear your voice. I've been worried."

"Hey, beautiful lady. I promised to always return, and I figured it applied to phone calls, too."

"Thanks. That means the world to me."

"Me too, honey. Could I speak to Ady?"

"She's been chomping at the bit to talk to you."

Dani called out to Ady. Trevor smiled when the little girl grabbed the phone and said, "Thank you so much for the bubble bath and the necklace. I have it on and everyone says it's so pretty. I miss you."

"I miss you too, sweetheart. Do you get to go to the beach every day?"

"Uh-huh. Tony takes me anywhere I want to go, except to see you."

"I'll get back to see you as soon as I can."

"Crash?" Ady continued without a break. "I sneaked down and saw Tony watching TV. They said someone shooted people at a court. I thought it was you."

"I am fine, Ady. I'll see you as soon as possible."

"I'm gonna take a bubble bath now. Bye."

"Do you need to get her in the tub?" Trevor asked when Dani picked up the phone again.

"No, Jana's taking care of that."

"I'm almost afraid to ask, but how is Jared feeling about us?" Trevor squinted his eyes as though expecting a blow.

"Jana says he's getting used to the idea, but I'm not too sure of the final verdict."

"Don't be too hard on him, Dani. He's only protecting the people he loves. It's the exact same thing I'm doing."

She sighed. "Maybe if we take things slow, he'll realize how good you are for me."

"There's no rush. I love you now, and I'll love you when you're ready."

"Or whenever Jared's ready?"

Trevor laughed. "Or whenever he's ready. How do feel about setting a wedding date twenty years in the future—when he's ready?"

"Okay, maybe not quite that long."

"Come see me, Dani!" shouted a little voice. "I'm so funny."

"You better go, sweetheart. Ady's calling," Trevor said.

"I love you."

"Right back at you."

§

"Señor Lasky, we expected you to provide us with the identity of the witness by now."

Zack huffed. "Hey, I'm doing my best. Not many people are privy to that information. Those who know are very tight-lipped. If you have any suggestions as to how I can acquire that information, I'm ready to listen."

"No, that is why we pay you. And you had better come through with the information."

"No problem, Mr. Rios."

Zack waited for the double beep before laying the phone on the night stand. He rested his head in his hands and moaned, "What have I gotten myself into?"

Twenty-Four

Trevor paced the length of the safehouse. *I'm going crazy—I have to get out of here.* His cell phone pinged with a text message was from a phone number he didn't recognize.

They're on to you.

The text sent a tremor down Trevor's spine. He went upstairs, removed his suitcase from the closet, and packed his clothes. *Today, I take back my life.*

He zipped the suitcase closed, then hid it behind the kitchen door and called out to the agents on protection duty. "Hey, get in here. I think someone is upstairs."

Agent Matthews pointed to the curtains billowing through the open attic window. "Look up there."

Several agents rushed into the house. Trevor grabbed his suitcase and computer from behind the door and hurried to the garage with keys in hand. Thankfully, the Corolla had been backed into the garage. He quickly loaded his things in the trunk, then opened the garage door and started the engine.

A few seconds later he peeled out of the garage. At the front gate, he punched in the code. His fingers tapped on the steering wheel as the gate crawled open. "C'mon, c'mon. If the house were on fire, it'd be a smoldering pile of ashes by now."

"Stop!" someone shouted.

Trevor glanced back. Three agents were running toward the car. He couldn't wait any longer. He crashed through the still-opening gate. In his rearview mirror he watched the agents halt at the pile of rubble.

He focused his eyes on the road except for a quick glance at his Rolex. It was 10:36 and 15 seconds. "I bet I'll get a call from Don in about three minutes."

At 10:39 and 39 seconds, Don's ringtone broke the silence in the car.

"Hello, brother. I figured you'd be calling about now."

"What's going on, Trevor? I understand you left the safehouse. Again."

Trevor made sure the left lane was clear and switched on his blinker. "I got an anonymous text telling me they were on to me. By they, I assume the texter meant Morales and his organization. I'm not going to sit there like a turkey waiting for Thanksgiving dinner."

"Trevor, you can't take on an entire drug cartel alone." With each word, Don's voice got louder.

"Maybe not, but I have a chance to take out Morales and his son. I refuse to spend my life running."

"Okay, I give in. If I can't talk you out of it, I might as well help you. What do you need?"

"I'll let you know later, but you'll have to get a new gate at the safehouse."

"You didn't!"

Trevor turned left onto I-5. "It was too slow. Also, you might want to increase the endurance training. The agents were huffing and puffing after a quarter-mile driveway."

"I'll consider the suggestion." Don chuckled, but then his voice choked up. "Be careful, Trevor. Traci would never forgive me if something happened to her favorite brother."

"Actually, I'm her only brother."

§

Several men waited outside the door of Trevor's Portland apartment. A tall man in a baseball cap pulled a key out of his pocket and put it in the lock.

"Whoa, how did you get hold of that? Did you heist it from the owner?" One of the men leaned over a large box resting on a dolly.

"Are you stupid, Juan? This is a bump key." The man hit the key with the heel of his hand and unlocked the door.

Juan shook his head. "I need to get me one of those."

The boss stepped into the luxury apartment. "Let me disarm the security system." He walked to the Honeywell Keypad and hit the start button. Pictures of young children moving across the screen almost made him hesitate. The man shook his head it and typed *H-A-1-7*. A green light flashed.

He motioned to the other men. "You—what's your name?

"David."

"Okay, David, set up the computer on the desk in the corner."

He checked a duffel bag carried by a stocky man in his early twenties. "Carlos, place the heroin between the mattress and box springs in the bedroom, and the meth in the medicine cabinet in the bathroom."

Carlos nodded. "Yes, sir."

Another worker entered the apartment with a Fred Myer grocery sack. "I thought you'd never get here," the man told him. "The safe is behind the painting on the bedroom wall. He pulled out a crumpled post-it note from his pocket. "Here's the combination."

"Got it, boss."

When all the men finished their tasks, they reset the alarm and left the building.

§

Don Townsend shuffled through the papers overflowing his inbox. He glanced at the door and absently tapped his pen on his desk. The intercom buzzed and he pushed the button. "Yes, Carole, what is it?"

"I have the Bureau chief on line 1."

"Thanks." Don hit the flashing button. "Lee, what can I do for you?"

"I'm giving you a heads-up, Don. We got an anonymous tip that Willis is involved in some pretty bad stuff."

"What do you mean?"

"The tipster said Willis is selling drugs out of his apartment. The person also mentioned embezzlement. We have a search warrant for Willis's apartment."

"I don't believe this," Don said in exasperation. "What kind of evidence did this anonymous tip provide?"

"I'm not sure."

"You're taking the word of someone who won't give you his name? Which crooked judge signed that warrant?"

"You better be careful who you accuse," growled the chief.

Don lost his cool. "This is a lawsuit in the making, with you as the main defendant."

"I'm just letting you know as a courtesy. Officers should be entering his apartment as we speak."

"It's a setup and you know it! Wait, did you say apartment?"

"Yes, why?"

"Never mind." Don hung up the phone and reached for his cell. "Answer, Trevor, answer."

"Hello," Trevor said in a mechanical voice. "You have reached the phone of Trevor Willis. If this is Don, you can reach me in six weeks. Beep."

"Very funny. Your robot imitation needs some work."

"I'm not coming in, Don."

"I know. In fact, I want you to stay far away from here. I think the repercussions have begun."

Trevor sighed. "What repercussions?"

"They're searching your apartment for drugs and anything else they can use to charge you with some serious crimes."

"You know they won't find anything."

"I wouldn't be too sure." Don's flat voice spoke volumes.

"What are you accusing me of?"

"Nothing, Trevor. Unfortunately, your loyalty doesn't buy too much when something is planted. The good thing is, they're not searching your house."

"They probably don't know about it. I buried my ownership under multiple layers."

"I'll contact you if I hear anything. Be careful."

"Thanks, Don."

Twenty-Five

"Ady, I'm going to the store. Do you want to come?" Dani slipped on her shoes and grabbed her purse.

"Aww, do I have to? I want to finish watching *Tangled*."

"Is that okay with you, Tony?"

"Yeah, sure. I've never seen this." His laugh followed Dani out the door. "A frying pan—who'd have thought."

Dani reviewed the shopping list before she fastened her seat belt and backed out of Jared's driveway.

A few minutes later, when she stopped at the intersection near Gardner's Deli, a man yanked open the back door of the vehicle and jumped in. He pointed a gun at Dani's head. Her entire body shook at the reflection of his cold gaze in the rearview mirror. "Wh–what do you want?" she mumbled.

"Drive to the highway." He pushed the gun barrel against her temple.

In the self-defense class, Trevor had instructed, "Be aware and take charge." As Dani and her captor approached the sheriff's office, she made her decision. With trembling hands, she yanked the steering wheel to the right. She hopped the curb, drove across the lawn, and stopped at the steps to the city jail. Her assailant lost his balance and fell to the floor in the back of the vehicle. Dani pressed on the horn. A deputy hustled out of the building and ran after the carjacker, who fled on foot.

Dani sat with her head on the steering wheel until the sheriff opened her door and helped her out of the car. Her legs buckled, but the lawman supported her.

"You all right, ma'am?"

She closed her eyes and took a deep breath. "I–I think so. I'm just a little shaky."

"Let's get you inside. Is there anyone I can call?"

"My brother, Jared Carpenter, please."

"Jared's your brother? He helped me get my leg back in shape a while ago. He's a good man."

Dani smiled. "Seems like everyone knows him."

§

Jared motioned for Tony to follow him. "What do you need, Jared?" Tony asked, keeping a close eye on Ady.

"I just got a call from the sheriff," Jared said in a low voice. "Someone attempted to abduct Dani. She drove the car up the steps of the sheriff's office, and the guy ran off. I imagine it has something to do with Trevor."

Tony sighed. "More than likely."

"I was afraid of something like this happening. First Jana was nearly killed because of Trevor—"

"I hate to disagree, but Trevor was the only one who believed in her. He almost lost his own life protecting her."

Jared stopped and stared at Tony, then continued with less conviction. "Now Dani's life is in danger because of him."

"You've got some things confused, Mr. Carpenter. Trevor Willis is one of the few really good guys left. There are a lot less criminals on the streets because of him. Trevor risks his life and never gets the glory."

"Sorry, Tony. I never thought about it that way. I'm just worried about my sister."

"Being with Trevor is probably the safest place to be."

Jared thought a moment. "You may be right. I'm heading down to the sheriff's office. Do you want to come?"

"I'd like to find the guy and let him know what I think." Tony's fists opened and closed. "But my job is to protect this little girl. I'm not leaving her."

"I figured you'd feel that way."

§

After the tail lights of Jared's car disappeared down the street, Tony grabbed his cell phone and dialed.

"Trevor Willis."

"Hey, boss. I've got bad news," Tony said.

"Are Dani and Ady okay?"

"Ady's here with me, and I think Dani's all right, but I haven't actually seen her."

"Tell me everything," Trevor ordered.

"This afternoon, she headed to the store. An armed man jumped in her car and attempted to abduct her."

"Attempted?"

Tony chuckled. "Dani doesn't back down from a challenge. She ran the car up to the door of the sheriff's office. Apparently, the guy took off running."

"She took charge. Yes! She actually listened in class." Trevor's voice held a hint of pride. "Where is she now?"

"She's with the sheriff. Jared went to get her."

"Oh, great. One more black mark by my name."

"You might be surprised, sir."

"Listen, Tony. Larry Preston called me out by name during the chaos in the courtroom. The FBI got an anonymous tip that I'm running drugs from my apartment and committing several other crimes. My guess is it will be on tomorrow's news. If Morales knows about Dani, the only safe place for her is with me."

"I agree. I just told Jared that."

"You did? How did he take it?"

"He said I was probably right."

There was no answer from Trevor.

"You still there, boss?" asked Tony.

"Yeah, did I hear you right?"

"As Ady would say, uh-huh."

"Speaking of Ady, I think she'll be safest with you, since Morales probably doesn't know about her. I'm sure Jana would let you stay there, or maybe the Grants will rent you their guest house. I'll be there late tonight. Let the family know."

"Sure, boss. Everyone will be safe until then."

The sheriff brought in two chairs from the lobby. "These might be more comfortable for you," he told Dani and Jared. "I ordered some sandwiches from the deli. They'll be here soon."

"Thank you, Sheriff," Jared answered.

"Now, Miss Carpenter, we haven't caught the man who attempted to abduct you, but in the rush to get away, he left his gun in the back seat, complete with a fine set of finger prints. We have an ID on him. We'd like to show you a few pictures. Do you think you can identify the man?"

"I think so. I'll do my best."

A knock sounded on the door and the deputy poked his head in the room. "Sheriff, we found something on the car."

"Well, don't just stand there. Bring it in."

He dipped his head slightly toward Dani and sidled past her. "This was under the wheel well."

The sheriff turned the object over in his palm. "Have you shown it to the lab?"

"Yes. It's some kind of tracking device."

"Thanks, son."

The deputy left the room. Holding up the device, the sheriff asked, "Have you seen this before, Miss Carpenter?"

"No, I haven't."

"We'll look into it. Right now, let's see if we can identify the kidnapper." The sheriff showed Dani a series of eight photographs, allowing her to study each as long as she needed. On number 8, she recognized the steely eyes of her would-be kidnapper. A shiver ran through her like an electric current.

"That's him," she mumbled.

"Are you sure?"

Dani met the sheriff's gaze. "Yes, that's him. I'll never forget those eyes."

The sheriff patted her hand. "Thank you, Miss Carpenter. The prints on the gun are his. He works for a drug cartel run by a man named Morales."

Twenty-Six

Dani brought Ady up for a bath as soon as they returned from town. "I think you must be the cleanest little girl in the country. We're almost out of bubble bath."

"I need a bath every night 'cause I play lots every day."

"Then why do you take a bath every morning, silly?

"It's warm at night and I get sweaty just like Daddy, so I need a bath again." Ady smiled a cheesy grin.

Dani wrapped a soft pink towel around Ady, lifting her out of the tub. Water swooshed down the drain in a mini whirlpool. "Let's get your PJs on. Then you can say good-night to everyone."

"I want to wear my purple pajamas."

"Purple it is." Dani tickled Ady's tummy.

A few minutes later, when Ady was dressed, Jana peeked around the doorframe. "Knock, knock! Ready for bed, Ady?"

She giggled. "Yes."

"We thought we'd come up here to tell you good-night." Tony peeked around the corner.

"Yay!" Ady jumped on the bed.

Jared rushed to tickle her. "Ha, ha. I got ya. Good-night." He kissed the top of her head.

Someone else walked through the doorway. "Crash! You came." Ady jumped into his arms and hugged his neck. "I missed you so, so much."

"I missed you too, Ady. I missed you too."

Ady touched his hair and beard. "You look funny. You look old, but I knew it was you."

"How did you know, sweetie?"

"Because I love you."

"I love you too, Ady. Now it's time to go to sleep."

"I know why you want me to go to sleep," Ady crowed.

"And why is that, little girl?" Trevor touched her nose.

She laughed. "Because you want to kiss Dani."

Everyone joined in Ady's laughter. Trevor walked over to where Dani sat speechless on the end of the bed. He tipped up her chin, and brushed her lips with his as gently as a butterfly lands on a flower. "She's right."

Her eyes filled with tears. "That's what I wanted, too."

Jared cleared his throat. "You're not alone."

"Oh, did you want to kiss him too, big brother?" Dani teased.

Jared shook his head. "I'm not touching that one." He left the room.

Together, Dani and Trevor tucked Ady into bed and walked downstairs.

Voices sounded from the TV as a news banner flashed across the screen.

"This is Miranda Rios at KATU News with a breaking story from downtown Portland." The reporter stood in front of Trevor's apartment building. "Today, government officials raided the apartment of renowned businessman Trevor Willis."

Trevor went stiff. "It's starting sooner than I imagined. I didn't think the news would break until tomorrow."

Dani stepped away. "You knew? What have you done?"

He put up his hands. "Dani, I haven't done anything."

"Along with the seizure of illegal drugs," continued the TV reporter, "all of the computers in the downtown apartment were confiscated as evidence in the investigation. Willis is also the suspected head of a child pornography ring."

"Whoa!" Trevor's sharp intake of breath drew everyone's attention. "I can't believe this."

Now the screen showed an officer removing a computer from Trevor's apartment. "Our sources at TW Industries claim Willis has embezzled funds from the company."

With each charge listed, Dani moved farther away from Trevor.

"A warrant has been issued for the arrest of Trevor Willis, whose current whereabouts are unknown. We'll bring you updates as they become available," finished the reporter.

Jared jumped up from the couch and punched Trevor in the jaw. "I can't decide whether to throw you out of my house or call the police."

Tony stepped in front of Jared. "You better think twice before you make another move."

The steel in Tony's voice brought Jared to himself. "All right. Trevor, you better explain yourself."

Trevor stood in front of Dani with his hand outstretched.

"Child pornography, Trevor?" she said angrily. "What about Ady?"

"Please, Dani, think. Who was living in that apartment before we left for camp?"

"I was."

"How many computers did I have?"

After several seconds, she said, "None."

Trevor opened his arms and Dani stepped into them, her tears starting to fall. "Shh, shh. Everything's going to be fine. It's going to work out."

"Boss, I hate to break this up," Tony said, "but we don't have a lot of time."

Trevor gathered everyone around the kitchen table and said, "We have to make a plan. I need to leave tonight. It's not safe around here. Dani"—he squeezed her hand—"there must've been something in the apartment that tipped them off to you."

She shrugged her shoulders. "My clothes are there, but that's about it." Another tear escaped.

"The deputy found some kind of transmitting device under the wheel well of your car," Trevor said. "They've targeted you, Dani. You're not safe here."

She rubbed her palms together and looked heavenward. "I don't know where else to go. Would I be safer at my parents' house?"

Trevor pushed a piece of her hair behind her ear. "No, you wouldn't. I think you should come with me. I can keep you out of harm's way."

Dani searched the depths of his eyes. "What about Ady?"

"Whoever it is, I don't think they know about her—yet. Her best bet is to stay with Tony." Trevor nodded to his friend. "He is very good at disappearing into thin air."

"Wouldn't Dani be safer with Tony, too?" Jared interrupted.

"No one's looking for Tony. If Dani's with them, it would compromise Ady's safety."

"But—"

Dani silenced her brother with the touch of her hand. "He's right. The most important person in this equation is Ady. No matter what happens to me or to Trevor, she must be protected."

"At least you have a choice, Dani. I didn't quite get that." Jana chuckled. "But Trevor did a good job guarding me."

"Hey," Jared complained. "What am I—chopped liver?"

"You've been watching those old comedians again." Jana leaned over and kissed her husband. "Jared, from the moment I met you, you've always been there for me."

Tony cleared his throat. "We've got to act fast. Do you have all the documents, Trevor?"

"Right in here." Trevor unzipped his computer case and pulled out a sheaf of papers. "I have identity papers for all of you. Jana and Jared, I don't know if you're safe or not, but since they looked for Dani here . . . " His insinuation hung in the air. "Here's a credit card and some cash. Consider it an opportunity to take the vacation of a lifetime."

"It looks like the planning's already been done." Jared pushed everything back toward Trevor. "We can't take this."

Trevor harrumphed. "This isn't a frivolous gift. It's yours and Jana's ticket to safety. Get over your pride." He pulled out another envelope. "Tony, here are yours and Ady's identity papers. You have everything else."

"Yes, sir."

"Dani, hurry and pack all of your things, and Ady's. We have to leave soon." Trevor took a deep breath. "Jared, here's a key for a storage unit. The address is on this card, along with the code and unit number. You'll need to exchange your car for the one in the storage unit."

Jared looked at the card. "What about my patients? I can't just leave them."

"Are all their records up to date?"

"Of course they are." Jared paused and added sheepishly, "Jana makes sure of that."

"Good," Trevor said. "I have a top-notch physical therapist ready to come in tomorrow morning."

"Trevor, I don't put my patients in just anyone's hands. He has to be exceptional."

"I know. That's why I asked Charles Armonas. He just retired, but he agreed to take over for a little while."

Jared gaped. "*The* Charles Armonas? His methods revolutionized physical therapy. How did you get him?"

"Let's just say he owes me a favor."

"I'm speechless. Thank you."

"I'm heading up to tell Ady goodbye. I hope she understands." Trevor ascended the staircase two at a time.

Ady sat on the bed in her purple pajamas and fuzzy robe. Her sniffles poked at Trevor's heart. "Hi, sweetie. Did Dani tell you that you're going with Tony?"

Another sniffle. "Uh-huh. Did I do something wrong?"

"No, you're such a good girl."

"Did you do something wrong, Crash? Uncle Jared yelled at you."

"No, I didn't do anything wrong, but some bad men want to hurt me, so Dani and I have to go away for a while."

"Take me with you." Ady propelled herself into his arms, and her tears morphed into sobs.

"You'll be safer with Tony." Trevor wiped away her tears with his handkerchief.

Her shoulders slumped but she nodded. "Okay." Bruce's disappearance had forced Ady to grow up too fast. However, in the last few weeks, she'd become a normal, happy four-year-old girl. Now, the weight of the past seemed to press on her shoulders, bringing back the frightened child.

Trevor hugged the girl who'd giggled her way into his heart. "I'll call you as often as I can. When this is all over, I'll come and get you."

Ady hugged him tight. "I love you, Crash. Please come home," her tiny voice whispered in his ear.

"I will, sweetie. I promise."

She dove into Dani's embrace. "Please come back."

"I will, Ady. I will." She clung to the little girl and kissed the top of her head. "Let's go. Tony's ready for you."

The three walked down the stairs, and Ady took Tony's hand. When they reached the door, Ady broke away for one last tearful hug from Trevor and Dani, then left with leaden feet.

Twenty-Seven

Dani watched the street long after Tony and Ady drove away. When she finally joined the others at the kitchen table, Trevor said, "We've got to change your appearance, Dani." He opened a bag and pulled out a box of hair color.

"I haven't dyed my hair since I was fifteen. A friend colored it purple. I learned my lesson."

"Suit yourself. We could go with a wig, but hair color doesn't blow off in the wind or make you sweat in hot weather."

Dani sighed. "Okay, I'll do it. What shade did you get?"

He read the label. "Burgundy black. Supposedly it washes out in twenty-eight shampoos."

"You're turning it purple again? I can't believe it."

"Hey, it could be worse. I'm a redheaded cowboy.

"Are you sure about this, Trevor?" Dani asked.

"Dead sure."

"Then let's do it."

Trevor pulled out a hair trimmer. "Okay. Jared, what kind of barber are you?"

Jared grabbed the trimmer. "You don't want to know, but I'd love to get a sharp instrument near your throat."

Trevor chuckled and took a step back. "Uh, Jana, will you tell your husband to behave? And then can you help Dani get ready? We need to leave as soon as possible."

"Honey, don't take any extra skin from Trevor," Jana teased Jared. Then she shooed Dani into the hall bathroom and showed her how to turn the knob just right to get warm water.

"Jana, I'm so scared. First that man tried to kidnap me, and now all these charges against Trevor. I don't know what tomorrow will bring."

Jana smiled. "Maybe just take one day at a time, I guess." She led Dani to a chair in front of the vanity and began applying the dye with gloved hands. "Do you trust Trevor?"

Dani opened her eyes. "Yes. In fact, I've fallen in love with him. He is so confident, and kind, and considerate. It's like he knows just what to do or say to make me feel better. He's amazing with Ady. I feel all giddy whenever I think of him."

Jana laughed. "You have it bad."

Dani looked up at her sister-in-law in the mirror and nodded.

Jana squeezed Dani's shoulders. "Then I'm happy for you both."

A knock sounded on the bathroom door and Trevor called, "Ready for your next hair-color client?"

"Come in. I'm about to set the timer for Dani's hair."

Trevor stepped into the room. As if he couldn't stop himself, he captured Dani's fingers and raised them to his lips. "You are beautiful," he said before moving to the tub to get his hair wet.

Dani handed him a beige towel. "Let's get going on you, cowboy. I'll take care of him, Jana, if that's all right."

"Let me know if you need anything." Jana left the room and closed the door behind her.

"Should I be worried?" Trevor asked Dani.

She put her hand on her hips. "It depends."

"Depends on what?"

"On how honest you are with me." Her voice shrank with every word.

He put the towel on his shoulders and sat on the chair in front of the mirror. "Um, how long do we have on that timer?"

"You're avoiding my question." Dani poured the color and developer into the plastic bottle. She replaced the lid, put gloves on, and shook the bottle to mix the two liquids.

Trevor frowned. "No, I just don't want to leave your purple hair color in too long."

"Yeah, right." She held the bottle above his head.

"Okay, start the process and we'll talk."

Dani squeezed the dye onto his newly shorn head. "It looks like this'll be easier than mine. He really took a lot off."

"How can I be a redneck if you can't see my neck?" Trevor winked at her in the mirror.

After applying color to his roots, she rubbed it into the rest of his hair. "Now, back to the question. Will you be completely honest with me? What you know, I'll know?"

He looked down for several seconds, then up at Dani in the mirror. "Yes, I owe that to you. What I know, you'll know."

"My first question is, how did you know about the arrest warrant if you're innocent?"

"Don told me. They obtained search warrants based solely on the accusations of an anonymous caller. Don is keeping me in the loop."

"Wow." Dani stopped. "Won't Don get in trouble for that? Couldn't he lose his job with the FBI, or even go to prison?"

Trevor studied the floor. "Yes, he could."

Dani peeled off the gloves and threw them in the trash can. She glanced at the timer. "I have a few more minutes." She moved to face Trevor. "It will be okay. I'm staying with you." She kissed him lightly. "But"—she touched his lips—"remember our bargain. Everything you know, I know. Capiche?"

"Capiche." He leaned in to kiss her, but the moment was shattered by the timer. Dani clamored to turn it off. Then Trevor led her to the tub and said, "Lean over and we'll rinse your hair."

"Oh, set the timer for nine minutes."

"I'll finish this and then set the timer for six minutes."

The door opened and Jared stuck his head in. "You two doing okay?"

"Yes. We're fine, big brother."

"Good. I thought I'd sit here and keep you both company." He leaned against the wall and crossed his arms.

Dani rolled her eyes. "We don't need a chaperone."

"It's fine, honey," Trevor said. "You need to get the dye out of your hair. It's getting purpler by the second." He rinsed her hair, then massaged in the conditioner and rinsed again. He wrapped the towel around her hair. Once he had dried his hands, he turned to Jared. "Do you have any questions before I take care of the goop in my hair?"

"Where are you going?"

"I'll find a place to lay low tonight, and then we'll try to make it to my place in Newberg. After that, I plan on flying to Phoenix to clear my name."

"You will watch out for my sister? Keep her safe?" Jared glanced at Dani.

"I give you my solemn promise." Trevor smiled and held up three fingers on his right hand. "Scout's honor."

"I'm trusting you, Willis. Don't make me come after you." Jared poked his finger at Trevor's chest.

Dani rolled her eyes. "Stop the dramatics. We'll see you soon. That's a hint, by the way."

Reluctantly, Jared left the room.

After rinsing his own hair, Trevor combed it out in front of the mirror. "There are some clothes on your bed. If you'll go change into them, I'll be done in a few minutes."

She had reached the door when Trevor called, "Hey."

Dani whirled around. "What?"

"Purple looks good on you." He winked.

She threw her towel at him and left.

Twenty-Eight

At the Newberg police station, Officer Mills dressed for duty in front of his locker. He checked in the mirror and straightened his collar before heading to the briefing room.

The police chief cleared his throat to start the daily meeting. "Good morning. The big news for today is the warrant for the arrest of Trevor Willis. It's not likely he'll be out here, but keep your eyes peeled."

Willis . . . I know that name, thought Officer Mills. *Why does it sound so familiar?* He drew a gasp of air. *The guy I stopped a few weeks ago.*

The chief continued listing the charges. "Embezzlement, child pornography, possession of narcotics with intent to distribute—"

Panic surged through Officer Mills. *Child pornography— he had a kid with him.* He jumped from his seat.

"Officer Mills"—the chief pointed at him—"did you have something to say?"

"Do you have a picture of him?"

"Yes." The chief clicked on a remote control, and Trevor's face smiled down from the screen.

"I stopped him a few weeks ago, Chief. He was dressed as a Scoutmaster, and he had a boy with him in the truck."

"Thank you. I believe this warrant is now our main priority. You're dismissed. Let's keep Newberg safe. Officer Mills, could you stay for a moment?"

"Yes, sir."

"Mills, I want you to talk to Martin, get him whatever information you have. Let's put this scumbag behind bars."

"I don't intend to let him go again.

§

A rusty, banged-up pick-up truck with Texas plates drove from the Oregon coast toward Newberg. Dani sat in the passenger seat wearing a blue-plaid button-up shirt and low-cut jeans. A cowboy hat rested on her lap. Dressed in tight jeans, a faded Western shirt with the sleeves rolled up to his biceps, and a pair of scuffed cowboy boots, Trevor drove with the windows down and country music blaring. He somehow managed to keep a white Stetson on his head.

Dani glanced at him and smiled. *He sure looks good like that. Maybe he should adopt the look in real life.*

"A penny for your thoughts," he said, bursting her reverie.

"I, well . . . I always thought I would marry a redhead." She bit her lip and blushed.

He winked. "Oh, and I thought you were admiring the way I looked."

She didn't reply but glanced out the window, embarrassed.

Trevor laughed. "You were thinking how good I looked?"

Dani glared at him. "How long till we get there?"

"About twenty minutes."

"Can we turn on the air and close the windows? I feel like I'm in a hurricane."

He looked at her windblown hair. "I guess I can do that. Maybe in addition to being a championship bull rider, I can be a master mechanic who can keep this bucket of bolts running with air conditioning."

"Thanks." She rolled up the window with an old-fashioned hand crank. "Freshly dyed hair really doesn't taste that great."

§

Two pairs of eyes watched a pick-up truck pull into Trevor's driveway in Newberg.

"Is it him?"

A man stepped down from the cab and slipped his arms into a denim jacket.

"Yeah, it's him."

"You sure?"

"Pretty sure."

"Let's go."

They scrambled down from the tree and approached Trevor as he perused the yard. He put his hand on the front door handle, but tensed at the crack of a twig. With a finger to his lips, he motioned through the window for the woman in the car to duck down. Then he reached into his jacket and pulled out his weapon. He moved quickly toward the sound and pointed his gun.

"Come out with your hands up."

The intruders stepped into the light. Trevor lowered his weapon. "Sean, Luke. What are you two doing out here? I might have shot you."

Sean stepped forward. "With your CIA-issued gun?"

Trevor chuckled. "I'm still not with the CIA." He lowered his voice. "It's FBI, but if you tell anyone, I'll deny it."

"Not even Jeff?" Sean ventured.

"No! He's got the biggest mouth around. Now, what are you doing here?"

"Uh, we heard the news report and knew it wasn't true, so we waited for you to see if you needed our help." Jeff stared at Trevor. "Wow. You look different, Brother Willis."

"Yes, I'm a master of disguise—at least if you believe shows like *Mission Impossible.*"

Luke chuckled. "Yeah, right. What can we do?"

"I'm touched, boys, both for your trust in me and for your willingness to help. There is actually one small thing you can do for me." Trevor opened Dani's door.

"Whoa, who's that?" Luke asked, obviously impressed.

Trevor growled. "She's too old for you, kid."

"Where'd you'd find her?"

"Luke, would you like me to throw you in the lake again?" Trevor helped Dani out of the car. "I'd introduce you, but then I'd have to kill you."

Luke gave a little smile. "Ha, ha. I get it, Brother Willis."

"It was a joke, but I'm still not going to introduce you. As I was saying, if you really want to help me, you can take this garbage sack and throw it away somewhere else."

Sean leaned forward. "Is it nuclear waste?"

"You need to stop watching all those spy movies. It's all the stuff from the hair dye."

"Aw, that's boring." Sean kicked the dirt. "Anything else?"

"Don't let anyone know you've seen us."

"We can do that. Uh, Brother Willis?"

"Yes, Sean?"

"We have something for you. Here's my super cool multifunction Swiss Army knife."

Trevor held out his left hand in a Scout handshake. "Thank you. I'll keep this and give it back when I return."

Luke glanced at the ground. "I don't have anything awesome, but I thought you might like my incendiary device."

Trevor accepted the Bic lighter. "At least you won't be setting anyone else on fire. Okay, I have to grab a few things inside before I leave. Thanks for taking care of the garbage."

"Bye." Sean wiped a speck from his eye.

Trevor stowed the items in his pocket. "Take care, boys."

He grabbed Dani's hand and they hurried into the house. "Can you go through the pantry and grab some food?" he asked her. "Granola bars, water, nuts, etc."

In his office, he downloaded a file onto a flash drive before moving his computer equipment into a hidden room. He replaced the computer with one that had been wiped clean. Then he removed cash and documents from his safe and dropped the items into a valise.

He had just exited the office when the front door slammed open and Sean rushed into the living room, shouting, "Brother Willis! Brother Willis!"

Trevor took hold of his shoulders. "Breathe, Sean. What's going on?"

"My mom just called me." The boy sucked in a lungful of oxygen. "Officer Mills is at my house and wants to talk to me." Another breath. "About you."

"Okay, where's Luke?"

"He's dumping the garbage sack before he heads home."

"Thanks. You're great. Now, go home and forget you ever saw us." Trevor grabbed Dani's arm. "Come on. We have to get out of here."

Police sirens rang through the air as they drove away.

Twenty-Nine

"I'm not sure how long I'll be able to elude the authorities," Trevor said quietly into his cell phone. He stared out the curtain of the hotel room. The green glow of the Vacancy sign flashed on his skin. "We had a close call this morning in Newberg."

"How's Dani holding up?" Don asked over the airwaves.

Through the door to the adjoining room, Trevor glanced at her still form on the bed. "She's sleeping now. I don't know why she believes in me, but I'm grateful she does."

"The same reason I believe in you," Don replied. "I've had a watch on your alias, and no one seems to have found it yet."

Trevor ran a hand through his hair. "Are there any leads on Dr. Miller's whereabouts?"

Don hesitated. "Not yet."

"What aren't you saying? They didn't find Ady, did they?"

"You tell me, Trevor. Tony disappeared into thin air. You're the only one who can contact him.

Trevor collapsed in the chair. "Good. Now just spit it out."

"It's just, well, I'm hearing rumors that the character assassination is linked to Morales."

"Morales? That's not really news."

"I know, but there are more substantiated rumors. They say he's also behind Dr. Miller's disappearance."

Trevor let out a low whistle. "Should Dani stay with me? Maybe I should send her with Tony."

"You know she's safer with you than with anyone else. You've both been through a lot, and she's still safe. It should only be a day or two before I can arrange the plane. I'll have a package for you to take to Aunt Ina in our Phoenix office. It'll put you in the clear and authorize assistance for you."

"Thanks, Don. I'll need that. Talk to you soon. Give Traci and the kids a hug for me."

§

Trevor's face stared back at him from the front page of the newspaper with the headline "Evidence Points toward Wealthy Portland Businessman in Murder of High-Profile Lawyer."

Quentin Stoddard, defense lawyer, was found shot to death in his home early this morning. The police have named Trevor Willis as a person of interest. In the past week, Willis has been implicated in numerous crimes including drug possession with an intent to distribute, embezzlement, and child pornography.

Trevor crumpled the page and threw it at the trash can, missing by a foot.

A shadow stepped between him and the garbage can. "I've never seen you miss before. Whatever you read must have really upset you." Dani reached down and picked up the errant ball of newspaper.

Trevor stared as the fluorescent light shone through her hair like a halo. He looked into her eyes. "You're an angel. Thank you for believing in me."

She sat in the chair next to him. "Anyone who knows you would never believe those allegations. They're completely ridiculous."

"After you read that"—Trevor inclined his head toward the wadded-up article in her hand—"you'll have a better idea who it is."

Dani flattened the page and began silently reading. "No doubt. It's Morales."

"That's my guess. After the shootout at the courthouse, Stoddard broke all ties with him."

"I can't believe they've already tried you in the media for murder." She read on, then declared, "Well, this is a bunch of garbage. They should be sued for printing it." She crumpled the page and tossed it at the garbage can. She didn't miss. "You were with me when it happened, Trevor. That's a solid alibi." She stood up and moved to the window. Her finger followed a raindrop zigzagging down the glass. "When is Zack supposed to get here?"

Trevor tapped his platinum Rolex. "In about five minutes." He crossed the floor to Dani and rubbed her arms. Glancing around, he caught his reflection in the window. *No one should recognize me as the man on the front page.* He wore mirrored aviator sunglasses, a Western shirt, and faded boot-cut jeans. He adjusted the brim of his cowboy hat, sending his eyes farther into shadow.

§

Larry Preston watched from the shadows of the parking garage as the ancient green Mercury Capri squealed around the corner and whipped into a parking spot near the executive terminal. A tall, lanky man wearing a baseball hat unfolded himself from the front seat and stepped out. He stretched, then walked around to the open the trunk. He reached inside and pulled out a package wrapped in plain brown paper.

Larry ran toward Zack. "Lasky! Hey, Zack, wait up!"

He turned. "Larry, what are you doing here?"

Winded from running, Larry bent down with his hands on his knees. "You're a hard man to track down, Lasky."

Zack glanced down at his watch before scanning the garage. "I'm in a hurry. What do you want?"

"Your phone." Still panting, he pointed toward Zack's pocket. "It's off. Your wife is trying to reach you."

"What?" Zack whipped his phone out of his pocket.

"Don sent me to get you. She's going into labor."

Zack opened the phone. "What are you talking about? It's on and I don't have any missed—"

Preston used the butt of his standard FBI-issue handgun to knock out his fellow agent. He returned his gun to his shoulder holster and pushed Zack's limp body into the trunk of the Capri. "Sorry about that, Lasky. I had no choice." He checked Zack's pulse. "You'll have quite a headache, but you'll be all right." He grabbed the package and shut the trunk. Walking casually to his car, he checked the writing on the tag proclaiming Aunt Ina as the recipient. He threw Zack's package on the back seat and retrieved one of his own, then carefully filled in the name and walked into the airport with his package tucked securely beneath his arm.

When he spotted Trevor, Preston squared his shoulders, stepped forward, and presented the parcel to him. "I believe you're expecting this package for Aunt Ina. You left it at home. Uncle Don said to bring it to her in Phoenix, and she'd know exactly what to do with it."

Trevor's eyes narrowed. "What are you doing here?"

"Lasky's wife went into labor, so he had to leave."

Trevor grabbed the package. "Well, thanks. We'll be taking off right away."

Preston waved, then watched Trevor walk out to a blue single-engine Cessna. Once the package was safely stowed in the cargo hold, Preston gave a mock salute and mumbled under his breath, "Have a pleasant trip, Willis."

Preston made his way back to the parking garage.

Suddenly, two men flanked him on either side. "Mr. Morales thanks you for your service, but he regrets that you are no longer useful to him."

Before Preston could react, a bullet silenced him.

Trevor and Dani left the terminal and headed for a small plane on the tarmac. The closer they got to the aircraft, the slower Dani walked. Her hands were shaking.

Trevor placed his valise in the back seat. "What's wrong, Dani?"

She opened the passenger door and climbed into the plane. "Where's the pilot?"

"I thought you knew. I'm the pilot."

She gasped. "What?" Her breaths came shallow and fast.

Trevor caressed her cheek. "It's all right. I've logged more than a thousand flight hours."

"I'm afraid of flying in these small planes. My cousin was killed in one when it crashed several years ago. I thought I could do this." She shivered.

"Honey, you *can* do this. I'm right here with you. Let me get everything ready to go and I'll be right back."

Trevor pulled the blocks from under the wheels and stowed them in the baggage compartment next to the package marked for Aunt Ina. He latched the bay and climbed into the pilot's seat. "I put your pillow and a blanket behind your seat."

A sniffle escaped from Dani. "Thanks."

"Everything will be fine. Don't cry."

The tears began in earnest. "Let's see. I was almost kidnapped, Ady was pried away from me, I heard terrible rumors about my boyfriend, and my hair is purple."

Trevor squeezed her hand. "So, you're considering me your boyfriend. Today can't be too horrible."

Dani punched him in the arm. "Don't make me laugh when I want to cry."

"Let's be on our way."

With the preflight checklist complete, he started the engine and drove to the runway. He accelerated until the plane's nose lifted. Then he pulled back on the yoke. The Cessna rose, soon to make the airport a distant memory.

He looked over at Dani and laughed. "You can open your eyes and relax your hold on that pillow. We've taken off."

A few minutes later, she screamed as a pocket of air caused the plane to dip sharply.

"It okay," Trevor assured her. "Why don't you try to sleep?"

Without a word, she pulled the blanket tighter and hugged the pillow until she drifted off.

Thirty

Trevor navigated the single-engine plane over the Mogollon Rim in Northern Arizona. The tension in his neck loosened when he gazed at Dani curled up on the seat beside him. She slept on her puffy frog pillow nestled against the door. *I hope Don's right and the information will clear my name.* Trevor reached out to touch Dani but stopped at the last second and grabbed his water bottle instead. *When all of this is over . . .*

A bang shook the plane, startling Dani out of her slumber. Trevor dropped the bottle and fought to control the pitching aircraft. The famous words of *Apollo 13* commander, James Lovell, replayed through his mind: *Houston, we have a problem.* "Dani, grab the radio," Trevor said through clenched teeth.

She fumbled with the microphone. "Got it."

"Call in a Mayday."

She shouted into the microphone, "Mayday, Mayday! We're going down. Mayday, Mayday." Dani's terror echoed his own. "It's dead, Trevor. The radio's dead!"

"That explosion came from the back—it shouldn't have knocked out power." He looked out the side window. Moments ago, scattered lights broke through the night on the ground below, but now darkness shrouded the earth. "It seems to have affected things on the ground, too."

Please help us, Trevor prayed. He scanned the horizon for a place to land. He nodded toward a fairly level canyon. "We're landing over there. Keep the blanket around you and cover your face with the pillow."

Trevor felt unseen hands guiding his as he manually aimed for his target. With all the electronics wiped out, he barely managed to control the descent. The trees sped past in a blur. His ears rang at the horrific noise as the wings clipped the tall ponderosa pines. Only the shoulder harnesses kept him and Dani from being flung violently around the cabin.

When the plane hit the ground, the control panel crumpled in front of Trevor, sending a fiery pain through his leg. The aircraft skidded through the underbrush with the roar of a freight train. He watched the trees in front of the plane part as easily as if a comb had parted the trees.

Finally, the plane stopped. The damaged propeller continued to scrape the nose, grating on the ears like microphone feedback. When the propeller finally wound down to a standstill, silence engulfed the cockpit.

A moan sounded next to Trevor. "Dani?" No response. Panic rose to his throat. "Dani!" He reached out to check her wrist for a pulse. Relief rushed over him as a rhythmic beat met his fingers. He patted her cheeks. "Dani, please wake up."

Trevor tried to move his legs, but they wouldn't budge under the mangled instrument panel. With the acrid smell of aviation fuel in his nostrils, he struggled to free himself. A few long minutes later, he managed to climb out of the pilot seat. Ignoring the pain that shot through his thigh, he unstrapped Dani and moved her as gently as possible. Adrenaline pushed him forward to the shelter of a large boulder. He carefully placed her on the ground before slumping against the rock.

Trevor closed his eyes and breathed deeply, gathering his strength. Time stood still in the quiet forest. *No, there's no time to rest—not until we're safe.* He forced his eyelids open and shook his head to clear the grogginess. His mind registered the unexpected position of the afternoon sun. He wiped his forehead, then stared at his hand, now covered with dark-red specks. He glanced down at his leg. A narrow, three-inch sliver of metal jutted out of his thigh.

His gaze settled on Dani's still form. He knelt by her side and searched for injuries. A large lump had formed at her temple, but there was no other obvious damage. "Dani, honey, please open your eyes." Trevor had helped Jared give a blessing to Ben Carpenter but had never given one by himself. *Will it work?* Praying it would, Trevor took a deep breath and placed his hands on Dani's head. He felt the words of the blessing flow through him as he spoke. When faced her once more, her warm brown eyes held his gaze. Gratitude washed over him, and he raised his eyes heavenward. "Thank you."

Dani stretched her arm toward Trevor and used her thumb to try to wipe the dried blood from his forehead. Then she noticed his thigh and gasped, "You're hurt!" She tried to rise but grabbed her head and sank back against the boulder.

"I know, honey. Just relax and don't try to move. If the plane hasn't blown up by now, it probably won't." He exerted the effort needed to stand. "I'm going back to get the first-aid kit, then I'll take care of my leg. I'll be back before you know it." He caressed her cheek, his hand lingering briefly. "I love you."

Trevor staggered back to the wreckage. He used Sean's knife to cut away the material around his wound, then found the first-aid kit. Fortunately, the narrow metal splinter hadn't hit any major arteries. With Luke's lighter, Trevor sterilized the knife blade and removed the splinter. Then he hobbled around to inspect the damage to the plane.

When he saw the hole in the fuselage, a wave of nausea swept over him. This was no accident. A blast had pushed the sheet metal outward with explosive force. Trevor spotted the remains of a familiar-looking device—the electronic pulse generator Bruce had developed.

The rumors were true. Morales had kidnapped Bruce.

Thirty-One

Trevor helped Dani through the dense brush as they made their way down the mountain. He carried the important items in a backpack, along with food and water. Occasionally Dani swayed as she walked. Trevor's leg had gone numb.

An old house with some run-down outbuildings appeared through the trees. Trevor veered in that direction. When they reached a gentle creek, he carried Dani across, splashing through the water. He gently set her down on the opposite bank. A cow lowed and two horses walked toward them, obviously hoping for a treat.

As the last sunrays slipped behind the mountain, Trevor and Dani crossed the fenced-off garden and entered the ramshackle barn through a large, doorless opening. He used dried leaves to clear the mouse droppings off the hayloft, then found an empty galvanized bucket to use as a step-up to the loft. Dani spread out her frog blanket, and they ate a couple of granola bars and drank a little more of their water.

"We'll check at the house in the morning and try to find a way down to Phoenix," Trevor said.

Dani snuggled against him. "I just want to sleep."

He wrapped his arms tighter around her. "Go ahead. Everything will work out fine. I promise." He stared up at the stripes of moonlight showing through the boards until he finally fell into an exhausted sleep.

The early morning sunlight touched Trevor's face. He opened his eyes and jerked back. A pair of ebony eyes watched him. Fear turned into relief. The eyes belonged to a girl about Ady's age. "Well, hello there. You startled me."

She glanced above his right shoulder. "There's a long daddy spider. I wanted to squish it, but it might have childrens."

"Yeah, childrens." A little boy stepped out from behind the girl.

Trevor inched closer to the edge of the shelf. "Let's let him live so he can take care of his kids." The spider scurried away.

Dani opened her eyes and smiled at the little girl. "I'm Dani and this is Trevor. What's your name?"

"Kaylee. This is my brother, Max. Why are you in Nanny's barn?"

Dani sat up and picked hay from her hair. "We were in a plane crash on the mountain. We walked down to get help."

"It was late and we didn't want to wake anyone, so we slept in here," Trevor added. He climbed off the ledge and then helped Dani down.

"Jeremy—he's my big brother, but not my biggest brother—went to get Daddy. We stayed to make sure you weren't dead or anything."

Trevor glanced at Dani, then back at Kaylee. "Well, thanks for watching over us."

"We're at Nanny's house 'cause there was a big boom and Nanny didn't have electricity," continued the little girl.

"Everyone lost power?" Trevor asked.

"Yep, even Nanny's neighbors. It's back now."

Trevor leaned over and whispered to Dani, "Bruce must have perfected the pulse."

Kaylee took Dani's hand and Trevor's and pulled them toward the open door. "Nanny's making pancakes, and she always makes too many so there will be enough for you."

Max cautiously took Dani's other hand.

On the way to the house, they met the concerned father. He maneuvered his children behind him. "Kaylee, Max, go wash up." He glared at Trevor and Dani. "What's going on here?"

Trevor explained the events of the last few days, leaving out the part about him being wanted by authorities. "Kaylee mentioned electricity going out. It almost sounds like an EP—an electronic pulse."

"I figured as much," replied the man. "That's why we came up to check on my mother. Everything is back to normal, though. A colleague of mine, Bruce Miller, was working on EP's with reversible effects."

Trevor's head popped up. "Bruce? He works for me."

The man's body tensed. "You're Trevor Willis?"

"Yes, that's me."

"From what I hear, you're quite the criminal."

"No, no!" Trevor stepped back. "I'm not guilty of any of those charges. I testified against Alejandro Morales. We think he had me framed to get revenge."

The man relaxed a little. "Well, I guess I'll give you a chance because Bruce trusted you."

"How do you know he trusted me?"

"Because he researched you—not just your company."

Trevor's foot stopped in midair over the flagstone steps leading up to the porch. "He researched me? Why?"

The man grunted. "He felt he was being followed, and he worried about what would happen to his daughter if something happened to him. He trusted you with Ady. That says a lot."

"Wow," Trevor replied. "I had no idea."

"I'm not one to believe in coincidences, but if you dropped out of the sky right here where my mother lives, and we both know Bruce, I'd say the chance of this meeting being a coincidence is about a million to one."

Trevor smiled. "I don't believe in coincidences either. Just divine plans."

"I agree with you there." The man opened the porch door.

"This is Dani Carpenter," Trevor said.

"Charles Hunt. My mother has breakfast ready. We might as well feed you before we decide whether or not to turn you over to the authorities."

§

While the breakfast dishes dried in the dish drainer, Trevor and Dani sat at the yellow Formica table. Via his computer, he accessed the security footage from the apartment.

Dani bit her fingernail. "My goodness, Trevor. Two types of drugs."

"That's not all. Look at the foyer shot."

She leaned closer to the screen. "He's pulling money out of that bag."

"And the leader just handed him a sheet of paper, probably the combination to my safe." Trevor clenched his fists and drew a deep breath. "No one should have that."

Dani's eyebrows lifted. "I didn't know you had a safe."

"Something's not adding up."

"What?"

"Look at that guy." Trevor pointed to the screen. "The leader. He keeps his face away from the camera, but does he look familiar to you?"

She leaned forward and squinted. The color drained from her face. "Zack?"

Thirty-Two

Charles Hunt leaned over Trevor's shoulder. "I take it you've found something important?"

"Yeah. It looks like a person we trusted may be on Morales's payroll."

"I don't understand," Dani said. "Why would he do this?"

Trevor sighed. "There are a lot of reasons. He might have needed the money. A government agent doesn't make all that much. And Zack's got a baby on the way. Or he might have been threatened. Or . . . "

"Could he be behind the explosion on the plane?" Dani's eyes bored into Trevor's.

"He could be, but I don't think so. I need to talk to Don." Trevor retrieved his phone from the backpack. "I need to call him right now."

She placed a hand on his arm. "Trevor, remember our deal? Everything you know, I know?"

"I don't *know* anything." He lifted her chin to look into her eyes. "When I find out, I'll tell you. I promise. Why don't you go lie down on the couch? You're looking a little pale."

"I'm feeling beat," she admitted.

He left her in the living room with a cool washcloth over her eyes.

On the front porch, Trevor dialed his brother-in-law's private cell. Eight rings later, Don's voicemail greeting came on. After the beep, Trevor left a message. "Don," he said with an edge of irritation, "I know you're there because you're never without this phone. Our plane went down, and I need some answers. I better hear back from you in two minutes or less."

Half a minute later, Trevor's phone rang. He accepted the call. "Took you long enough."

"A plane crash? Are you okay?" Don demanded.

"Yeah, we were lucky. I managed to crash-land the plane and we walked away—well, I carried Dani out unconscious, but she's okay now."

"What about you?"

"I'll have a pretty nasty scar on my leg—it'll ruin my swimsuit look." Trevor touched the hole in his jeans.

"Where are you?"

"Somewhere around the Mogollon Rim in Arizona. I think the town is called Pine."

"So, you might have been right about Larry Preston. He was found dead at the airport—shot in the head. Zack had been knocked out and shoved into the trunk of his car."

"You mean Caitlyn wasn't in labor?" Trevor asked.

"What are you talking about? She's still holding on."

"Larry brought the package for Aunt Ina. He said Zack couldn't deliver it because Caitlyn was having the baby." Trevor stopped as realization struck. "Larry must have placed the EP in the package. He brought the plane down."

"The original package Zack had was in Larry's car. We wondered why you left without it." Don paused. "Were you able to look at the security footage from your apartment?"

"Dani and I just scanned it. Several men entered my apartment and planted evidence."

"I know you, Trevor. What aren't you saying?"

"Dani and I feel the lead man looked an awful lot like Zack."

"Are you kidding? He was actually on camera?"

"Well, he wore a hat and always stayed in the shadows, but both Dani and I thought we recognized his mannerisms."

"Okay, okay." Don gave a disgusted huff. "I can't believe he'd betray us like this. I'll keep an eye on him. You and Dani be careful. Try to get the surveillance video to the Phoenix office. I will overnight the evidence to the SAC, and email an official request for assistance.

"One more thing."

"Go ahead, Trevor."

"This man on the video had the combination to my safe. It's not written down anywhere, and you and Traci are the only people who know it."

"Are you accusing me of something?" Don asked tightly.

"Just think about it, *brother*. And remember that Dani and I nearly got killed."

Trevor disconnected the phone and gazed out at the beautiful Mogollon Rim.

§

Charles's mother—Nanny, as Kaylee called her—walked onto the porch. "Well, young man, we're going to need to take care of that leg of yours."

"No, I'm fine," Trevor said. "But thank you, Mrs. Hunt."

"Call me Nan like everybody else. And about your leg, I don't plan on taking no for an answer. Follow me." She led him into the bathroom and pointed to a pink fuzzy robe draped over a hook. "Take your pants off and slip that on."

"I'll be fine, really." He began to back out of the room.

"Put your pride in your back pocket where it belongs and get those pants off. Now."

Trevor stared at his feet. "Yes, ma'am."

Nan left the room while he discarded the pants and donned the feminine robe. She returned a few minutes later with a blue metal Craftsman tool box. "Growing up on a ranch far away from the big city, you have to be your own doc." She opened the box and removed a pair of medical scissors. "Let's see what it's like under that bloody gauze."

Trevor forced his gaze to the first-aid kit. "I've never seen a tool box that color."

"I used to have a rusty old red one, but when they came out with this color a few years ago, I thought it was prettier." Nan pried up a piece of gauze and inserted the scissors.

Trevor gasped involuntarily.

"I'm sorry. We may need to soak the bandages to get them off." She placed a warm washcloth on his thigh. "So, do you think your plane crash and the electricity being knocked out are related?"

"I didn't hit any power lines."

"I wasn't talking about that." Nan removed the gauze from his leg and finished wiping off the dried blood. "There was something odd about that outage. Even my watch stopped."

Trevor gave a small nod. "Yes, there's something odd. And yes, it had something to do with the plane crash. Ouch!"

"Just a little hydrogen peroxide to clean everything out." She took a closer look with a magnifying glass. "It's deep, but not very wide. I think a few butterfly strips will work to close it up." She dried the area and met his gaze. "You were lucky."

"Actually, I wasn't lucky. I was blessed."

§

The green Chevy Astro van pulled onto the country road and headed toward Strawberry and the Verde Valley. From there, they would take Interstate 17. Trevor, Dani, and most of the Hunt family sat in the van. Joshua and Lana followed with Nan in a gold Ford Taurus. Kaylee and Max occupied car seats in the middle row. Jeremy and Dani settled in the back bench seat. Trevor crouched on the floor between the middle seat and the sliding door.

"You comfortable down there?" Charles glanced over his shoulder.

"Feels like I'm riding on a cloud with all these pillows." Trevor put his hands above his head and leaned back on the soft stack of bedding.

Kaylee sighed. "I wish I could sit there instead of my car seat."

"Me too." Jeremy put his feet up on either side of her head.

"Daddy, Jeremy put his stinky feet by me."

"Put your feet down, Jeremy," Charles ordered.

Dani touched Trevor's head with her toes. He reached back and rubbed her foot.

"Trevor doesn't mind if Dani does it to him," Jeremy said.

Trevor laughed. "Her feet aren't stinky."

"Neither are mine." Jeremy lifted his foot to his nose and drew back. "Eew. Sorry, Kaylee. They do stink."

Charles's wife, Anne, pointed to a line of cars up ahead. "Charles, what's happening?"

Trevor made his way to his knees and looked out the windshield. "It's a police barricade." He turned to Dani, who met his eyes. "I'm giving myself up," he told her. "I don't want you all to get in trouble."

"You aren't giving yourself up alone!"

Trevor knelt before her in the cramped space and stroked her cheek. "Honey, please stay here."

Dani shook her head. "We're in this together and we're staying that way." She touched his lips with her finger to stop his objection. "No arguments."

His eyes shone with unshed tears. "How did I ever get blessed enough to find you?"

"Stop it with that stuff," Jeremy interrupted. "We're almost to the roadblock."

"Quick, Trevor, sit here." Dani patted the place by her.

He took a seat. "What now?"

"This." She put her arms around Trevor's neck and kissed him. "Hopefully, they'll just ignore us."

"We're next," Anne called.

Trevor drew back enough to speak. "You think we'll need to keep this up till we get to Phoenix?"

Dani rolled her eyes. "Nice try. Just through the roadblock."

"Darn."

Officer Brighton leaned his head in the driver's side window. "We would like to check your vehicle. There's a fugitive and we have reason to believe he might be coming this way. Have you picked up any hitchhikers?"

"No, sir," Charles replied.

"Mom, Lena and Brad won't stop kissing," Jeremy complained. "It makes me want to ralph."

Anne didn't even pause. "Lena, do I have to separate the two of you?

"We're just kissing, Mom," Dani whined.

The officer looked in the back and waved them through, until a man in a dark suit put a hand on the officer's shoulder and whispered to him.

"Sir, can I have you and your family exit the vehicle?" Officer Brighton said. "The younger children can stay in their car seats." He touched the handle of his gun.

Charles glanced in the rearview mirror. Trevor nodded. "Okay."

Max and Kaylee started crying when everyone got out of the van. "It's all right," Anne soothed as she leaned through an open window.

The suit walked directly to Trevor, who stiffened when the man grabbed his chin and turned his head to examine him from different angles.

Trevor stood ramrod straight with daggers shooting from his eyes. The suit nudged him toward the officer and then grabbed Dani's arm, which caused Trevor to break contact with Brighton and remove the man's hand from her. Officer Brighton drew his weapon. Trevor stepped in front of Dani.

"You can put that away, Officer." The suit motioned to Officer Brighton, then addressed Trevor. "Mr. Willis, I will ask nicely—once. Please come with me. Do you have anything in the van?"

"Yes I do, but I don't know who this Willis fellow is. I think this a case of mistaken identity."

"I don't think so, Mr. Willis. Get your things and follow me."

"What if I refuse? What are you charging us with?"

The man leaned close and whispered, "I would rather not use force in front of the children."

Trevor glanced at Kaylee and Max, and then at Dani. "Do you need both of us?"

"Yes, we do."

Trevor removed his backpack from the cargo space in the van while Dani hugged Kaylee and Max. They thanked the Hunt family and followed the suit to a white van. Trevor helped Dani inside but remained outside the vehicle.

"Have a seat, Mr. Willis," ordered the suit.

Trevor frowned. "The name's Flynn. I'll just stand here until you tell me why you've detained us."

"Like I said, please have a seat."

Trevor crossed his arms and stared down the man.

"Mr. Willis—"

"Flynn."

The man shook his head. "All right then. I am special agent Percival Graham. Don Townsend asked me to find you and bring you to the Phoenix office. We wanted it to seem as though you were still under suspicion in case someone was watching you. Do you have the surveillance video?"

After a pause, Trevor said, "I do."

"Now, if I can get you in the van, we can be on our way."

"I'll need to let the Hunts know we're okay. You sure picked a lousy way to bring me into the Bureau."

Trevor pulled out his cell phone and sat next to Dani on the bench seat. She unbuckled her seat belt and moved to one of the captain's chairs.

Thirty-Three

In the FBI office in Phoenix, Trevor and Dani sat on straight-back chairs at a steel table. A mirrored window occupied a good portion of one wall of the interrogation room .

Trevor reached for her hand, but she jerked it back and faced away from him.

"Dani, please talk to me." He touched her shoulder.

"You don't want to hear what I have to say." Her foot tapped on the floor in a staccato pattern.

"Yes, I do."

She turned the full force of her anger on him. "Why did you try to keep me from coming?"

Trevor got to his feet. "I love you, Dani. I want to protect you—keep you away from the evil people in this world. Life wouldn't be worth living without you." He sat again and buried his head in his hands. "Especially if it was because I didn't protect you."

Her anger seemed to deflate as she let out a slow breath. She stood behind him and kneaded the tension from his neck and shoulder. "I feel the same way about you. I love you and would shrivel up and die if I lost you. I depend on you and discover new and amazing things about you every day. But Trevor—"

"Uh-oh. Here it comes."

She leaned in and whispered, "I mean it when I say we're in this together."

"But, I—"

"No buts. You either love me enough to trust me in everything, or we're through."

"I'll do anything to keep us together—even telling you everything." His eyes narrowed. "But that doesn't mean I'd let you get in a dangerous situation."

"I'd rather know what's going on than not know."

He stood up and kissed her. They broke apart when a knock came at the door.

Agent Graham entered the room. "Good. It looks like you've kissed and made up. Things were getting pretty tense in here. Now, Ms. Carpenter, would you follow Special Agent Sandoval. He'll take you to get something to eat."

Dani glanced at Trevor, who shot her an understanding look and approached Agent Graham. "Sir—"

"Call me Percy."

"Okay, Percy. Why don't you have Sandoval bring some sandwiches in here? I would prefer Dani hear whatever we have to say."

Graham looked over his glasses at Trevor. "Are you sure?"

"Yes."

Later that evening, Special Agent Graham dropped Trevor and Dani off at the Tempe Mission Palms Resort. He and Trevor unloaded a large number of shopping bags from the trunk. "Here's the room key. I got you the one-bedroom suite since you're supposed to be a newlywed couple. You can sleep on the sofa, and she can lock the bedroom door." Graham paused a moment. "You know, I almost didn't recognize you with that close-cut red hair. Good disguise."

"Thanks. What tipped you off?"

"For a teenage boy making out with his girlfriend, you had too many muscles and a pretty good five-o'clock shadow. "

Trevor flexed his muscles. "I'll take that as a compliment." He offered his hand to Graham. "You'll pick us up at eleven?"

"Affirmative." Graham's gaze bored into Trevor's. "Tomorrow is the beginning of the end for the Morales empire."

Trevor's eyes reflected the steel of the agent's. "Tomorrow."

Trevor put his arm around Dani's waist., and the two watched Graham exit the circular driveway

She veered toward the fountain in the drop-off zone and pointed to the water. "Hey, cowboy. Let's get a picture." She pulled out her special-issue secure phone and pushed it toward Trevor. "Here, you take it. You have longer arms."

After glancing around the parking lot, Trevor pulled down his Stetson and snapped a picture of Dani and himself. Hopefully it would be the first of many.

He checked the key envelope and steered her toward the elevators. While riding up, he looked over all the bags. "Do you happen to have a bathing suit in one of those?"

"Of course. We'll be at a resort." She looked down and blushed. "You might like it."

When they entered the suite, Dani glanced around, then hurried to the bedroom. "This is very nice. Do you want to flip for the bed?"

"No, senior agents always get the bed." He brushed past her into the bathroom. "Yes, this should do fine for me."

Dani stared at him with her mouth open.

His laugh echoed through the bathroom. "I'm kidding, of course. No flipping necessary. You take the bed." He pushed a lock of purple hair behind her ear and kissed her cheek.

"Thanks." She put her bags on the floor and looked over her shoulder. "I might even consider letting you use the bathroom sometime."

Trevor scooped her up and brought her into the bathroom, then dangled her backward over the toilet. "I think it might be time for you to get a swirly."

"Trevor, no. Don't you dare." Her head dipped closer to the toilet. "I'll let you use the bathroom. Now put me down."

"Is that a promise?"

"Yes, yes it is." Laughing, she clung to his shirt.

He carried her into the bedroom. "Would you like to go for a swim after we talk to Ady?"

"We can talk to her?"

"Of course. Graham provided me with a secure Wi-Fi card. We can use my laptop to call her. You go change while I get the connection started."

"I really miss her," Dani said as she headed into the bedroom.

The magic of Ady's laughter floated over the screen. "You look so funny, Crash. Why do you have orange hair?"

"That's nothing. Wait till you see Dani."

"Where is she?" Ady bounced up and down on the couch.

"Oh, she'll be here in a second. How are you doing?"

Ady looked as though she might cry, but she said, "Good. I guess."

"Hey, there. What's wrong? Isn't Tony being nice to you?"

"Uh-huh." She nodded, but a tear escaped. "I miss Daddy and you and Dani."

The door from the bedroom opened, and Dani stepped into the room. Trevor motioned her to the computer. "Look who I found, sweetie."

Ady squealed when she saw Dani. "You look so different. I like your purple hair."

"Thanks. It's so good to see you."

"You're lucky." Trevor interrupted the two girls. "She laughed out loud at my new look."

Ady giggled again. Trevor feigned an angry face. "What are you laughing at?"

"You belong in Phoenix," Ady said matter-of-factly.

"What do you mean?"

"'Cause everybody"—Ady spread her arms wide—"wears purple and orange when the Suns play. Even if they're not very good. Which is always."

Trevor fought to contain his laughter. "Maybe we can go to a game sometime."

"Can I get popcorn and lemonade and nachos and cotton candy?"

Dani smiled. "Maybe one or two of those. We don't want you to get sick."

"Okay." The little girl's shoulders fell. "Dani, go so I can tell Crash something?"

"I won't be far," she said, then stepped out of camera range.

Ady dropped her voice to a whisper. "Crash, if just you and me go to a game, can I get all of that?"

"I'm afraid I agree with Dani," Trevor said. "I mean, those things are good, but not all at the same time."

"Can you tell Tony I need popcorn?"

Trevor winked. "I'll do that."

Dani popped her head back in camera range. "Did you hear that, Tony?"

He appeared on the screen behind Ady and gave a two thumbs up.

"We need to let you get to bed. I love you, sweetie." Trevor blew her a kiss.

Dani blew a kiss and raised Trevor a hug. "I love you and miss you."

Ady gave a big sigh. "Goodbye. I love you." She blew kisses until the screen went black.

Dani stared at the blank screen. Trevor reached over and closed the laptop. "Are you ready to head to the pool?"

"Yep. And you?"

"Just give me a minute to change." He grabbed a shopping bag from his pile and disappeared into the bathroom. A few minutes later, he reappeared wearing a T-shirt and knee-length red and black swim trunks.

Dani let out a huge breath. "What a relief. I was afraid your taste would run toward Speedos."

"I felt uncomfortable in those when I swam in high school. I'll never wear them again." He shuddered. "Let's go."

He opened the door just as a hotel employee raised his hand to knock.

The young man stepped back. "Sorry, sir. I didn't expect the door to open."

Trevor waved off the apology. "No problem. What can I do for you?"

"These were delivered for you." He pushed a couple of ordinary black suitcases into the doorway.

"Wait just a minute." Trevor grabbed his wallet from the table and pulled out a twenty-dollar bill. "Here you go. Thanks for bringing them up."

"Thank you." The young man bowed and retreated down the hallway.

"Now, we should be ready to go." Trevor held out his arm for Dani and then locked the door behind them.

After winding around the hotel and going up and down several staircases, they finally found the deserted pool. Trevor jumped right in, while Dani subscribed to the test-the-water-with-your-big-toe method. She had progressed to her knees when he glided through the pool and surfaced in front of her.

"You know, you can jump in by yourself. Or" —he winked at her—"you can give me the opportunity to help you."

"Trevor. No!"

"I am motivated to help you because I can tell you want to experience the perfect temperature of the water."

Dani backed up to the previous step. "I promise you won't have access to the bathroom if you go through with this."

"I have my handy-dandy lock-picking tools to help me." Trevor clasped her arm.

"Please?"

"Of course I'll help you in." He lifted her above the water and walked toward the deeper end of the pool.

Her futile kicks just sent water into her own face. He reached the deepest part of the pool and tripped on an imaginary obstacle. "Oops!"

Dani screamed as she flew forward, her arms and legs flailing. She landed with a splash and sank to the bottom of the pool. Trevor waited for her to float to the top. His mirth morphed into fear when she didn't surface. He dove down and lifted her limp body out of the pool. He pushed himself out of the water, then bent his head to perform mouth-to-mouth. He jumped back when a stream of water hit him in the eye.

"You scared me to death!"

She giggled. "You should've seen your face."

"I'm sorry, Dani. Next time, I'll let you go at your own pace. Don't scare me like that again."

A shaky hand pushed away the hair from her eyes. "How did you hold your breath for so long?"

"Jared and I used to have contests all the time. I think I'm up to about two and a half minutes. I actually beat him a few times. Well, maybe once."

Trevor got to his feet and helped Dani up. "Let's try the hot tub." He locked his arm around her, afraid to let go. After they stepped into the swirling water of the Jacuzzi, she laid her head on his shoulder. The bubbles seemed to melt away the tension.

"I'm sorry for scaring you," Dani said after a few minutes. "Like Jared says, sometime my impetuousness will get me into trouble."

Trevor squeezed her shoulders. "It's okay. I deserved it." He climbed out of the hot tub and grabbed a towel for himself and one for Dani. "Here you go. I don't want you getting chilled."

"Thanks," she said softly. "Will you forgive me?"

"Always." He brushed her lips with his finger. "Again and again. Will you forgive me?"

She blinked away tears. "Always. Again and again."

Thirty-Four

"We'll be right down." Trevor set down the phone and called to Dani, "Are you ready?"

"Almost. Just a few last-minute things to throw in the suitcase."

"Didn't you do that last night?" He placed his luggage by the exit.

She poked her head out the door and smiled. "Not the last-minute things. By definition, they're packed right before you go."

"Well, if you're not out here in thirty seconds, I'll just leave without you. You'll be safe . . ."

"No such luck. I'm ready." Dani zipped the suitcase, yanked it off the bed, and walked right by him into the hallway. "Well, don't just stand there."

Trevor glanced around the room and hustled after her.

"It's a good thing this elevator is slow. Otherwise, I might have left without you," she said, then cast a sideways glance at him. "You would have been safe . . ."

Half a minute later, they stepped out of the elevator.

Special Agent Graham stood outside the front doors where he alternated between watching the time and the hotel lobby.

A clock in the lobby chimed eleven times. "Getting nervous, Agent Graham?" Trevor asked. "I think we're right on time."

Graham popped the trunk and loaded their luggage. "I have a feeling we're being watched. Hurry."

They piled into the vehicle, circled the fountain and pulled onto 5th Street toward Mill Avenue. Graham glanced in his rearview mirror every minute or two. He took a few side streets, meandered through the Arizona State University campus, and continued on toward to Sky Harbor. "It's not looking good. That navy-blue Mazda has stayed with us on every turn. I'm calling headquarters."

Trevor looked over his shoulder. "I've been watching him in the side mirror."

Graham reached for the radio. "Saguaro, this is Jackrabbit. Wiley Coyote is on our scent. What do you suggest?"

"Take him on a scenic route to the destination. We'll let you know when you can return to the burrow."

"That's a go." He turned to his passengers. "Is there anywhere you've never seen around here that you'd like to?"

Trevor shrugged. Dani mimicked the gesture. "I wouldn't mind seeing Chase Field, where the Diamondbacks play." He looked out at the cityscape. "Phoenix has sure grown. I'm surprised all the buildings don't melt in this heat."

Graham laughed. "California is built to withstand the earthquakes. Phoenix is built to withstand the heat."

"Trevor, they're still following us," Dani reported.

He reached back and patted her shaky hand. "It's okay. There's a plan for this."

"But if they're following us, they must know who we are."

"Don't worry. My guess is they're on a fishing mission," Graham said, keeping his eyes on the road. "They don't know anything for sure."

Dani shivered. "They're getting awfully close for fishing."

"You know things are only going to get worse," Trevor said gently, stroking her face with the back of his hand. "I won't feel betrayed if you stay behind."

She clasped his fingers and gave a half smile. "I know." She took a deep breath. "I'm ready. We can face anything together."

"You know I love you." He kissed her hand.

"Right back at you."

"There's the stadium. They've built up the area nicely." Graham pointed to the right. "Talking Stick Resort Arena is right next to it."

Dani huffed. "That's quite a mouthful. I'm not sure about this corporate names trend."

"I miss when they played at Veteran's Memorial Coliseum." Graham snorted. "Much less of a mouthful."

"We all know that knowledge is power," Trevor said. "What's the plan?"

"We have agents ready to whisk you away to a car, and you'll head to the Goodyear Airport, where a private jet is waiting. If they try to follow you into the executive terminal, I'll delay them long enough for you to get away. Ideally, I'll do it without blowing my cover."

Trevor pulled a pen and notebook from his shirt pocket. "How do I get to Goodyear?"

"There's a GPS with the information programmed in."

"Good. How long does it take?" He looked at his watch.

"About 30 to 40 minutes—depending on traffic."

The radio crackled. "Jackrabbit, this is Saguaro. You read?"

Graham grabbed the mike. "Affirmative, Saguaro. We're awaiting instructions."

"Proceed to the burrow. We're ready for the bunnies." The voice ordered.

"Will do. Our ETA is about twenty minutes. Over and out." Graham put the microphone back in place. "You heard Saguaro.

Our plan is in play." He veered toward the I-10 and the 202 Loop for Sky Harbor International Airport. "Dani, when you say goodbye, act as though I'm your father. Willis, respond appropriately."

"I'm not sure referring to me as a bunny is a compliment." Trevor mumbled.

Dani smiled. "At least we're bunnies together."

"True."

Graham exited the freeway and turned left into Sky Harbor's Executive Terminal. He parked in the drop-off area near the front door. Everyone piled out of the car and pulled the suitcases out of the trunk.

Graham opened his arms to Dani. "Well, sugar, this is goodbye."

She leaned into his embrace. "Bye, Dad. Love you." She wiped at the corner of her eye.

He shook Trevor's hand. "Son, you take good care of my little girl."

"Yes, sir."

"Goodbye, darlin'. Call when you get in."

Graham waved as they blended into the crowds in the terminal. When he turned around, two men were climbing out of the blue Mazda. The blood chilled in his veins.

Thirty-Five

Inside the building, FBI agents surrounded Trevor and Dani. They provided the two with wigs and baseball caps, while agents wearing cowboy hats walked out to the tarmac pulling look-alike black suitcases. Within three minutes, Trevor and Dani were on their way to Goodyear in a gray Ford Focus.

His cell phone beeped. "Can you please read me that text?"

She tapped the message icon. "It's from Agent Graham. It says, *'Following me, not you. Heading to Bureau and safety. Meet you in Goodyear. Be safe. PG.'*"

"He's doing the right thing, going to base." Trevor glanced over his shoulder before zipping into the left lane to pass a semi truck.

"I'm worried," Dani said softly.

"He'll be fine. You'll see."

The scenery along the route alternated between industrial complexes, housing tracts, sports complexes, farmland, and desert. After a straight shot on the I-10, Trevor exited on Litchfield Road and made a left turn onto South Central, heading to the airport. The GPS continued giving instructions until

Trevor stopped at an out-of-the-way hangar. A man wearing sunglasses and a dark suit approached the car. He opened the door for Dani.

"Good afternoon, Miss Carpenter. Would you follow me?" The older man extended his hand.

Dani glanced at Trevor, who nodded. "Thank you," she said, accepting the agent's assistance.

"You're welcome." He transferred her hand to the crook of his arm. "My name's Art Toscano."

"Not Special Agent like everyone else?" Dani said.

"I figure it's implied in this scenario."

She smiled. "Where are we going, Art?"

"Don't worry." He patted her hand and moved toward the hangar. "We just need to make sure all your papers are in order. Mr. Willis is usually thorough, but he was in a hurry. We don't want any problems when you land in Mexico. A Mexican jail is no place for a woman like you."

Dani nodded. "No arguments from me."

He ushered her to a makeshift desk inside the hangar. "Can I have your passport and driver's license?"

She retrieved the items from her bag and handed them over.

Art passed the passport and license under a light. "These are indistinguishable from official documents. Like I said, Mr. Willis is quite thorough. I'm impressed."

Heat rose in Dani's cheeks. "He is impressive."

"I have a feeling he's pretty smitten with you, too." Art's smile reminded Dani of her grandpa Joe. "The most important thing to remember now is you are no longer Dani Carpenter. You are Gina Salerno from Melrose Park, Illinois. You're on your honeymoon in Puerto Vallarta with your new husband, John Flynn. Things should be quite interesting, with your fiery Italian spirit and John's Irish temper." Art winked at Dani.

"If I can survive purple hair, I can survive anything."

"Keep a sense of humor and you'll get far in this business."
Art stood up and offered Dani a business card. "Here are our
contacts in Mexico if you hit any snags."

She accepted the card and stood. "Thank you." She scanned
the room till she caught Trevor's eye. He hurried over.

"Make sure you memorize those names and numbers," Art
told her. "You can't take this card off the plane."

"Got it."

Trevor put his arm around Dani. "Are you done with this
beautiful woman yet?" He kissed her cheek.

"I am. You know, if you don't treat her well, you'll have to
answer to me." Art bowed to her. "Good luck and be safe."

"Thanks, Art," she said, then followed Trevor to the plane.

Dani hesitated only a moment before she climbed the steps
of the government-owned Embraer Legacy 500 jet. With Trevor
behind her, she walked through the wood-laminate galley. She
turned right and entered the passenger cabin. Admiring the
white-leather captain's chairs, she couldn't resist collapsing in
one of them. *I may never fly commercial again.*

♯

Trevor turned left and walked into the cockpit. "Hi, I'm
Trevor Willis, or John Flynn if you check my passport."

The pilot shook his hand. "I'm Tom Logan. This is my
copilot, Sam Goodson."

"It's good to meet you both. If you two would like a break
during the flight, I'd be glad to fly this baby for a bit." Trevor's
eyes traversed the cockpit with the look of a spider preparing
to devour its prey.

"Thanks for the offer, Mr. Willis."

"No problem. And please call me Trevor."

"Okay. Thanks for the offer, Trevor, but I heard what you
did to the last FBI plane," Captain Logan replied with a stone
face. "I think you'll be fine in the main cabin."

"You know that wasn't my fault." Trevor paused. "Anyway, if you need me, I won't be far away."

"Unless we activate your ejection seat, sir," Goodson deadpanned.

Trevor nodded. "Okay, I get it. Stay in my place."

§

Joining Dani in the cabin, Trevor said, "We've got a couple of comedians flying this plane."

She tried not to smile. "I take it they wouldn't let you fly it?"

"Very funny," he huffed, then grinned sheepishly. "You're right, they wouldn't. How do you know me so well?"

"I don't know you nearly well enough, but I'm beginning to notice some trends." She stood on her tiptoes and kissed his cheek. "Did you know that even the toilet has a seat belt? What will they think of next?"

He looked out the window, then at his watch, then out the window again.

"Trevor, extraterrestrials are invading," Dani declared, testing his attention.

"That's great." Trevor leaned closer to the window.

She touched him on the arm. "Trevor?"

He whirled around. "What?"

"Are you okay? You haven't heard a word I've said."

"I'm sorry. What did you say?" He looked out the window one more time before concentrating on her.

"What's wrong?"

"I'm worried about Graham. He was supposed to lose his tail, check in at HQ, and meet us here. We may have to leave without him." Trevor glanced at the tarmac again. "Art's coming over, and he's not smiling." Fifteen seconds later, Trevor took a couple of steps on the soft gray carpet, meeting Art at the doorway.

"I've got bad news about Graham," Art said.

Trevor leaned against the galley. "Tell me."

Art sighed. "The Bureau says he was run off the road. His car flipped several times."

"Is he . . . is he alive?" Dani asked from behind them.

Both men turned to her. "He'll recover . . . eventually," Art said. "But it may be the end of his field work."

Dani let out a long breath. "I'm so glad he's alive."

"He was an integral part of this operation to capture Morales," Trevor muttered. "Who's taking his place?"

"You're looking at him," Art replied.

"You?"

"I do more than check paperwork. I'll give you my résumé when we return with Morales."

Trevor rubbed his palms together. "Okay. We can do this." He closed and latched the outer door, then called to the captain, "We're ready for takeoff."

"Ten-four," said Logan. "Make sure everyone is secured in their seats. We're completing our final checklist and should be off the ground in less than ten minutes."

Trevor guided Dani toward the seats. "Where did you want to sit, hon?"

"I'll sit right here, sweetie," Art teased in a falsetto voice.

Trevor rolled his eyes. "I think we'll sit as far from you and your inner-woman as possible, Art. Maybe you should take the seat in the restroom."

Trevor chose two chairs facing each other. Several minutes later, as the plane taxied down the runway, Dani closed her eyes and took deep, calming breaths. He held her hand until the plane leveled off.

"It's been a long day." She covered her yawn and stretched her arms. "I'll be ready to crash tonight."

"If you thought the seat-belted toilet seat was exciting, watch this." Trevor turned their seats to back up to each other and then reclined them to make a flat surface. "You can lie down and take a nap."

"I wish the airlines I fly had seats like this. Although, the last time I took a nap on a flight, I woke up to the plane crashing."

"Yeah, I know."

The plan lurched downward and Dani gasped. Trevor embraced her. "It's okay. Just a bump in the road."

"I hate turbulence." She gave a grunt and sat on the edge of her berth.

Trevor brought her a pillow and blanket and tucked her in. "You'll be better off if you can sleep through this."

§

Dani lay on the converted bed and snuggled under the blanket. The men's voices faded and she drifted to sleep. About an hour later, she sat up and sniffed. "Cinnamon rolls?"

Trevor held out his plate. "Would you like me to get you one or are you satisfied watching me eat mine?"

She swung her legs over the edge of the converted bed. "I want one, please." Trevor left the cabin. Dani tried in vain to turn the bed back into a chair. Finally Art showed her the trick. By the time Trevor returned, the two chairs faced each other with a table between them.

"Here you go. I brought some milk," he said. "These can get messy, so I brought a napkin, too."

Dani looked at the china plate, crystal goblet, and cloth napkin. "They don't spare any expense, do they?"

Trevor's laugh resounded off the cabin walls. "This plane is usually reserved for the bigwigs. It was the only one available, so we lucked out."

"I'll say. Did you get any sleep?"

"No. Art and I have been ironing out details. I've been filling him in on Graham's role."

Captain Logan emerged from the cockpit. "Willis, I need a break. You want to take over for a while?"

Trevor rushed to the control center before Logan could change his mind. "Sure thing."

Logan laughed. "I couldn't resist pulling his leg about flying this aircraft." He placed a cinnamon roll on his plate and microwaved it. "I couldn't resist these rolls, either."

Soon he returned to the cockpit to trade places with Goodson, who grabbed a couple of cinnamon rolls for himself.

A while later, Trevor returned to the main cabin, his eyes shining. He pumped his fist. "That was great! I may look into getting one of these for the company."

"You look like you won the lottery." Dani chuckled.

"I did. I've always wanted to fly one of these. I could die happy right now."

The atmosphere in the cabin changed in a flash, and she turned away from him.

He stepped behind her and held her shoulders. "I'm sorry, hon. It was a careless comment."

She refused to look at him. He turned her to face him and lifted her chin to meet her eyes. "Dani Carpenter, you are my reason to keep living, the reason I'll make it through this whole thing. Flying is fun, but being with you brings me real happiness."

She leaned into him, her tears escaping in torrents.

"It's going to be okay."

"What if it's not, Trevor? What if I lose you?"

"You're not going to lose me. You might decide to get rid of me, but I'll be sticking around as long as you'll let me."

The captain's scratchy voice came over the speakers. "We're about forty-five minutes out of Puerto Vallarta. We'll begin our descent in about twenty minutes."

"Do you want anything to eat before we land?" Trevor moved to the galley. "There are salads or sandwiches, chips, water, fruit. Any takers?"

"What kind of salads?" Dani asked.

He pulled out a prepackaged entree and held it up to the light. "This is Asian chicken and the other one is . . ." He squinted at the label. "Chef's cobb."

"I'll take the Asian chicken. After that cinnamon roll, or two, I need something lighter."

He tossed the package slightly above her head. She reached up like an outfielder and caught it. "Whoa, Dani, where'd you learn to do that?"

"Oh, just another talent not listed on my résumé." She winked at him.

"What kind of sandwiches?" Art walked up behind Trevor.

"Ham and Swiss on wheat, or chicken salad on ciabatta." He held out one of each.

"I'll have the ham and Swiss."

Trevor tossed it to him. "Great, I wanted the chicken salad." He took grabbed more goblets and added ice and water and squeezed a slice of lemon in each, then put the glasses on a tray alongside his sandwich. He gave a glass to Art, and one to Dani. Trevor raised his and made a toast. "To the success of this mission and to our reunion at the end."

Dani and Art raised their glasses. "To the success of this mission."

Silence continued for the rest of the flight. Dani thought of what the next few days would hold. She took a sip of the water to swallow the dread that rose in her throat.

Thirty-Six

Trevor and Dani strolled hand in hand down the Malecón. The heart of Puerto Vallarta beat in this twelve-block, car-free promenade of shops, restaurants, statues, and ocean views. Dani scanned the area, attempting to take it all in. For today, they were John and Gina Flynn, regular tourists on their honeymoon.

Trevor chuckled. "Don't try to see everything at once. You'll go crazy. We'll come back here later and see the night life."

She raced to the seawall. "Look at that sand sculpture. The details on the horse are amazing, especially the braided mane."

He reached his arms around Dani's waist and kissed the top of her head. "You open my eyes to the joy of life."

She leaned her head on his chest, then pulled him forward, pointing. "Trevor, there are men on top of that pole." She felt herself being jerked backward when he suddenly stopped in the walkway. "What?"

"Trevor was your last boyfriend," he snapped. "I'm John, the man you just married. Do you think you can keep us straight?" His wink softened the feigned rebuke.

Real tears welled in Dani's eyes. "I'm so sorry, John. You know I love you." She reached out to touch his stiffened jaw. "Forgive me?"

Trevor's stony features melted like a chocolate bar on a sun-drenched windowsill. "Always. Again and again. Let's go check out that pole."

They leaned against the seawall and watched the five men dressed in orange pants and white shirts. Colorful, hand-embroidered scarves crossed their chests and encircled their waists. They wore elaborate beaded hats. The man in the middle played a flute and the other four anchored themselves to one of the ropes before jumping off the platform in unison, swirling around the pole in an inverted position.

A man stood next to Dani and pointed up. "Los Valadores de Papanlata."

Trevor maneuvered her to his other side and spoke to the man. "Thank you. We were wondering about them."

"Sí." The man leaned around Trevor to address Dani. "They are called the birdmen. This is an ancient ritual. According to a Totonac myth, 450 years ago, there was no rain for a very long time. The gods were angry because the people ignored them." He looked back at the performers. "Five *jovenes*—"

"Five youths," Trevor clarified for Dani.

"Yes. They were chosen to represent the bird gods," the man continued. "The boy in the center plays the flute to imitate the singing of birds. He is my son. The other four, who—" He held up his finger and whirled it around.

"Spin," Trevor offered.

"Sí, spin. They spin around the pole as the directions north, south, east, and west. As they turn, the earth is reborn. The god Xipe Totec allows the rains to nourish the land once again."

"What a beautiful legend. Thank you for sharing." Dani smiled at him.

"De nada, señorita."

"That's señora," Trevor corrected.

"Sí, señora." The man took her hand. "I apologize."

"No problem. You speak English quite well."

"I went to the universidad in Michigan." The man raised Dani's hand to his lips and gently kissed it.

Trevor put a protective arm around her to lead her away. "We've got to be going. We have reservations."

"Oh, señor? The Valadores accept tips." He dipped his head toward the ground.

"Yes, yes. Of course." Trevor reached into his pocket and handed the storyteller a couple of bills.

"Gracias. You are most generous."

Dani and Trevor continued down the Malecón..

"Slow down, John," she said after a minute. "I can't keep up with you."

Trevor adjusted his pace. "Sorry, hon."

"He was a very nice man. So knowledgeable, too."

Trevor turned to put his hands on her shoulders. "You are such a good person. You feel that everyone is as good as you. They're not. You can't trust anyone right now."

Dani sighed. "My head knows that, but my heart is having trouble grasping the concept."

He hugged her in the middle of the throng of people swarming through the Malecón, then guided her through the crowd. "Just a short way down the path and we can catch a cab. I've got reservations for dinner. This will be one of the most memorable meals you've ever had."

"You're sure building up this place, Trevor. What kind of food do they have?"

"The food doesn't matter."

"It doesn't matter?" Dani stopped and gave him a quizzical look. "How could the food not matter?"

He chuckled. "The food's good. The view is spectacular. Especially at sunset."

They reached the street to find a line of cabs. "Taxi." He raised his hand, and a cab cut off another driver to pull in front of them. The determined driver jumped out of the car and ran around to open the door. Dani slid in first and scooted to the middle seat, while Trevor sat near the door.

"Where to?" the cabbie questioned.

Trevor put his arm around Dani.

"Hotél Los Cuatros Vientos."

"Sí. A good place to bring a woman beautiful." He glanced in his rearview window.

Trevor glared at the man. *"Sí, soy un hombre suerte."* He intertwined his fingers with Dani's and whispered in her ear, "I am definitely a lucky man."

They drove through the streets of Puerto Vallarta, where grand hotels and beautiful restaurants coexisted with hovels. Children played ball in the confines of their adobe-fenced yards. They looked up from their game and waved at the gringos. The cab continued upward until they stopped at a vine-covered building. Welcoming tropical flowers hung in baskets around the covered walkway. Trevor paid the driver.

"Señor, I no have change."

"That's okay." Trevor helped Dani out of the cab and waved goodbye to the driver, who kept repeating, *"Muchos gracias, muchos gracias!"*

The cool, darkened interior of the restaurant felt wonderful after the Malecón, where the hot Mexican sun beat down on the cobblestones. A hostess greeted Trevor and Dani. "Hola, may I help you?"

"We have reservations. The name is John Flynn."

"Yes." She smiled. "Our best table on the terrace. Maria will escort you."

A young woman motioned for Trevor and Dani to follow. She led them up a stone staircase to the rooftop. Their table faced the ocean and boasted a stunning view of the town and the iconic crowned church—Nuestra Señora de Guadalupe, or Our Lady of Guadalupe. The vibrant oranges and reds painted the sky and reflected on the calm ocean. Trevor and Dani ordered limonadas. As they sipped the tart drinks, the sun seemed to stop a moment on the horizon before it plummeted through the colors and disappeared into the sea in a blaze.

"I can hardly believe how quickly the sun set," Dani remarked. "This will be one of the most memorable meals ever." She squeezed Trevor's hand. "Because I'm with you."

He smiled and draped an arm around her shoulders. "Tonight, we enjoy being together. Forget about what will happen in the next few days."

They enjoyed a delicious dinner. Afterward, they shared an order of fried ice cream and then reluctantly got up from the table. On their way to the street, they passed the fountain in the courtyard. "Can we take a picture, John?" Dani asked. "I'd love to remember this night."

"Sure thing." They posed in front of the fountain. Trevor held Dani's cell phone at arm's length and snapped the photo. He glanced out the gate. "Wow, there's our taxi. Someone in the restaurant must've let him know we were finished."

The cabbie stepped forward and opened his arms. "Señor, I am here to take you wherever you like. No charge."

"Thank you. We wanted to see the Malecón at night." Trevor led Dani to the cab. The driver opened the door.

"Como se llama?" Trevor called over the seat.

"Miguel."

"I'm John, and this is my wife Gina."

"Mucho gusto. At the Malecón, go to the glassblower's shop. Tell him I send you and he gives a good price."

"We'll do that." Trevor leaned forward. "Were you born in Puerto Vallarta?"

"No, I grow up in a very small village not far away. I am lucky. I receive a education."

"Then why are you a cab driver?" Dani asked.

"It is because of my education that I get such a good job. Taxi drivers must speak English and know many things."

A few minutes later, Miguel stopped the cab and hopped out to open the door. "Here is the Malecón. Would you like me to pick you up at the other end in a couple of hours?"

"Sure, that'd be great," Trevor replied. "We'll meet you near the amphitheater at 9:00. We're going on the *Marigalante* tomorrow and have to be up early."

"Sí, señor. Nine o'clock at the other end. Enjoy."

Trevor handed him a twenty-dollar bill.

"No, no. There is no charge," Miguel protested.

Trevor put out a hand. "Please keep it."

"Gracias."

§

Miguel watched the two Americans disappear into the crowd. *They are good people. I wonder how they came to be involved with Don Francisco.* Miguel pulled out a cell phone and dialed.

"Tío, they are coming."

Thirty-Seven

Occasional white caps illuminated the blackness of the bay. Palm trees stood between the ocean and the brightly lit shops. Neon lights and loud music blared from the clubs. Strolling by the ocean to avoid the crowds, Trevor and Dani came upon a table where two men sat playing chess.

One of the men looked up and said, "Señor, come drink with us." He patted a sand-covered chair. "Or your lady?" He stood and took Dani's elbow.

She sat down. One man handed her a sandy goblet while the other man held a sandy wine bottle. He poured a stream of sand from the bottle. Dani beamed. *"Muchas gracías."*

Trevor snapped a picture. He took her hand and escorted her back to the sidewalk. He deposited a bill into their equally sandy tip jar before moving on.

"I wonder if all that sand itches," Dani said.

Trevor chuckled. "Now you'll be scratching your arms all night."

She pulled him toward the crowded shop area. "Oh, there's the glassblower's shop. Let's check it out."

"I'll follow you to the ends of the earth—even into a store."

They watched a portly man shape molten glass into a palm tree. He glanced up and motioned for Dani and Trevor to enter the shop. A blast of heat met them as they passed the artisan's workstation on their way to the display shelves. Dani's gaze fell upon a small red dragon with exquisite detail.

"I think I can tell what your favorite is." Trevor picked up the delicate dragon and admired the workmanship.

"I always wanted to be a princess with a pet dragon."

"I have the perfect item for you," said the glassblower, who suddenly stood behind them. "Follow me." He led Dani and Trevor to his workspace. "I finished just this morning. Now I know it is for you." He placed a miniature glass figurine in Dani's palm. An intricate turquoise dragon reached out his head to eat an apple from the palm of a short-haired young girl.

"It's beautiful. I'm glad Miguel sent us here."

A smile broke out on the man's face. "Miguel? My nephew?" He opened his arms wide. "Then you are *familia*. I wish to give you this dragon as a gift."

"Oh, I can't accept it. Please let me pay you." Dani set the dragon on the counter and reached for her purse.

The man placed his hand upon hers. "No, I insist. May all the dragons in your life be tame."

Dani smiled. "Thank you."

He wrapped the figurine in layers of tissue paper. He leaned toward her and whispered. "This one is a gift, but if your husband would like to buy you another present, I would not object." He winked at her.

Dani picked out a dolphin. "For Ady?"

Trevor nodded. "Sure."

They walked out to the noisy boardwalk and sat on one of the park benches, watching the people pass by. The locals, dressed in their finest, approached the night clubs, tourists in tropical shirts, Bermuda shorts and sandals examined the wares in the shops, and young children peddled small packets of gum for a nickel.

One little girl approached Dani with her little brother in tow. "Chicle?"

Dani's heart melted at the sight of her. She must have been Ady's age. "How old are you?"

She looked at Dani with a question in her face. *"Cómo?"*

"Cuantos años tienes?" Trevor translated.

The girl swayed back and forth and held up five fingers.

"Y tu hermano?"

Three fingers went up.

"Sí." Dani nodded. She opened her purse and handed the girl five dollars.

"Gracias, gracias!" She ran across the boardwalk to her ever-watchful mamá, showing her the money. Her mother waved. The girl ran back to Dani and handed her a package of Chiclets before returning to her family.

Trevor stood up and pulled Dani away from the bench. "Come on. If we stay, every street urchin will descend upon you and we'll never get out of here."

They approached an unusual statue. A ladder rose ten feet into the air. A pillow-headed alien mother raised her hands to two alien children ascending the ladder. Each child's left hand and foot were anchored to the structure. Their right hands stretched up and their right feet left the safety of the ladder.

"Where do you think they're going?" Dani wondered.

"To the mother ship. You know, 'ET phone home.'"

Dani's thoughts turned to Ady. "I imagine their mother will miss them." Her shoulders slumped.

"Ady is fine. We'll see her soon." He hugged her. "Now, go over there and climb up. Let me take your picture."

"Are you sure? Are we supposed to touch it?"

"If we weren't supposed to, it would be fenced off."

She looked at the ladder and then back to Trevor. "Okay." She walked through the sand and climbed a few rungs.

"Go higher." He shouted to her.

Dani gazed upward and took a breath. She inched up a couple more. "This is as far as I go."

"Okay, now pose like the statues." He snapped the picture. "Now you get one of me." They passed and he gave her a quick peck on the cheek. He climbed the ladder as far as the first alien. "I'm ready."

She snapped the photo. An overwhelming feeling encompassed her. She dropped to sit on the curb. Her hands shook and heat enveloped her body.

Trevor descended the ladder without touching the rungs. He hurried to Dani and wrapped her in his arms. "What's wrong?"

"It's . . . it's not the mother ship. It's . . ." A shiver raced through her. "It's heaven. The children are going to heaven." She closed her eyes and reached up to touch his cheek. "I had a feeling—just for a moment—I was watching you leave this world. Without me."

"Hey, it's okay." He held her tighter. "We're both going to make it through this. I promise you. We'll get through this."

"Can you promise that?"

He took a deep breath and closed his eyes for a second. "Yes." The conviction in his voice calmed her. "Yes, I can."

They rested there a few minutes. Trevor looked at his watch. "It's almost 9:00. Let's see if Miguel is waiting for us."

Thirty-Eight

Trevor and Dani walked through the lobby of the Sheraton Buganvilias. The elevator took them up to the penthouse. He handed the package to her and pulled the key from his pocket.

Dani stood before the door. "Isn't three bedrooms a little much for us?"

"We could get a one-bedroom unit . . ." Trevor teased.

"No, this is fine. I'll feel a little lost in it, though." She entered the room and gasped. "Someone's been here."

Trevor slipped past her and called out, "Hello?"

The terrace door slid open and Jared stepped through. "You're kind of late tonight, aren't you?"

"What are you doing here?" Dani walked over and slugged her brother in the arm. "You don't have to babysit me."

Trevor stepped forward. "I asked them to come. I'll be gone a few days and I don't want you to be alone. Okay?"

She nodded her head. "I'm sorry, Jared. Forgive me for jumping to conclusions?"

He ruffled her hair. "No problem." He lowered his voice. "Are you really okay after the crash?"

"I'm okay. There are no residual effects. How long have you been here?"

"Only about forty-five minutes. Our flight got in pretty late." Jana took her husband's arm. "We're heading out to the hot tub. Want to join us?"

"Sure. Trevor?" She looked toward him.

With his attention focused on his cell phone, he said, "Uh, I'll join you there later." He walked into his bedroom and shut the door.

Dani, Jared, and Jana stared open-mouthed at the door.

"I wonder what that was about," Jared muttered.

Dani sighed. "Is that something I have to get used to?"

"I'm afraid so." Jana hugged her shoulder. "Get your bathing suit on and let's go."

Dani hurried into her bedroom and changed into another new swimsuit, a gray one-piece with turquoise draped across each shoulder and three accent beads on each strap. She glanced at herself in the full-length mirror. *I bought this for Trevor, not my brother. Hopefully, he'll make it out to the Jacuzzi.*

She joined her brother and sister-in-law in the living room. When they walked past Trevor's room, he opened the door and let out a low whistle.

"I'll be sure to get there quickly." He winked at her.

Dani was about to dive into the pool to swim a few laps when her brother stood next to her. "Race you to the other end and back," he challenged.

"Okay." She jumped in before Jared had a chance to say "Go." He didn't catch up with her until the turn. Their strokes glided through the water, and their bodies hit a rhythm. Jared beat her by a hand length. He hopped out of the pool and turned to help her, but Trevor appeared out of nowhere and pulled her out, then wrapped a towel around her.

"Let's hit the Jacuzzi." He tightened his hold on Dani as they all headed to the hot tub. After they got in, Trevor leaned back in the warm water, and Dani rested her head in the crook of his arm.

"Thanks for coming down," Trevor said to Jared and Jana. "I owe you both one."

Jana moved to a better position against the water jets. "Let's see. We flew first class to Puerto Vallarta and are staying in a penthouse on the ocean. And we're not paying for it. That might make us even."

"Uh." Jared leaned closer to his wife. "I think you're forgetting we were forced out of our home because our lives were threatened."

"We got to spend time at mountain cabin on a lake, all alone," Jana countered.

"I had to turn my patients over to another therapist."

"Who happens to be the best in the field." A smile played at Jana's lips.

"Jana! Will you stop seeing the best in the situation when I want to see the worst?" As if realizing the ridiculousness of his own words, Jared let out a hearty laugh. "I'm sorry, honey. Thank heavens you're here to see the best in everything."

Their feet were dry by the time they entered the lobby. A blast of cold air assaulted them as they left the warmth of the tropical night. Silently, they rode the elevator to the penthouse.

§

Trevor slumped into a deck chair on the flagstone terrace. The moon reflected its light across the surface of Banderas Bay. He leaned his head forward into his hand and groaned.

"Sounds like you have the weight of the world on your shoulders."

Trevor jumped to his feet and spun around. He let go of the breath he'd been holding. "What are you doing here?"

"You asked me to come, remember?" Jared pulled a chair next to him

"I'm beginning to reconsider," Trevor growled.

"Look." Jared stood up and rubbed his hands together slowly. "I know I haven't been very supportive of you seeing my sister."

"That's an understatement."

Jared leaned against the railing of the balcony. "Jana pointed out to me that Dani is old enough to make her own choices."

"She does a pretty good job of it, too."

"I keep forgetting she's not the little girl I protected all my life."

"No. Now she's the woman I will protect for the rest of my life, if she'll let me." Trevor stood and took a couple of steps to the railing.

Jared chuckled. "I forget she's got a mind of her own."

"Me too. She reminds me all the time."

"Ever since what happened with Jana, I'm worried what might happen to Dani."

Trevor ran his fingers through his hair. "I understand. I'd do anything to take it back, but it's not possible. I promise you I will treat Dani like a queen. I've told Don I'm done. No more FBI jobs. I'm settling down to raise a family."

"If anything happens to her, you'll answer to me."

"I know." Trevor pointed to the left. "Over there. On the peninsula jutting out at the end of the bay."

Jared stepped closer and leaned over to see where Trevor indicated. "What about it?"

A shiver ran through him and his heart lurched. "Over to the left is where Morales and his men infest the jungle."

Thirty-Nine

Dani dressed in a tankini with an orange-paisley-print top and solid coral shorts. *This is my last new swimsuit. Hope Trevor doesn't mind repeats after this.* She walked into the living room where Jared and Jana talked on the couch.

Jana hugged her sister-in-law. "Three of us are ready. Have you heard anything from Trevor?"

"No. That's strange. He's always up at the crack of dawn." Dani turned and found only a shut bedroom door.

Jared mumbled. "Maybe that's when he went to sleep?"

"What? Maybe I should check on him." Dani paused at his bedroom door, poised to knock.

Trevor stumbled through the door, closing his eyes against the light. His short red hair stuck straight up and he wore only a pair of long shorts. He ran his fingers through his hair. "I guess I overslept. Can I use the shower in your room, hon?"

"Yeah, sure."

He kissed her on the forehead and then brushed by her into the bedroom.

He returned a couple of minutes later with a towel around his shoulders wearing the same swimsuit he wore in Phoenix and last night. *He only has one swimsuit? I would think his swim wardrobe would match the rest of his clothes.*

"I'll just get my shirt, then we can go. Miguel should be waiting for us downstairs."

Jared cocked his head. "Who's Miguel?"

"Oh, he's a taxi driver. He's been taking us around." Trevor waved his hand in dismissal. "No one to worry about."

They left the penthouse and entered the elevator. "Did you find him or did he find you?" Jared pressed.

"I gave him a great tip; he's interested in the money. He's just a kid."

"Alejandro Morales isn't much older than a kid." Jared's tone stopped Trevor in his tracks. "Did you let down your guard with him?"

"I . . ." Trevor's face paled. "I might have." He leaned against the elevator wall, then slowly slipped down to a squatting position. "I can't believe I took that kind of chance—especially with Dani here."

"We all make mistakes. It happens to the best of us." Dani pulled him up.

He raised her chin, looking her in the eye. "Not to me. I'm sorry." He kissed her forehead.

"What should we do?" Jana intertwined her fingers with Jared's.

"Stop the elevator so we have a chance to think." Trevor pointed to a button. "That one."

Jana hit the button. The elevator stopped with a jerk. "Done."

"Okay." He paced back and forth in the small space. "I'll call Art. He'll move us to another hotel. He can check out Miguel. By the time we get back, it will be worked out."

"I'm not sure I want someone else packing my things." Dani reached for the button to start the elevator.

"I agree with Dani." Jana said.

"No. We don't have time. Let me call him." He dialed the number. "Art, we have a problem. We need to change hotels." He waited a moment. "We have a cabbie who is kind of attached to us. I need you to check him out. His name is Miguel. I'll get the taxi information to you when we get to the marina."

Trevor's foot tapped the carpeted floor as he waited for Art's reply. "Yeah. I'll meet her today. Tomorrow night is the real deal. Keep in touch."

The speaker on the elevator crackled to life. "Hello? Is everything fine in the elevator?" asked a heavily accented voice. "We show you have stopped."

Jared leaned toward the speaker. "We're fine. We hit the button on accident. I think we finally figured out how to start it again." He pushed a button. The elevator shuddered, finishing the downward journey to the lobby.

Miguel waved at the group. "Over here, Señor John."

"Give me your read on him, Jared." Trevor waved back and smiled. "Hola, Miguel. *Listos?*"

"Sí, señor. You are late this morning." Miguel opened the doors for his passengers. When they were situated, he hit the gas, pulled into the traffic, and swerved in and out of the congested lanes. "Almost there." He looked at the passengers in the back seat and flashed them a toothy grin.

Trevor turned his head toward the cabbie. "Where did you say you were from, Miguel?"

"A small village near Las Caletas."

Dani, Jana and Jared slid over with each lane change. They gave up attempting to stay upright.

"Too bad you're not back here, Trevor. Two beautiful women keep sliding into me—even if one is my sister."

Trevor chuckled, "I'll have to sit there on the way home."

"We are here, señor." Miguel pointed. "Go through the gate."

Trevor paid Miguel and thanked him.

The driver stuffed the money in his pants pocket. "I meet you here after?"

"No, not today. A friend is meeting us. Adiós."

After Miguel left, Trevor addressed Jared. "What's your take on him?"

Jared guided his wife through the gate. "He looked scared."

The group headed to the pirate ship *Marigalante*. They paused to take the obligatory tourist pictures in front of the gang plank with a curved cutlass as a prop. Their own pirate, Skull, greeted them with orange juice and escorted them to a seating area with long, narrow benches. Trevor glanced around until his eye rested upon a female pirate who beckoned him to join her. Hot jealousy rushed through Dani. When Trevor actually rose, her feelings threatened to explode and take the ship down with them.

"Excuse me, Dani. I have to meet someone for a minute," Trevor said, then left without waiting for a reply.

Her arms stiffened at her sides as she clenched and unclenched her fists. She began to stand.

Jared yanked her back down and whispered, "Sis, I think you're forgetting this isn't exactly a pleasure cruise."

Dani whirled to face her brother. "What?"

"Everything he does is to further his objectives. His *professional* objectives."

She let out a long breath. "I'm sorry. You're right."

Jana put her arm around Dani's shoulder. "I can see it in his eyes. You don't have to worry about other women, even if they're beautiful pirates."

The jealous monster returned when Trevor took the pirate's hand and kissed it. Dani harbored thoughts of knocking the lady buccaneer overboard, but then Trevor shoved something into his pocket and descended the stairs to return to her.

Trevor squeezed her and spoke into her ear. "I got what I needed. We're ready to launch the plan tomorrow." He kissed her cheek and turned his focus to the pirate issuing instructions for the tour as the *Marigalante* threaded its way through the marina to Banderas Bay.

A short time later, Skull escorted them downstairs and took their orders for breakfast. Dani marveled at the speed of the crew serving the entire ship full of people. Jared and Jana chose the American breakfast while Dani and Trevor opted for the spicier Mexican version. When they returned to the deck, tarps shaded the entire area, and Skull showed them to their seats.

While the ship journeyed to the Marietas Islands, the crew of the *Marigalante* presented a swashbuckling show with sword fights and pirates falling from the deck into the water. They included many of the children in the audience.

Dani pointed to a precocious five-year-old and sighed. "She reminds me of Ady."

"I was thinking the same thing. We're going to have to bring her here some time." Trevor squeezed Dani's shoulders.

The rest of the tour felt like a normal touristy day. Almost. They snorkeled, kayaked, and rode the banana boat. When the long, yellow raft came to a stop, the passengers relaxed their grip, and the speedboat driver jerked to a quick start. Jared and Jana flew off, their arms and legs flailing before they landed in the ocean. Trevor and Dani managed to hang onto the handles, refusing to be knocked off until the driver made a quick turn, sending Trevor into the water. The driver stood up and applauded Dani as the last woman sitting. She slid gently into the bay and the group swam to the white-sand beach.

They lounged under a grouping of coconut palms and enjoyed ice cold passion fruit juice. Trevor shook his head. "I can't believe you clung to that raft when I was thrown off."

"I can believe it." Jared sipped his drink. "As a kid, whenever I tried to get something from her, it was like taking a steak from a pit bull."

"Personally, I think it's my gymnastic training. The only trophy I ever won was for participation, but . . ." Dani held up a finger. "My toes were strong enough that I never fell off the balance beam."

"Except once." Jared muttered under his breath.

She narrowed her eyes. "Jared Carpenter, you promised to never mention that. Ever."

"It was—"

Her tone oozed menace. "Jared."

Jana shook her head.

The teasing deflated with a look from his wife. "Okay, sis. I won't tell . . ." He stood up, his eyes darting back and forth. "That the captain and star quarterback of the football team passed by and winked at her."

"You are in so much trouble." She pushed herself up from the sand and her brother took off. "I'll let him run a while before he realizes I'm not chasing him."

"So," Trevor pulled her back to the sand. "What happened when this football-playing hunk winked at you?"

"I don't want to talk about it."

She turned away from him and spoke to Jana. "What did you two do before you got here?"

"We rented a beautiful cabin in the Rockies and—"

"Señora *Flynn*," he said, emphasizing the alias. "You know I'll find out. You might as well just tell me."

"Nope." She shook her head. Her lips formed a thin line.

Trevor leaned close and whispered to Dani, "I will find out."

She scratched where his breath tickled her ear. "Don't bet on it," she hissed back.

"They're getting ready to ferry everyone back to the ship." Jared called from a safe distance.

Trevor waved and helped both women up. "Let's go. Just remember, I have ways of making you talk." He wriggled his eyebrows at Dani.

§

Art met them at the Marina and drove them to their new hotel. They unlocked the room and explored the suite.

"I think this might actually be nicer than the last place." Jana opened the patio door. "Look at this fountain."

"What did you find out about Miguel?" Trevor asked, bringing up the so-called elephant in the room.

Art hesitated and looked toward the women. "We need to talk."

"They need to know what's going on," Trevor said.

"Okay, Miguel is the son of Enrique Rios—Morales's right-hand man."

Trevor threw his arms in the air. "I can't believe I let my guard down. I could have ruined the entire operation."

"The good news is that he doesn't seem to be part of the organization," Art continued.

"Where does this put Dani?" Jared asked angrily.

Dani squeezed Trevor's fingers. "Right where I belong, by his side."

Trevor kissed her cheek. "I'll be putting her in your care, Jared. I still believe she's safer with us."

Forty

Dani stood in front of the bathroom mirror, dressed in a gauzy white top with purple flowers embroidered around the neckline. Trevor had bought it for her that morning at the Mercado on the river walk. She paired it with denim capris and dressy sandals. Tonight they were heading to see the show "The Rhythms of the Night" at Las Caletas.

A knock sounded on the door of her suite. "Come in." Dani turned for a last look in the mirror, then stepped into the main part of the suite just as her sister-in-law entered the room. "Hi, Jana. Is everyone ready?"

"Not quite." Jana looked over her shoulder. "Jared and Trevor are having a powwow on the terrace. You look great, by the way."

"Aw, thanks. You look good yourself. What are they talking about?" Dani clipped a silver bracelet onto her wrist and grabbed a light jacket.

Jana chuckled. "I'm not sure, probably top secret plans."

"I'm ready to find out what it's all about." Dani led the way through the French doors onto the terrace. The men's conversation turned off like a faucet.

Trevor smiled and kissed Dani on the cheek. "Let's go."

She refused to move. "No, not yet. I think Jana and I deserve to know what's happening tonight."

"Um, we're going to Las Caletas for a romantic dinner and show. Everything is candlelight."

Jared sighed. "You might as well tell them, Trevor. If they don't know the plan, how will they know to act instead of react?"

"Okay, you're right. Keeping the girls in the dark could be dangerous."

Dani crossed her arms. "Women."

Trevor frowned. "What?"

"We're women, not girls."

"Whatever! Now, during the show . . ." Trevor strode across the room and looked out at the patio, then came back to where the others stood. "I'll make my way to a rendezvous point. Someone will be joining you for the boat trip back—"

Dani hit his chest with her palm. "Wait a minute. You're not coming back tonight?"

He held her shoulders and said gently, "Hon, you knew I had to go into Morales's compound, and you knew you couldn't come with me."

She nodded, still captured by his eyes.

"That's why Jared's here." Trevor wiped a tear from Dani's cheek. "Now, let's get going or we'll miss the boat."

The two couples climbed into a taxi. Miguel followed them through the streets of Puerto Vallarta until they reached the marina. When they boarded the catamaran to Las Caletas, he pulled a phone from his pocket and dialed. His foot tapped the floor of the car while he waited.

"Tio, I have followed them. They are traveling to 'The Rhythms.'"

He paused. "Yes. I will be here when they return."

A sigh escaped his lips. "Yes, yes, I know what to do."

He threw the phone on the passenger seat and cradled his head in his hands.

§

The catamaran set sail in the early evening with the music and entertainment of a party cruise. Dani plastered a smile on her face and pretended to listen to the history of Las Caletas. Words such as *John Huston, jaguars,* and *no electricity* tickled at her consciousness, yet she paid no attention. She sat on a bench, encircled by Trevor's strong arm, allowing the ocean breeze to calm her terror. The sun dropped below the horizon and the moon dared to show its light as they neared the end of Banderas Bay. Thousands of candles beckoned them to the surreal beauty of Las Caletas.

Drums and flutes lured them from the boats. Dani struggled to soak in the romantic mood. *Will he make it back to me? What if he doesn't? How will I go on without him?*

"Let's enjoy this time we have together." Trevor whispered in her ear and kissed her cheek.

His smile infused her with courage. She returned the smile with a lighter heart. "You're right—as you occasionally are."

"Oh, really? Just occasionally?"

"Yes, just occasionally."

He squeezed her hand as they followed the endless line of people. "Things will work out. Nothing will keep me away from you. After all, I need to show you that I'm right a lot more than occasionally."

She took a deep breath. "If you don't come back to me . . . I'll . . . I'll . . . never talk to you again."

Trevor's laughter turned a few heads as they reached the terraced restaurant.

"There are other people here." Jared prodded Trevor.

The waiter seated them at a table overlooking the bay. Candles cast a soft glow on the fresh-flower centerpiece. The waiter took their order sand served tall glasses of passion-fruit juice mixed with Sprite. Then he escorted the party to the buffet.

Jana pointed to some chicken, and the attendant placed a piece on her plate. "This looks delicious."

"I might eat too many of these fresh tortillas." Jared held out his plate, and a woman served him a tortilla right off the grill.

"I'm ready for the desserts. I think I see chocolate-dipped strawberries and pineapple. Dani kept sneaking peeks at the end of the buffet to ensure the treats were still available.

The conversation veered toward home, Ady, and the town of Puerto Vallarta—all the things a tourist would talk about. Dani excused herself to find the restroom.

Jana pushed away from the table. "I'll go with you."

"Jared, did you ever notice that women can never go to the bathroom alone?" Trevor commented as the girls headed off. "It's always a group activity."

Dani turned back to glare at him. "Ha ha. You're quite the comedian."

Jared chuckled. "You're in real trouble now, Trevor."

The two women wound their way along the path until they reached the most beautiful outdoor restrooms Dani had ever seen. Inside, the glow of candle flames danced on the flower-covered vanity complete with running water. And the toilets actually flushed.

"Whoa, can you believe this?" Dani exclaimed. "I would love something like this in my apartment."

"Maybe I'll finally get rid of Jared's pink dotted-swiss shower curtain and redo the bathroom." Jana paused to touch Dani's arm. "How are you holding up?"

She closed her eyes and took a deep breath before she answered. "I'm scared to death, but then Tr—I mean John—

looks me in the eye and says everything will work out." She looked down. "And I believe him."

"What happens when he's not around?"

Dani's shoulders fell. "The spell breaks and I'm scared to death again."

Jana gave her a quick hug. They took the path they thought led to their table, but had to ask for directions before they finally made it back.

Trevor stood and took Dani's hand. "We were just about to send out a search party for you two."

"Then I remembered your nonexistent sense of direction, Sis," Jared put in. "I assumed my wife would get you back here somehow." He pulled Jana to him.

"Like I said, you two are just so funny," Dani mumbled, trying to push away from Trevor.

"Not so fast. You're stuck with me," he said as he embraced her. "This is it. Everything is set in motion." He kissed her cheek. "I have one question before I go."

"Ask anything."

"What happened when the captain of the football team winked at you?" Trevor whispered in her ear.

Dani stepped back a little. "I can't believe you just asked me that."

"It might be a last request."

"Okay, okay. When he winked, I fell and broke my wrist and was out for the rest of the season. Are you satisfied?"

Trevor smiled. "Yes. I love you and I'll see you in a few days. Stick with Jared."

"Love you back.. Please stay safe." She threw her arms around Trevor's neck.

They finally let go when "Rhythms of the Night" was about to begin.

Trevor cleared his throat. "I think I had a few too many of those fruit drinks. I'm going to find the little boys' room. You all go ahead and save a seat for me." He winked at Dani. "I'll find you."

Words failed Dani, so she simply nodded. Trevor waved and headed on the path toward the jungle.

Jared physically turned Dani around to lead her away from Trevor. "Come on, Sis. Let's go watch the show."

Art Toscano joined them on deck for the endless ride home. The thrum of the engine pulled Dani farther from Trevor and stretched her tenuous heart strings. *Without him, life is as dark as a moonless night.* At that realization, she stopped pretending everything was all right.

Art shooed Jared and Jana away from Dani, then sat beside her and pulled her into a fatherly embrace. "He'll be back, especially with you to come home to."

"What if this is the time he doesn't come back?"

"I want you to close your eyes and listen to the waves lapping against the hull. Take a deep breath. Now release it."

With the exhale of air, Dani's shoulders relaxed. "Okay, I'm feeling calmer," she said.

"Now, clear all your fears from your mind."

With her eyes still closed, she nodded.

"Now, pour your heart out to God and listen to what he says."

Dani opened her eyes and looked at Art. He nodded and she leaned against the railing.

Heavenly Father, I am so afraid of losing Trevor. Please keep him safe and bring him home to me.

Warmth spread through her body and her skin tingled. She opened her eyes and sat up straight. Tears cascaded down her cheek and she smiled and gave Art a hug. "Thank you so much for reminding me to have faith."

They disembarked from the boat to a seemingly endless line of taxis. Miguel brushed up beside Dani, separating her from the others.

He grabbed her arm with an unyielding grip. "Señora Gina, I have a taxi waiting."

Dani struggled to free herself. "Miguel, what are you doing? Let me go!"

"I am taking you home." He pushed her inside a taxi with the rear door open and followed her in. He closed the door and shouted to the man at the wheel. *"Vamos, ahora!"*

The force of acceleration plastered her to the seat. She watched through the rear window as Art pulled his gun and chased after the escaping vehicle. Jared pushed a driver out of the way and commandeered a cab to chase them. He stayed in sight until a few wild turns in the neighborhoods lost him.

With her final hope for rescue gone, she wiped away her tears. She confronted the boy they had considered their friend. "Why are you doing this, Miguel?"

He ignored her and dialed his cell. "I have the girl."

"Woman," Dani hissed under her breath.

"No, he was not there." Miguel flinched. "I do not know why. I will question her." He hung up without another word.

Dani slid as far away from him as possible, but he moved closer to her until her spine crushed against the door. "Why did you kidnap me?"

Miguel's hardness melted away. He became a boy instead of the man he was trying to be. His voice lowered. "I am sorry, Señora. I am your friend, but I am also my father's son. He ordered this."

"Your father?"

"Yes, Enrique Rios. He is the man Don Francisco puts in charge of his business."

"Who is Don Francisco?" Dani asked.

"Don Francisco Morales."

Her blood froze in her veins. She fought against Miguel and pushed him away. The cab squealed around a sharp corner and threw Miguel at her. She reached behind his ears and brought his head down on her knee. Blood spurted from his nose and he jerked back. Dani clawed at the door, but there was no handle.

"Tío, la cuerda." Miguel yelled to the man in front.

The driver reached onto the seat next to him and threw a rope to his nephew.

Dani gasped. "You're the man at the glassblower's shop!"

"Sí, how is my dragon?" He laughed. "She tells me where you are."

"How?" She sucked in a small breath. "A tracking device?"

His grin reflected in the rear view mirror.

Miguel began wrapping the rope around Dani's wrists. She thrust her bound hands into his chin.

"Stop!" he commanded. He shook his head, silently begging her to stop. His mouth brushed against her ear and she barely heard the words "I am trying to help."

Dani gave up and lay limp against the door. Miguel gagged her with a bandana after quietly assuring her that it was clean. Then a stern expression overtook his features. He stared straight ahead as the car moved through the city and south toward the jungle.

Forty-One

As Jared led Dani away, Trevor turned around once. He could barely resist the urge—no, the instinct—to take her and run far away from Morales. Trevor shook his head. *We'll never be safe until he rots in prison.*

He reached a fence marking the end of the Las Caletas grounds and unlocked the gate with the key he received on the *Marigalante,* then followed tags scattered through the jungle until he reached his first stop on the way to infiltrate the compound. He searched the jungle. *My guide should be—*

A strong arm clothed in camouflage reached around his neck, and a hand clapped over his mouth. "Señor Willis?"

Trevor twisted from the grasp and opened his mouth to speak, but the man put his finger to his own lips. "Shh. I am Mateo. Put these on and follow me. In silence."

Trevor nodded and changed into the camouflage clothing. He and Mateo began the first of many switchbacks descending from the mountains to the jungle floor. The sound of animal chortles and rustling leaves unnerved Trevor. When he came eye to eight eyes with a spider the size of his fist, he jumped back three feet. He took a deep breath and clenched his hands. When he exhaled, his shoulders and fists relaxed. *I hate spiders.* Mateo glanced back with flint-like eyes and once again put his finger to his lips. The duo continued their trek up and down the mountains.

A few hours later, they reached the top of a ridge. Mateo spread himself out on the ground and army-crawled to the edge. Trevor followed his lead. Below the ridge, a brightly lit compound repelled the animals of the night, yet held a greater danger from the human creatures who hid like scorpions ready to strike.

They retreated from the overlook where Mateo pointed out a fissure in the mountain. "We will sleep in there. There are provisions and observation materials. Before first light, we will sneak into the compound."

Trevor nodded. "Thank you. I'll take the first watch."

He settled on the ridge, resting his night vision goggles on a makeshift tree-branch platform. His mind wandered to the last week he spent with Dani. *When this is over, I'm not wasting a minute. It's time to pop the question.* The lights of a vehicle entering the compound drew his attention away from the future and focused it on the present. It stopped in front of a low-profile Quonset hut, and several men carrying weapons exited the building. Enrique Rios, Morales' assistant, opened the driver's door and embraced the man emerging from the car.

Trevor shook his head and looked once more. *It's the glassblower. What's he doing here?* He pushed closer to the edge of the ridge and gasped. The glassblower reached into the backseat of the car and yanked out a woman. Trevor's face paled, his pulse quickened and his hands shook violently. He croaked out a single name. "Dani."

He sucked in a breath of air. If he was going to get her back, emotions had no place in the operation. *She is not the woman I love. She is just the objective of this operation.*

He continued to observe as Miguel exited from the vehicle. *When I get my hands on that street rat, he'll wish he never gave us that first ride.*

Miguel took Dani's arm from the glassblower and helped her across the compound to another nondescript bunker-type building. They descended the stairs, disappearing from view into the bowels of the building.

§

Dani looked back as Miguel escorted her down the concrete stairs and into an underground room. *If I only knew where Trevor was, I'd feel safe.* Miguel closed the door and pulled a string in the middle of the room that was attached to a light bulb. A worn table and chair sat in the middle. Two doorways led off this main room. Miguel untied her and removed the gag.

"What are you going to do with me?" Dani asked breathlessly.

"I do not know why you are here. I think it is my old friend Alejandro."

"Alejandro Morales is your friend?"

"Not anymore." Miguel stared at the ground. "I grow up here and we play together as children. My father is Enrique Rios, the assistant to Don Francisco."

She sat against the one table in the room and leaned her hands on her knees. With her eyes closed, she said a silent prayer. A warm feeling came over her when she looked at Miguel. "You didn't want to do this, did you?"

"No. Don Francisco threatens my mother. He does not say it, but I know."

"I understand. They want me because Trevor is the one who arrested Alejandro."

"I do not understand. Who is Trevor?"

"Señor Flynn is an alias—a made-up name." She paced the space in front of the table. "His real name is Trevor Willis and I'm Dani Carpenter."

"You are not married?"

"Not yet, but soon." Dani gave a slight smile. "That's why Don Francisco wants me, to hurt everyone Trevor loves."

Miguel put a finger to his lips. "They are coming. Sit here, fast." He brought the chair to her.

Dani complied just as a group of men emerged from the stairwell. Dani looked into the eyes of the man in the middle. Ice chilled her blood, and her lungs betrayed her when they refused to draw in air. She had no doubts, evil filled the heart of Don Francisco Morales.

His charming smile never dispelled the steel in his eyes. "I have waited a long time to meet you, Señorita Carpenter. Our mutual *friend*, Señor Willis should be joining us before too long."

"I don't know what you're talking about." Dani lied.

"I think you do not tell me the truth. It does not matter. The truth will come. I do not think Señor Willis will appreciate the hospitality I am showing to you. Do you know what they call me?"

Dani nodded. "The Scorpion."

"When he arrives, you will see why." Don Francisco reached out and lifted up her chin with a surprisingly gentle touch. "I will show you how I strike my enemies again and again until they beg for death."

Dani jerked her chin away.

"Apparently, you do not appreciate my hospitality, too. You will, *mi carina,* you will." The smile dropped from his face. "Or you will face the terror of my inhospitality." He turned and beckoned a man behind him. "I want to introduce you to my son, Alejandro."

"Mi padre, I could convince her to enjoy our hospitality if I were alone with her."

Without warning, Don Francisco slapped his son across his face. "Alejandro, we are not people who do such things."

"No, you just kill people in cold blood," Dani murmured under her breath.

Miguel gave a quick shake of his head and she closed her mouth.

Don Francisco turned a seething gaze to his captive. "Would you repeat that, señorita?"

"I was just clearing my throat, sir. I didn't say anything." Dani focused her eyes on the floor.

"To say nothing would be a wise choice." He snapped around and started up the stairs. "Put her in the cell, Miguel."

Alejandro passed by slowly and stroked Dani's cheek. She spat at him. He raised his hand as if to strike her, but Don Francisco ordered, "Alejandro, come."

"I will see you again," he informed Dani with a growl before hurrying to catch up with his father.

§

"Mateo, wake up." Trevor jostled the sleeping man. "Get up. Hurry."

"¿Cómo?" Mateo's disorientation lasted only a moment before he jumped up. "What is happening?"

He jerked his head toward the compound. "They just brought in another prisoner."

"Who is it?" Mateo strained to see over the ridge.

Trevor's hands began to shake, his professionalism evaporating. "Dani Carpenter. My girlfriend."

"Señor, we will find her."

"I know where she is." Trevor kicked a pile of leaves on the jungle floor.

Mateo grasped his shoulders. "Amigo, if you do not keep calm, we are all in danger. And then who will rescue her?"

"Dani. Her name's Dani."

"But for you, she is nameless. Just another person in the custody of Don Francisco."

"You're right, you're right. We need a plan." Trevor led the way into the small cave. Mateo joined him with a flashlight and a map of the compound. They poured over the map, and Trevor pointed to a building near the center where Miguel lead Dani. "That's it. That's where they're keeping Da—the woman."

"That is good. According to our contact, that is where Dr. Miller is kept."

Trevor nodded. "But it's also bad. It's the brightest spot in the compound."

"What is the American saying? 'Two birds with one rock'?" Mateo rubbed his chin.

"It's 'two birds with one stone.'" Trevor chuckled. "How do we get our birds?"

"You are correct. Many lights surround it. Our contact will cut the power to the compound. We will have only a few minutes to enter the building and find the doctor and woman."

"Okay. I can see how we get in, but how do we get the hostages out when the power comes on?"

"The buildings are old army; they are of metal. We cut through the back of the building and stay close to the walls." He pointed to the left. "Right there."

"Good plan." Trevor clapped him on the back. "Where do we head to get away from the compound?"

"At the far end, someone waits with transportation." Mateo pointed to the map. "You leave when the policía and FBI begin the assault."

"Wait." He closed his eyes and held out his palms. "I leave? What about you?"

"I go back and capture Don Francisco, and I crush the Scorpion."

Forty-Two

Miguel led Dani through the first door into a concrete room with wall-to-wall metal-barred cells. At first glance, they were all empty, but Dani noticed a blanket-covered mound in the last cell. It moved at the sound of the closing door.

Miguel selected a key from a row of hooks and opened the cell next to the occupied one. "I am sorry. There is no choice."

"I understand." Dani peeked through the bars, straightened her shoulders, and entered the cell.

"I am in the other room. Make noise and I come."

"Thank you."

When the door closed, the mound turned over. A man limped to the wall of his cell and squinted. "Miss Carpenter?"

She closed the distance. "Yes? Dr. Miller? What are you doing here?"

"They—they made me finish the development of the EP. They said they had my little girl."

"Ady's safe. She misses you, but she's safe."

Bruce sat on the cot, held his head in his hands, and wept with relief. "Is she with Willis?"

"No, Trevor's here in Mexico. She's with his chief of security."

"Where?"

"Only Trevor knows how to get in touch with Tony. I can't let the information slip if I don't know."

"That's true."

"Dr. Miller, they used the EP to bring down Trevor's plane."

He stood and clutched his head. "But you said he's here? He's okay?"

"We were both on the plane, and we're both doing fine."

"How is Ady?"

Dani smiled when she thought of the little girl. "When we were in Washington, we roasted marshmallows and she scolded me when I burnt mine."

A chuckle came from the adjoining cell. "My wife used to put her marshmallow in the fire and blow it out when it was charcoal."

Soon, they reclined on their own thin mattresses and drifted off to sleep.

§

Trevor and Mateo half-climbed and half-slid down the cliff to reach the bottom. They crouched in the underbrush and surveyed the compound about thirty feet away. The jungle hid their approach for the first twenty feet, but the final distance crossed a barren moonscape gutted of all vegetation. Further to the East, Trevor noticed the spotlights stopped short of a stream that flowed underneath the fence.

"Hey, what about over there?" He pointed. "The light doesn't reach it and we might be able to swim through the pipe."

Mateo craned his neck and squinted his eyes. *"Sí, está bien."*

They made their way to the stream. Mateo used a stick to check the clearance through the pipe.

Trevor frowned. "What's wrong, Mateo?"

"I do not know. There is a . . .something blocks the way." His eyes widened. "Quick, the fence. Climb!"

Without hesitation, both men scampered up the chain links just as a large crocodile glided through the water and lunged at them with open jaws.

"Whoa. I can see why they didn't think they needed guards or lights over here." Trevor straddled the top of the fence before descending a few links and dropping to the ground. Mateo followed his lead. They sprinted toward a covered area between the fence and an outbuilding.

Trevor leaned against the metal shed and slowed his breathing. "We made it, just like in the movies."

"I do not like to be in movies."

Trevor chuckled softly. "Me neither, Mateo. Me neither."

With their breathing and heart rates slowed, they moved to the clearing and assessed the layout. "How long before the lights go out?"

"Right now," growled a familiar voice.

A hand reached out and grabbed Trevor by the shoulders. He struggled until the unseen assailant place a cloth over his mouth. The last thing he remembered was a man lowering him to the ground.

"Zack?"

Forty-Three

Early the next morning, Dani sat up straight at the sound of a commotion in the other room. She moved to the far edge of her cell and jumped when the door opened.

"I . . . I can bring her, Roberto." Miguel stood in front of a burly man who pushed him aside.

"Don Francisco gave orders for me to bring her. Do you want to tell him differently?"

"No." He hung his head.

"Now, quick, boy. Unlock the cell."

Miguel shuffled through the keys on the hooks, avoiding the actual key. "Try this one." He tossed the ring to him.

After testing the lock, Roberto threw the key at the boy. "Stop stalling and give me the right one."

Miguel slowly bent over and retrieved the ring. He placed it on the hook and hovered over the correct key before giving it to Roberto. Dani met the sorrow in Miguel's eyes and retreated to the back corner of the cell. Roberto opened the door and stepped toward her. She ducked under his arm, but he caught her and manacled her wrist with his hand. She struggled and collapsed to the ground as deadweight. Anger flared in his eyes. He reached down and grabbed her by the waist, flinging her over his shoulder. Dani kicked and yelled as he carried her across the compound. He stopped at the single non-army structure in the compound. The beautiful hacienda-style home shone like a lantern in the dreary compound.

Roberto carried her into the courtyard while Dani continued to struggle. He set her down and she ran. His arm shot out, stopping her progress. He hissed in her ear. "Stand still and do not make a sound."

Dani looked him in the eye and screamed. With no notice, he slapped her. She fell to the ground, holding her cheek but refused to cry.

Don Francisco opened the door himself and turned his red-faced wrath on Roberto. "How dare you use force on one who is my guest—unwilling as she may be. I will deal with you later."

Dani looked up to see the terror in Roberto' eyes.

Don Francisco reached down and took her hand, helping her to her feet. "I apologize for his actions. He will not lay a hand on you again, as long as you are under my protection."

For a man who routinely showed ruthlessness in his daily dealings with people, his voice mesmerized her. Instead of fighting back as she had with Roberto, she followed Don Francisco like a docile sheep to his opulent office. She sat in the chair across his desk and waited for him to speak.

"Señorita Carpenter, may I call you Danielle?"

Every fiber of her being screamed no, but her voice betrayed her. "Yes," she said.

"Thank you, Danielle. You may wonder why I have asked you here."

"Yes."

He stood up and walked around his chair. "Señor Willis seems to have arrived a little sooner than we thought. He is being brought here as we speak."

She bit her lip, looking him right in the eye. "I already told you, I don't know who you're talking about."

"Mi carina, we shall see."

A knock sounded at the door. Roberto carried Trevor, bound and unconscious, over his shoulder. He dropped Trevor to the ground in a careless manner. Dani bit her bottom lip, closed her eyes and clung to the chair in an effort to not flinch, but nothing prepared her for the voice in the hallway.

"Hey, what do you call a man with a rubber toe? Roberto! Get it? Ro-ber-toe."

Roberto glared at Zack.

Dani sprung from her chair and lunged at him. She pounded his chest with her fists. "How could you do this?"

Zack pushed her away. "Mr. Morales pays better than the FBI."

"Señor Lasky, be gentle with my guest. I need her unharmed."

Zack averted his eyes from Don Francisco. "Yes, sir. I understand. Willis only has one heart to break. We might as well start with his bones. He has 206 of those." He glanced at Dani. "We'll save the heartbreak for later."

Morales laughed. "You see life as a joke, Señor Lasky. It is a shame these two will not find things so humorous."

He nodded to Roberto who leaned down and broke open a small packet, releasing the smell of ammonia. He waved it under Trevor's nose. Within seconds, he regained consciousness and struggled against his restraints. His resistance stopped abruptly when he saw Dani. She dropped to the ground and stoked his hair.

He looked into her eyes. "I'm so sorry, hon. I thought I could keep you safe."

"I love you." She kissed his forehead.

Morales clicked his tongue, shaking his head in mock sadness. "Such a heartwarming reunion. I am afraid that it will not end happily. You, Señor Willis, will die slowly as Señorita

Carpenter watches. You need not worry, though. I will take care of her—for the rest of her life. She will never leave this compound."

Trevor pulled himself up with his abdominal muscles and scooted between Dani and Morales. "I'll bring you and your organization down, then I'll watch you rot in a prison cell."

Don Francisco's belly laugh echoed off the paneled walls. "You think you have help here? I own the loyalty of every man in Jalisco. They know their families will suffer if they betray me. How do you think I knew you were coming here? He called out through the office door. "Mateo! Come."

Trevor's guide limped into the office. "Si, Don Francisco?"

"How much assistance did you offer this man?" He pointed to Trevor.

"Nada. I bring him to you." He refused to look at Trevor.

"Thank you. You may leave." Morales turned to his captive. "All the people you thought were your friends are working for me." He pointed To Zack. "Even your FBI friends. Someone was needed to plan Alejandro's escape."

Anger sparked from Trevor's eyes to the man he thought of as a close friend. "You won't get away with this."

"Sorry, Willis. I already have." Zack spat out the words. "I'll make sure your remains get back to Special Agent in Charge Don Townsend." He turned his back and stormed from the room.

Morales stood before Trevor and looked at the man who brought him in. "Roberto, untie him and stand him up."

"Sí, Don Francisco." He yanked him to his feet to face the ruthless man.

"I will now demonstrate why I am the Scorpion." Morales fished a small metal device from his suit pocket. "This is my stinger." He turned a dial and touched it to Trevor's chest.

"Is that all you've got?" Trevor goaded him. "That's no worse than a mosquito."

Morales grinned, turning the dial up. He touched it to Trevor's chest again. Trevor took a step backward. A grunt escaped his lips. The man adjusted the strength again and touched Trevor's shoulder. He flew backward with a groan.

Dani ran to him and cradled his head in her lap. "Stop!"

"Mi carina, had I touched his chest, all would have stopped. That would have been too quick."

She leaned over Trevor, shielding his head and torso. She pleaded through her tears. "Please stop."

Roberto yanked her away from Trevor. She immediately elbowed him with all her strength. When he let go of her, she stomped on his instep. He grabbed his foot and let out a string of Spanish curses. She grabbed the gun from his belt, shoving him away. She took a step toward Trevor when Roberto gained his footing. She turned the gun on him.

"Stop! Don't take another step."

"*Chiquita,* you will not shoot." Roberto held out his hand, palm forward, and stepped closer. "Your hand is shaking."

"Stay back." She tightened her grip and released the safety.

"Give me the gun." He took another step.

Dani fired the revolver at his feet.

"*Ay! Gringa loca.*" He jumped back behind the desk.

She kept the gun aimed at Roberto and eyed Trevor. "Can you get up?"

"I . . . I think so." He struggled to push himself to a standing position. He held his arm and hobbled toward her. "No!" He reached out his hand.

"Do not move, Señor Willis." Morales held the stinger to Dani's neck.

She froze as though touched by winter's frost.

"Señorita, please drop the gun." The charm left Morales. Only the eyes of a cold-blooded killer remained.

Her eyes locked with Trevor's. He blinked and gave a small nod. "Do as he says."

"But—" A jolt of electricity shot into her neck. She gasped and dropped the gun. She whirled toward Morales, jamming her elbow into his ribs. He dropped the stinger and fell to his knees. Trevor grabbed the device and took a deep breath to regroup his strength. He turned the dial up two notches and touched Morales's leg. When the current hit his limb, Morales cried out.

"You're not using this against anyone ever again. Especially not my girl."

"I have learned a lesson. Next time I will hit her with the full strength. No mercy."

Trevor threw it on the floor and crushed it with his heel. "I will crush you like the insect you are."

Out of the corner of her eye, Dani saw Roberto pick up the gun. Before she had a chance to call out, he brought the butt of the gun down on the back of Trevor's head. He crumpled to the thick burgundy carpet. She jumped up and clawed at the assailant's arm. He swatted her away like a mosquito.

Morales struggled to his feet. He stood as tall as possible while clinging to the desk for support.

"Roberto, take our guests to their cells." He spoke with great effort.

He slung Trevor over his shoulder and reached for Dani. She dodged him and stepped out of his reach. Her resistance stopped when the venomous voice of Don Francisco pierced her soul.

"Mi carina, it would be a shame if Roberto were to accidentally crush the bones in your delicate wrist because you struggled to extricate yourself. Or, if he injured Señor Willis further because you did something rash."

Defeated, she nodded and allowed Roberto to grasp her wrist.

"And señorita,"

She turned to face the evil in Don Francisco's eyes.

"I will never underestimate you again."

She glared at him, allowing Roberto to lead her across the compound.

When the door of his office closed, Don Francisco jammed the button on the intercom system. "Get in here, now." He hobbled to the couch in the corner of the room.

Enrique rushed into the office without knocking. "What is it, Don Francisco?" He took five steps to his boss. "Are you hurt?"

"Of course I am hurt. Our guests are dangerous—even when in captivity." Don Francisco's expression darkened. "I planned to allow Señorita Carpenter to live, but that has changed."

"What happened?"

"She disarmed Roberto and almost escaped." Don Francisco's fists clenched, venom dripping from his words. "And Señor Willis used the stinger. On me."

"No! I will get the doctor to take care of you." Enrique left the room and barked orders to men in the hallway.

When his assistant returned, Don Francisco said, "I have not decided whether I will make him watch her die, or if she will watch him die."

"Sí, Don Francisco. Who do you wish to punish more?"

"Good question. Watching Señorita Carpenter die would be punishment for Señor Willis, but he would suffer more to die knowing she will never leave here. That is what we will do. You make the arrangements, mi amigo."

"Sí."

A knock on the door signaled the doctor's arrival. Enrique opened the door and escorted him to Don Francisco, who lay on the couch.

Enrique bowed his head to his boss, then walked out of the room and closed the double doors.

Forty-Four

When they reached the cell block, Roberto released her arm and pointed his finger at her. "Do not move."

I could push him down the stairs, Dani thought, then looked at Trevor and squashed the idea. She preceded him down the steps, her heart lighter at the sight of Miguel.

"Open the cells." Roberto pushed her ahead. "Watch out for this one."

"She is too little to cause trouble." Miguel scoffed.

"Es loca!" He sent her a withering look.

Dani returned the glare without flinching. She opened the bars and walked into her cell. "Put him here."

He raised his open hand in a threatening manner. "Do not give me orders."

"He needs attention." She glared at him. "You don't want him to die before Don Francisco has a chance to kill him, do you?" She removed the thin blanket off the stained mattress. He dumped Trevor on the cot.

"Watch them, cockroach. If they escape while you are in charge, even your father cannot protect you."

"Do not worry." Miguel tapped his temple. "I am much smarter than the Americanos."

He escorted Roberto out of the room. Dani sat on the cot next to Trevor and gently tapped his cheeks.

"Trevor, wake up." She probed the back of his head and found a large goose egg. She prodded the area and he stirred. "Trevor?

He arched his back and attempted to sit up, but fell back on the cot. Miguel came back with a first aid kit and a bowl of warm water.

"Señora, this is for him." He inclined his head toward Trevor.

"You realize we're not the Flynn's, and we're not married.

"Sí, but you are always la familia Flynn for me."

Dani touched the boy's cheek. "Thank you. Bring that here and let's fix him up." She cleaned the area around the goose bump and crunched the instant ice pack. She found an elastic bandage to secure it to his head. "Miguel, help me get his jacket off."

Trevor took a sharp breath and said through clenched teeth, "I always thought you were gentle. I've changed my mind."

"Only women can change their minds." She tucked her hair behind her ear, exposing the mark left by Don Francisco.

"Señora—your neck!" Miguel pointed to an angry welt.

She shrugged it off with a crooked smile. "I got to feel the scorpion's sting. It's not as bad as Trevor's wounds."

Bruce paced in his cell. "Let me out of here so I can help. I am a doctor, you know," he yelled.

Dani stared at him. "You're not a medical doctor—"

"Yes, I am. I graduated from med school when I was 22. After I realized I had to actually talk to my patients, I went back to school and earned a doctorate in physics. Now, instead of checking my credentials, let me out of here."

Miguel brought the key and freed Bruce. He attempted to treat Dani, but she insisted he take care of Trevor first. Her burn paled in comparison to the wounds on his chest and arm.

"Oh, Trevor, I'm so sorry. I should have found a way to stop him before he did this." Tears fell down her cheeks.

"Hey, it's fine, hon. Just a few more in my collection of scars. I guess I won't be doing any swim suit modeling." The smile she fell in love with appeared on his face.

"I love you."

"I love you back." He closed his eyes, setting his jaw against the pain.

"We need a plan," Dani said.

Miguel smiled. *"No problema.* We have a plan."

"What plan?" Dani looked up.

"We wait for the lights to go out and you follow me."

Bruce and Dani shared a look before he examined the worst burn. He searched the first aid kit for some ointment and applied it to the burns on Trevor's chest. When he slathered it on Trevor's arm, he clicked his tongue and wrapped the wound with gauze. "If that's our plan, then we better get him strong enough to walk." He shook out three tablets. "Take this ibuprofen. It will work wonders."

"I'll be ready. Just let me rest a bit." Trevor swallowed the pills, then closed his eyes and fell into a restless sleep.

Bruce walked to the edge of the cell and motioned Dani to follow him. "The burns are serious, but they'll heal. It's the concussion that has him out of it."

"Will he be okay?"

"Don't worry, he's tough." Bruce paused and lowered his voice. "So are you."

Forty-Five

Dani jumped when the outer door slammed. Miguel hurried Dr. Miller into his cell and then locked both doors. He rushed toward the main room with the bucket and first aid supplies. He reached the door as it opened, spilling the water on Roberto's shoes.

"Lo siento." Miguel crouched down to wipe up the moisture with the already-wet rag.

Roberto kicked him over. "Don Francisco desires the company of those two." He pointed to Dani and Trevor.

Dani clutched the bars in her hand. "He's not ready to be moved yet. He needs to rest."

Roberto walked slowly to her and sneered. "He does not need strength to die." He handed two pairs of hand cuffs to Miguel. "Make them tight."

Miguel took the cuffs, then unlocked the cell. He approached Dani first and motioned for her to put her wrists out. When she complied, he attached the cuffs loosely with her hands in front.

"Ouch!" She stood with her back to Roberto and winked at Miguel.

He began to cuff Trevor the same way when Roberto stopped him.

"His hands behind his back."

"Of course." He helped Trevor up and cuffed him with his hands behind his back. "Do you wish me to bring them to Don Francisco?"

"No. He has requested you to bring your mother to the room. Now."

"Mi madre? Por qué?"

"You can ask him yourself, or you can do as he says."

Miguel hung his head. "I will do as he asks."

The big man marched them out of the room. Dani glanced over her shoulder when she heard Bruce yelling and shaking the bars in a vain attempt to free himself. Roberto prodded her on.

"Just remember, chiquita, Don Francisco no longer cares how I bring you to him. He does not even care if you are conscious."

She glared at him one more time before moving ahead, trying to support Trevor. After he fell to his knees the second time, she knelt in front of him. He raised his head a fraction of an inch and winked.

Happiness flooded through her, and she bit her bottom lip to keep from shouting out. *He's stronger than he's acting.*

Roberto uttered a curse and lifted Trevor over his shoulder, then used his foot to prod Dani to her feet. "Keep moving."

They passed the Morales home and turned left. At the sight of a bunker with windows painted black, an ominous darkness shattered Dani's relief. Unbelievable suffering had taken place in that building. Her feet refused to take another step.

Roberto pushed her forward. "Move!" When she didn't, he gripped her wrist with crushing force.

"Stop!" Dani cried out.

He laughed and pulled her toward the building. "I told you, Don Francisco does not care what condition you are in when he sees you."

He let go of her long enough to open the door. She bolted away from him. Trevor grunted when the henchman dropped him to chase Dani. Her athletic background provided no help in escaping Roberto's giant strides. He caught up to her and slapped her across her cheek. Trevor shoulder-butted him to the ground.

"Come on." Trevor used his head to point the way they should run.

As they passed the blacked-out bunker, an arm reached out and grabbed Dani, pulling her between the buildings with his hand over her mouth. She recognized Zack and bit him.

He released her and held his hand to his chest. When he put his finger to his lips and motioned for Trevor and her to follow him, Dani drew in a breath, ready to scream.

Trevor whispered in her ear, "Just follow him."

Zack opened a bulkhead door and shone a light down the steps. Once Dani and Trevor descended into the musty room, Zack produced a key and ordered, "Turn around." He unlocked Trevor's cuffs and handed the key to him. "Unlock her."

Dani's mouth dropped open. "Wait! You're not one of the bad guys?"

"Nope, always one of the good guys." Zack tipped his hat to her.

Trevor unlocked Dani's restraints and said, "I started to wonder when I realized you used the security code that turned on the cameras instead of the other one. How did you get the combination to my safe?"

"That information is classified."

Trevor gave an irritated huff. "Okay. Am I allowed to ask what the plan is?"

"When you were captured, I postponed the operation until tonight. Now I'll get back before they miss me, and you'll wait for someone to lead you out of the compound."

Zack bounded up the stairs but turned at the top. "Catch." He threw the flashlight down into the room and closed the door.

Trevor grumbled, then panned the room with the flashlight beam until he found a light bulb and pulled the string to switch it on. He took in their surroundings and said, "Looks like a storage room." He found a couple of crates and pulled them beneath the light source.

He patted the crate. "Come here and sit down, hon. Let me check your arm."

"I can't move it." A tear escaped Dani's eye as she sat down.

Trevor gently touched her wrist. She gasped in pain. He pulled her head to his chest and stroked her hair. "Shh, shh. It's okay. It's okay."

"It hurts so bad. I guess I'm just a wimp."

"You've been far from wimpy. Let me see if there's something I can splint it with."

He tilted several bins until he found some paddles used to stir paint, paper towels, and a roll of duct tape. "I feel like MacGyver." He winked at her. "The paper towels should protect your skin."

Dani winced.

Trevor kept talking. "I've heard of people who can break someone's wrist by squeezing, but it's rare."

"Ow! I'm beginning to believe that Roberto might be one of those people."

He tore off several long strips of duct tape. "I'm just placing these paddles to keep your wrist immobile. Can you hold right here with your other hand?"

"I think so," Dani said.

Trevor used the silver tape to wrap the makeshift splint around her forearm. "How's that?"

"It feels better." She lifted her arm.

"Now come over here where you belong."

Her smile lit the dank space as she scooted into his embrace. "You're right. I do belong here."

He sat up quickly. "Let me see your ring."

She slipped it off her finger and handed it to him. He took it and knelt on one knee in front of her.

"Will you marry me—when this is all over?"

For the first time today, she cried tears of joy. "Of course I will—once we get out of this situation. I'm not sure the FBI will appreciate using their ring for personal business."

"It's not theirs, it's yours."

Her eyebrows furrowed together. "What do you mean?"

"I mean I bought it for you. I love you. I want to spend the rest of my life with you, and I promise I will never say 'yes' to another job from Don."

She kissed him quickly. "I'll hold you to that. Now, I don't know about you, but I'm kind of tired of waiting for someone to lead us out of here."

"I knew there was a reason I fell in love with you. We think alike." He helped her up and kissed her cheek. "Let's figure this out."

Trevor spotted a metal door with no handle. His fingers probed the edges for some kind of latch before stepping back. He shook his head. "I'm sure this is some kind of exit. I just can't find a way to open it."

Dani searched and got the same results. She leaned her elbow on a rock shelf, stumbling forward when it moved under her weight. The gears sounded as the door lock released.

"You've done it!" He kissed her. "Take the flashlight." Trevor squared his shoulders. "Here goes."

He wiped his hands on his pants, then set his feet and pushed with all his strength. He pushed until the rusted hinges groaned with his weight pressed against the door.

"It looks like a passageway." Dani shined the flashlight through the opening.

§

Miguel rounded the corner with his mother behind him. He stopped before colliding with Roberto.

"Where are they?"

He looked around Roberto. "Who?"

"The prisoners. Where are they?"

"I do not know. We arrived just now. Don Francisco will not be happy when he knows you have lost them."

"I did not lose them." Roberto snorted, looking like a bull ready to charge the matador.

"What do you want me to tell Don Francisco?" He guided his mother to the door.

Zack sauntered around the corner whistling an abstract tune. "Why are we all gathered here?" He looked around. "Are they in there?"

"They are lost." Miguel inclined his head toward Roberto.

"What do you mean they're lost?" He threw his hands in the air and grunted. "I risked my life and my career to bring them to you, and you let them escape?"

Roberto's huge hands clenched and unclenched. He charged at the American. At the last moment, Zack crouched to the ground, spinning around in a Russian coffee grinder, and knocked Roberto to the ground.

"And my nephews thought folk dancing was for wimps. Now would you like to continue this fight, or would you prefer I help you locate them before Don Francisco finds out they're gone?"

Roberto pushed himself up. "We will find them."

"Miguel, take your mother inside." Zack searched down the street.

"And say nothing." Roberto raised his fist.

Miguel nodded and opened the door for his mother. He pulled her behind him before entering the large room where his father and the don waited.

Don Francisco stepped forward with his hand outstretched. "Ah, Carolina, it has been much too long since I have seen you. When Rosalinda returns, we will invite you for the evening meal."

She lowered her eyes, "Sí, Don Francisco."

"Come and sit over here, mi carina." He led her to a chair against the wall and directed his attention to her son. "Where are the prisoners? Did you see them on the way in?"

Miguel shuffled his feet and studied the ground. "I . . ."

"Miguel!" The one word from Don Francisco pulled Miguel's head upward, and he met the eyes of the legendary Scorpion. "Tell me what is wrong."

"They . . . they escaped from Roberto. He threatens me if I tell you."

Don Francisco clicked his tongue and patted the boy's cheek. "Miguel, Miguel. Do not keep anything from me. You are right to report this treachery. Where is Roberto?"

Miguel caught his father's steel gaze. "He is searching on this end of the compound."

"Enrique." Don Francisco's face darkened.

"Cómo?"

"Alert the camp and begin the search for them."

"Sí." Enrique reached his hand out for his wife. "Come with me, Carolina."

The calm in Don Francisco's voice chilled the room. "Bring Roberto to me."

Miguel exited the building with his parents and saw Roberto searching the out buildings. "Don Francisco wishes to see you."

"You told him?" He picked up the boy and shook him.

"I did not have a choice."

"Stop!" Enrique clamped Roberto's shoulder and applied pressure. "Go to him. Now."

Roberto threw Miguel to the ground and stomped to the building, but stopped with his hand on the doorknob.

"Enter."

Roberto twisted the knob with shaking hands.

"Did I not give you a second chance after you allowed my son to be captured?" demanded Don Francisco.

"Sí."

"You repaid me by allowing my prisoners to escape?"

"No." Roberto shook his head. "I will locate them now."

"It is too late. Come in."

The door closed and Miguel heard nothing more.

Forty-Six

The passageway grew more primitive the further Trevor and Dani moved. They followed the supports that ran through the tunnel. Tree roots jutted out through sections of the packed dirt wall. Trevor used the flashlight to push away spider webs and their occupants. Dani appreciated his efforts when she brushed against the occasional threads of web. She laughed when he hit a strand and used his flashlight to brush it off his arm. He stepped to the other side of the tunnel, repeating the motion when he encountered the other side of the web.

"I think you might be more skittish around spiders than I am." She teased.

He shivered. "I agree with Ron Weasley, I wish these were butterflies rather than spiders."

"I've found your kryptonite, Superman." She chuckled.

"Have you seen the size of some of these spiders? Even the Hulk would think twice about confronting them."

"Of course." She patted his shoulder, muttering "Wimp."

They reached a Y in the tunnel. "Well, this is an exploratory expedition. Let's go this way." He turned to the right.

Shivering, Dani stood staring down the branch of the tunnel. She slowly shook her head.

"What's wrong, hon?" Trevor said.

"It's dark down there."

"We're under the ground, it's dark everywhere. That's why we have a flashlight."

"When I try to walk that way, my heart feels cold. It's the same as when we approached the awful building. I am not going down that tunnel."

"It's okay," Trevor replied. "If there's one thing I've learned, it's to listen to your intuition. We'll go the other way." He kissed her forehead and they walked down the other branch of the Y.

§

Chaos ensued in the aftermath of the prisoners' escape. Spotlights flashed from the towers around the compound. Miguel hurried, searching for Trevor and Dani, hoping they hadn't been found. He turned the corner and ground to a stop.

"We'll be sending Willis and company out shortly. Synchronize your watches. Thirty minutes before we launch Operation Scorpion." Zack disconnected the communication, taking a step before he saw Miguel. He drew a deep breath. "Good thing it's you. What about your mother—is she safe?"

"Sí. My father took her to safety. Have they found them?"

"No, but I did. They're in the storage room."

"That leads to the tunnel?"

"Yes. I figured they would be safe there." Zack finished packing up the shortwave radio, then motioned for Miguel to follow. He opened the padlock and signaled for the boy to enter.

Miguel stepped down and allowed his eyes to adjust to the light. "Señor Flynn?" He pulled a flashlight from his pocket and shone the beam around the storage room. "They are not here."

Zack jumped down the stairs. "Trevor? Dani? Where are you?" He threw his arms up in the air. "Why didn't they just stay put?"

"I will check the tunnel for them?"

"Okay. I don't have time to search. Get them and Dr. Miller to the rendezvous point."

"Sí." Miguel followed the tunnel and heard the doors close behind him. "Señor Flynn," he whispered loudly.

Only silence answered. He hurried his pace, continuing to call out in a hushed voice. When he reached the Y," his heart leapt in his chest. If they went right, they would walk into Don Francisco's trap. He aimed his flashlight at the dirt floor. Two sets of footprints continued to the left. He let go of the breath he'd been holding and jogged down the tunnel until the light from his flashlight touched their backs.

"Señor Flynn, it is Miguel."

Dani peeked out from behind Trevor. She walked to the boy and hugged him. "Is your mother okay? I've been worried about her."

"She is fine, señora, but what happened to you?"

"Roberto," Dani replied, her gaze on the floor.

Miguel lifted her chin. "He will never hurt you again."

She nodded her head and blinked back tears.

"It is good you go this way. If you go the other way, you end up in the Scorpion's den." He watched the look pass between his two friends and cocked his head to the side.

Trevor took hold of Dani's hand and pointed down the tunnel. "Where does this take us?"

"To Dr. Miller."

"Good. How long do we have before the authorities get here?"

Miguel looked at the cheap plastic watch limply hanging from his wrist. "Twenty-one minutes. Hurry."

Miguel led the way, forging the trail through the spider webs. Trevor still jumped when the strands brushed his arm, but there was no time to pick his way through the tunnel. When they reached the end, Miguel handed his flashlight to Trevor.

"One minute. I check." Miguel touched his finger to his lips and climbed a crude ladder, then pushed the hatch open slightly to survey the room above. "I be right back." He hoisted himself up through the floor into the front room of the cell block and searched the cells. At the sound of movement in the lab, Miguel crept to the door and peeked in to see Dr. Miller gathering papers, and Mateo rigging explosives to the various pieces of equipment.

"Are you ready?" he called into the room.

Mateo spun around with a gun aimed at Miguel's heart. "Oh, it's you! I could have shot you."

"I knew you would not." Miguel slapped his friend on the back. "I have the other two in the tunnel. We have only nine minutes."

"We'll be ready," replied Mateo.

Miguel ran to the trap door and signaled for Trevor and Dani to come.

She climbed the first couple of rungs and looped her elbow over the next one. "I can't possibly hoist myself up there."

"Okay, I'll climb up right behind you." Trevor cupped his hands and shouted. "Miguel?"

The boy stuck his head through the opening. "Sí?"

"When she gets up there, help support her. She can't climb through on her own."

Dani began her climb with Trevor following. When she neared the top, Miguel reached down and grabbed her under her arms until she was able to step off of the ladder. Trevor followed her into the room.

"Where's Dr. Miller?"

"In the lab." Miguel pointed.

Trevor hustled the other two through the door but stopped short. "Mateo?"

The man hung his head. "I am sorry for what I was forced to say."

Trevor patted Mateo's shoulder. "I know. I never really doubted you, friend."

"Thank you. I have everything hooked up to the explosives."

"Good. We've only got a couple of minutes before all . . ." He paused. "Before all chaos breaks loose."

Bruce held up a worn satchel. "I've got all my notes. And, by the way, you look much better than you did a few hours ago."

Trevor nodded. "Okay, Miguel. Get us out of here."

"Sí." The boy walked to a crate on the outer wall and pulled it back, revealing an exit cut through the corrugated steel.

An explosion shook the ground, and the electricity flickered off. When the small group entered the narrow space between buildings, the crescent moon filtered through the clouds and lit their way.

"Follow me." Miguel slunk around the corner without waiting to see if the others followed. They flattened themselves as much as possible against the sides of the buildings. They reached the next opening. Miguel took a step out when a man shoved a gun into his chest.

"How do you come to be in possession of the prisoners?"

"La policía are looking for them. I—"

Mateo snuck behind the man and rendered him unconscious.

"Did you . . . did you kill him?" Dani clutched her uninjured hand to her throat.

"No, he is not dead. Although, he would not have hesitated to kill you." Mateo huffed before retaking his place at the end of the line.

They continued their journey to safety with no further incidents. Helicopters and gunfire roared as the combined United States/Mexican task force began their assault on the heart of Don Francisco's drug operation. Their last obstacle was a gate covered with jungle growth. Miguel pulled away the vines and produced a key to the padlock.

"There is a ATV over there." Miguel pointed down a path.

"I need you to take Dani and Dr. Miller to the extraction point." Trevor held the boy's shoulders and looked into his eyes. "Can you do that?"

"Sí, señor. I will keep her safe." He nodded.

Dani stood before Trevor with her hands on her hips. "You're not coming with us?" She angrily brushed a tear away.

His eyes pleaded with her. "I can't. I have to make sure Morales doesn't get away."

The anger melted away and she stood on tiptoes to kiss his cheek. "I do understand. Come back to me."

He drew her in for a kiss before clinging in a last hug. "I love you."

"Love you back."

Trevor and Mateo turned back toward the compound. Mateo pulled out a handheld radio.

"We are sending the hostages down the Northern trail to the extraction point. There are two men and one woman riding a green ATV. I repeat. We are sending two men and one woman down the northern trail. Confirm their arrival."

The radio crackled to life. "Copy. We are expecting two men and a woman down the Northern trail. We will watch and confirm their arrival."

While Mateo spoke to the control center, Trevor turned and ran over to Dani, kissing her one more time, then ran to catch up to his friend.

"I understand why you have such a hard time thinking of her as just a mission. You are a man lucky." Mateo winked at him.

A crooked smile broke out on his face. "I definitely am lucky."

Forty-Seven

Trevor disappeared into the dark compound, while Miguel jumped on the front of the ATV. Bruce helped Dani into the cargo space, and they began the descent to the extraction location. They ducked to avoid low-hanging branches as the vehicle sped through the jungle.

"Can you slow down, Miguel?" Dani shouted.

"No, I must get you down quickly." Never letting up on the gas, he headed for the unprotected portion of the trail just before the final switchback.

As the nose of the ATV enter the clearing, a gunshot reverberated through the jungle canopy. Miguel slumped over the handlebars, and the ATV slowed to a stop against the hill.

"Miguel!" Dani jumped from the cargo platform. "Miguel? Are you okay?"

He attempted to raise his head, but didn't have the strength. Another bullet whooshed over their heads. Bruce pulled the boy out of the driver's seat, laid him in the cargo space, and unbuttoned his shirt. Dani gasped at the gaping wound in Miguel's chest.

"Dani, give me your sweater," Bruce demanded quietly. "We need to stop the bleeding."

She peeled off the sweater and handed it over. Bruce placed the fabric directly on top of Miguel's wound and applied pressure. Another bullet chipped a section of green paint off the ATV.

"We're partially hidden now," Bruce said, "but they'll soon move within shooting distance. Can you drive this thing?" He cradled Miguel's head in his lap, still using the sweater to try to staunch the bleeding.

"Trevor taught me once. I think I can remember." Dani jerked away from their partially protected spot and climbed onto the seat. The pain in her wrist caused her to pull back, killing the engine. She took a deep breath, restarted the ATV, and maneuvered the machine onto the narrow path.

"Can you make it a little smoother?" Bruce called.

"I'm doing the best I can." She glanced back. "How's he doing?"

"Not good. I'm afraid we might lose him."

Dani braced herself before pushing the accelerator to the highest speed. "Keep him alive till we can get help. I don't think it's far."

She made a right turn around the path and hit a bump. The ATV caught some air, then came down with a thud at the base of operations. She jammed on the brakes as armed FBI agents surrounded them.

"Quick, we need medical help," Dani shouted. "He's been shot."

Within seconds, a medical team pushed between the agents. They gingerly loaded Miguel onto a stretcher. Dani jumped from the vehicle and matched her stride to the medics.

Holding up one end of the stretcher, Bruce demanded, "What type of medical facilities do you have here? This boy needs immediate surgery."

"Nothing here, sir, but we can airlift him to the ship."

"Then do it now." Bruce's voice left no room for debate.

By the time they reached the rocky beach, a helicopter waited. Dani and Bruce loaded Miguel, still on his stretcher, into the copter, then got in.

A young blond woman sat next to Miguel's head. "Hey, there." She patted his hand. "Can you hear me?"

The boy opened his eyes. "I see an angel," he said slowly, sounding drugged. "Am I dead?"

She smiled. "No angels, just me, your nurse."

"You are beautiful." His eyes closed again, but a smile remained on his lips.

She touched his shoulder. "Miguel. Open your eyes."

"Sí. Anything for you."

"My name is Aubrey. I need to start an IV." She cleaned the back of his hand with an antiseptic wipe. "You'll feel a prick." She quickly found the vein and started the IV fluid, then said, "They'll take you right into surgery when we get on the ship."

"Will you stay with me, Aubrey?" Miguel's words were slurred.

"If they'll let me."

"Good." He held her and then his eyes closed.

The helicopter descended to the deck of the United States Navy vessel. They transferred Miguel to a gurney and rushed him into the bowels of the ship before the helicopter blades stopped their rotation. Dani and Bruce jumped from the door, following Miguel and the trauma team until he disappeared behind the surgery doors. Aubrey led Dani and Bruce into an alcove with a couple of chairs.

"I promised Miguel I would stay with him, but I'll be out again when he's under anesthesia." She left them to their own devices.

"Bruce, is he going to be okay?" Dani touched his arm, searching his eyes for answers.

He sighed. "I'm . . . I . . . I really don't know. He's lost a lot of blood, but he's young and strong. I just don't know."

§

Trevor and Mateo dodged federal troops engaged in battle with Morales' men.

"What's our next step?"

Mateo crinkled his eyebrows. "Right in front of you, amigo?"

Trevor stifled a laugh. "I meant, what do we do next?"

"We make sure Don Francisco does not escape."

They continued through the darkened compound until they approached the blackened windows of the bunker.

A chill shook his frame. "I understand why Dani felt such revulsion when she approached this building. I feel the same way."

"Most prisoners of Don Francisco walk into the building. What is left of them is carried out."

"We better check in there. It's the last place I know he was."

Mateo opened the well-oiled door. "I do not think he will still be here, but I would not want to be the one who let him escape."

The thought of how close he and Dani were to being in this building made him weak, yet he still put one foot in front of the other. He stood to the side of the door with his weapon drawn to cover his partner as he entered the room.

Mateo stood straight and lowered his weapon. "No one in here is alive." He shook his head slowly and looked down. "He was a favorite of Don Francisco. The don even forgave Roberto when Alejandro was arrested. What could he have done to make the don so angry?"

Trevor entered the room and recognized Roberto. "He was the one we escaped from."

He nodded. "I understand. Don Francisco might forgive one mistake, but never two."

"I won't mourn for Roberto, but no man has the right to kill another man at will. I'm going to make sure Morales never kills again." Trevor backed from the room, and they made their way to Don Francisco's home.

Mateo approached the Mexican authorities herding a group of people through the front door. "Have you found Morales yet?"

"No. We have the servants of his house."

"What will happen to them?" Trevor scanned the group.

"They will be questioned to determine if they are active in Morales' organization."

He nodded, but then noticed a gray-haired man hugging the shadows. Something about him seemed out of place among the humble servants. The deference the others showed to the man struck Trevor like the sting of a scorpion. "It's him. You have Morales." Trevor pointed to the man trying to blend in with the other servants.

All guns raised toward Don Francisco Morales. Trevor noticed Morales's slight glance to the roof top, so quick that Trevor thought he might have imagined it. He followed the gaze and saw Alejandro Morales disappearing over the crest of the roof. He nudged Mateo and the two rushed to the other side of the house in time to see Alejandro limping into the jungle. Trevor jumped into the dense greenery after him. He dodged branches and jumped over fallen logs. Alejandro's old leg injury slowed him down allowing Trevor to catch up with him. He lunged the final few feet to grab the fugitive's ankle and dragged him down to the ground.

Mateo appeared from a different direction and jammed his gun into the prisoner's back. "Move a centimeter and I will shoot."

Trevor held Alejandro to the ground with his foot while he fished out the same handcuffs he'd escaped earlier. He pulled the prisoner's hands behind his back and cuffed him. "There won't be anyone left to break you out of the courtroom this time."

Alejandro spat at Trevor. "You will need to look over your shoulder for the rest of your life. You will never again feel safe."

He ignored Alejandro's rant and marched him over to the police waiting nearby. "I'm heading to the extraction point. Let them know I'm on my way."

"I am sure there is one person who will be happy to see you." Mateo chuckled as Trevor jogged away.

"Wait!" One of the authorities called him back.

Trevor faced the policeman. "What's wrong?"

The man smiled and held out an FBI jacket. "You will get through easier if you wear this."

"Thank you." Nothing else would stop him reaching Dani.

Forty-Eight

Trevor ran down the jungle path where Dani had disappeared a couple of hours ago. He burst through the brush, coming face to face with several rifles. He raised his hands and stared down the man in charge.

"I'm Trevor Willis—one of the people you came here to rescue."

"Sir, place your hands against the tree behind you." The sergeant nodded to one of the marines. "Search him."

A young woman with short brown hair picked her way through the sand. "Just a minute. We have confirmation that Mr. Willis was on his way. I have a picture."

The sergeant compared the picture to Trevor. "You're free to go, sir."

"Hello, Mr. Willis. We've been expecting you. I'm Special Agent Mackelprang. Please follow me."

"I wish you'd have told those guys about it."

"It was my fault. I just arrived on duty." She led him into a tent furnished with two folding chairs and a table masquerading as a desk. She pointed to one of the chairs. "Have a seat."

"Thank you. Where are the others who came down earlier? Two men and a woman?"

Agent Mackelprang searched through a file box. "We had to air evac them to the ship. One was shot and in pretty bad shape."

Trevor sprung from his chair, knocking it to the floor. "One was hurt. Who?" His heart raced at the thought of Dani being injured.

She looked confused. "I'm sorry, it was before I got here."

"You better get me on that ship before I decide to swim there." He glowered at her.

She pushed back from the table and rushed outside. She returned a few minutes later. "Hurry, we have a helicopter about to leave. I'm sorry. I had no idea they were friends of yours."

"More than friends. The woman is my fiancée."

Five minutes later he was in the chopper and off the ground.

§

There was a commotion in the outer hallway as Dani waited for the doctor to examine her.

"Please, sir."

That's Aubrey.

"You have a choice. Move aside and let me in, or I will physically move you and enter anyway."

Dani's heart leapt at the sound of Trevor's voice. She clutched the thin robe around her. The entire room faded away when he stepped through the door. He paused for a brief moment before crossing the room with his long stride and wrapped her in his arms. Somewhere, her mind registered Aubrey apologizing for allowing this man inside, but Dani didn't care about anything else except being with Trevor.

"Excuse me, but I need to examine this woman." A doctor in a white lab coat tapped on Trevor's shoulder. When he didn't respond, the doctor tapped harder. "Do I need to call in the MP's?"

Trevor slowly pulled away from her. "Who's been injured?"

Tears welled up in her eyes. "Miguel. He was shot and lost a lot of blood."

"Where is he?"

"In surgery."

"Okay. I'll find out more about Miguel while the doctor gets you get checked out." Trevor turned to Aubrey. "Can you help me find out what's happening?"

"Yes, sir."

Aubrey and Trevor left.

"Your x-rays are back," the doctor told Dani. "It looks like your wrist isn't broken. When we dock, we might want to do an MRI to see what damage was done. How did you hurt it?"

"A man tried to crush it." Shivers raced through her body.

The doctor squeezed her other hand. "You've had a rough time."

She nodded.

"That was quite the on-the-fly splint."

"Trevor did it."

"He sounds resourceful. Let me check your ears." The doctor brushed Dani's hair out of the way and concern creased his brow. "What happened to your neck?"

"Some kind of Taser? Don Francisco called it his stinger."

"We might want to include this in the MRI. No telling how much damage was done."

"It was only a second or two. Trevor's the one who has the worst injuries—other than Miguel." Her shoulders slumped. "Now Miguel is hurt, and might not make it. He kept a close eye on me, and it's my fault he got shot."

"Young lady, look at me. He was shot because of an evil man, not because of you. Don't you ever forget that." The doctor applied a salve to Dani's neck and bandaged it with gauze and medical tape. "We have some clothes for you to change into. Get dressed, then you can wait for news on that brave young man."

Dani wiped a tear from her eye, something that seemed to be happening far too often these days.

"Oh. When you get out to the niche pretending to be a waiting room, send your boyfriend in for his turn." The doctor winked at her before closing the door.

Aubrey watched through a large glass window as the surgical team worked on Miguel. The head surgeon looked concerned. When the patient went code blue, Aubrey leaned against the class and muttered, "C'mon, c'mon, Miguel! Fight!"

A minute later, the monitor blipped, signaling a heartbeat. The next time Miguel's heart stopped, Aubrey held her breath till the comforting rhythm once again danced across the screen. The third time, she left the observation room, unable to watch any longer.

Forty-Nine

Dani entered the waiting area, flinching at the scene before her. Aubrey faced the corner, her shoulders shaking. Bruce extended an arm around her shoulder while Trevor sat in an uncomfortable metal chair with his elbows propped on his knees and his head cradled in his hands.

"Is . . . is Miguel . . ." she choked out.

Trevor sprung from his chair and hugged her in his arms. "No. We haven't heard anything from the surgeon, yet. You know what they say, no news is good news."

Dani pushed him away. "Then why is Aubrey crying?"

The nurse left the corner, looking Dani in the eye. "I was observing the surgery and he kept coding—his heart kept stopping. I couldn't watch anymore."

"So, he's—" Dani backed toward the passageway shaking her head.

"No hon, he keeps fighting back. Every time." Trevor pulled her back and led her to a chair.

"The doctor wants to see you next."

"He'll just have to wait until we find out if about Miguel. I really don't need a doctor."

Dressed in surgical scrubs, Dr. Andrews stepped from the passageway and entered the alcove. Biting her bottom lip, Dani approached him and asked, "How is he?"

"He's alive, but pretty weak. We thought we lost him a few times, but he's a fighter."

She let out a sigh as the tension left her body "Thank you. When can I see him?"

"In a few hours. He's in recovery."

Dani flew into Trevor's arms and soaked his shirt with tears. "Thank heavens he's okay."

He pulled back from her and wiped a drop from her cheek. "I think it's time we do that right now," he whispered in her ear.

The four people in the room clasped hands and gave thanks that they made it through this ordeal alive.

Dani followed Aubrey down the passageway to the recovery room. Aubrey motioned to an uncomfortable chair that would have been at home in Morales' torture chamber.

"His parents are in there now."

"His parents? I guess that explains the MP's." Dani popped up when the door opened.

Miguel's parents exited. Enrique stopped, taking Dani's hand in his. "Señorita Carpenter."

She pulled her hand away from Don Francisco's top advisor as though his touch burned her skin.

"I am told you are much responsible in saving Miguel. I am always in your gratitude." He bowed his head slightly, maintaining a comfortable distance from her.

Dani cradled her hand. She stared at him with fear in her eyes and nodded.

"Come Carolina, it is time to leave." Enrique put his arm around his wife and they followed one marine as another soldier fell in place behind them.

"Dani." Aubrey tapped her on the shoulder. "Dani?"

She shook off her semi-trance. "Yes, I'm sorry."

"It's okay. He's ready to see you."

With a deep breath, Dani entered the cabin filled with machines beeping in steady rhythms. In the middle of everything, Miguel lay on a bed with white sheets. The medical equipment dwarfed him, reminding her of a little boy. The ever-present nurse adjusted a few knobs before recording the information in a metal-clad chart. Aubrey nodded to the attending nurse, who left them alone.

Dani wiped a tear from her cheek. She touched his arm. He blinked open his eyes and smiled when he recognized her.

"Señora Flynn?"

"Hello, Miguel."

His brow furrowed. "Is Señor Flynn . . ."

"He's fine."

The smile returned. "Then that tear was for me?"

Dani nodded. "You had me worried."

"Gracías." Miguel's cheeks colored.

Aubrey stood on the opposite side of the bed. "You had me worried, too."

"Ah, dos angeles. I am a man lucky." He basked in the attention of two women.

"I hate to burst your bubble, but I'm heading back to Puerto Vallarta in a few minutes. Thank you for protecting me." She leaned down and kissed his cheek.

He dipped his head. *"Vaya con Díos, señora."*

The seaman assigned to Dani led her topside to a waiting helicopter. Trevor stood on the deck and smiled when she came into view. The noise of the thrumming rotors precluded verbal communication until they landed on the tarmac in Puerto Vallarta. They watched as the chopper began its return journey to the ship. An FBI agent led them into a small building at the edge of the airport. Jana squealed and ran across the room, and the two embraced amid tears. When Jana finally released her hold on her sister-in-law, Jared hugged her.

"I'm so sorry, Sis. I've been on Trevor's case for all that's happened, but as soon as you're under my protection, I couldn't keep you safe."

Dani squeezed her brother hard. "It wasn't your fault."

"C'mon. Let's sit over here and you can tell us about your ordeal." He led the two women to worn chairs along the back wall. "Let me get you something to drink."

Trevor approached Jared with trepidation. The men stared one another down until Jared offered his hand. "Thank you for bringing her home."

Trevor cleared his throat and shook Jared's hand. He blinked a few times. "Um, yeah." He clapped his hands and then rubbed them together. "You all want to spend a few more days in Puerto Vallarta, or do you want to go home?"

With no hesitation and in complete accord, the vote sounded. "Home!"

A new voice agreed when Zack entered the room. "Home is great. Time and the stork wait for no man—not even the FBI. I have to get back to Cait."

"It's great to have you back on the side of the good guys." Trevor shook his hand.

"So, is Caitlyn ready to pop?" Jared asked.

"She says she is. I'm through with the Mexican side of the debriefing. The FBI will have to wait until after Zack junior makes his appearance."

Art Toscano and Bruce entered the room and called for the group's attention. "We're just waiting for the pilots to show up," Art explained.

Trevor jumped up from his seat. "We don't need to wait—I can fly the jet."

"Nice try, Willis. They need to get home too. Oh, here they are. Let's go."

As Trevor's foot touched the first stair to the plane, his phone buzzed. He moved away and answered, "Willis."

"It's okay to come in from the cold?"

"Yes. How long will it take you to get to the rendezvous spot?"

"Tomorrow morning."

"We'll be there."

Trevor bounded up the stairs, pulled them up behind him, and secured the door. He popped his head into the cockpit and greeted the crew, then said, "Remember, if you need a break—"

"Yeah, yeah, we know, Willis."

Fifty

On Trevor's computer screen in his living room, Zack, still clad in hospital scrubs and surgical cap, bobbed up and down with his new son in his arms. A shock of red hair poked out from a little blue beanie, while a tiny hand escaped from the receiving blanket. "He's lucky—he looks like Cait. I made it just in time to see Doc Eric catch him."

Dani leaned close to the monitor and touched the baby on the screen. "How's Caitlyn?"

"She was a real trooper. The good news is—drum roll, please—the fingernail holes in my arm won't need stitches!"

Dani joined in the laughter from the people behind her. "Can we see her?"

The computer image spun around the room, stopping on a hospital bed where Caitlin slept peacefully.

Zack's voice softened. "If I wake her up, my mother-in-law will ban me from the hospital. I'll talk to you all later."

The screen went dark and everyone filtered into the kitchen. Trevor grabbed a chocolate-chip cookie off a platter on the breakfast bar. "These are great, Jana. Thanks for commandeering my kitchen."

"No problem." Jana dipped a potato chip into some french-onion dip.

"Grab something to eat and meet me in the living room," Trevor said, then headed to the fireplace.

Jana and Jared sat in the crook of the sectional couch. Dani chose the chair closest to Trevor, and Bruce perched on the edge of an end table. All attention focused on Trevor.

He cleared his throat. "Art briefed me on the outcome of the raid, and I wanted to share it with you."

"We're ready to hear," Jared prompted .

"First of all, Morales and Alejandro are in custody. They're being held in an undisclosed maximum-security location. They won't be getting away this time. The entire Morales cartel has been broken up. The FBI retrieved records about their dealings in the States, and raids are happening as we speak."

"What'll happen to Enrique Rios?" asked Dani.

"He's in custody too. He'll be debriefed and possibly spend some time in prison, but because he made this operation possible, he'll likely be given a new identity and enter the Witness Protection Program."

"I don't understand," Bruce stood up and scratched his head. "Why would Rios turn against Morales? Wasn't he his right-hand man?"

"You're right, he was. Morales cut off his own arm as soon as he threatened Rios's wife. Rios came on board after that."

"What about Miguel?" Dani reached for Trevor's hand.

"The ship will dock in San Diego and he'll be transferred to Naval Medical Center. Afterward, someone might be in the right place at the right time to offer him a job and find him a place to live." Trevor winked at his fiancée. "Oh, I almost forgot. Bureau Chief Lee Evans is on administrative leave pending an investigation into his dealings with Morales."

The door chimes interrupted their conversation. Trevor excused himself and opened the front door. He laughed out loud when Ady jumped into his arms.

"Crash! I'm so happy you're here!"

He twirled her around. "I kept my promise," he whispered in her ear.

"Daddy?" she gasped.

"Go in there and see."

He set her on the wood floor and she rushed into the living room. She paused a moment until she saw Bruce. "Daddy! Daddy!" They held each other while Bruce kissed her head.

Not a dry eye remained in the room when Tony slammed the front door open.

"There's someone out there hiding in the tree."

Trevor took charge. "Jared, bring everyone up to my bedroom. The closet is secure." He entered the office and pulled a gun from the safe. Jared returned to help.

"No." Trevor held Jared's shoulder an arm's length away and looked in his eyes. "You have to protect them."

Jared nodded.

Trevor and Tony left the house from different exits and closed in around the intruders. Trevor nodded toward a piece of fabric visible in a tree. They aimed their weapons at the branches.

"You're surrounded. Drop your weapons and show yourselves," Tony called.

The branch rustled. Two sets of arms raised into the air, followed by two wide-eyed faces.

"It's okay, Tony." Trevor lowered his weapon. "Sean? Luke? What are you doing here?"

Tony kept his gun pointed at the two. "Who are they?"

"Two of my scouts."

With his eyes trained on the boys, Tony lowered his gun.

"We've been keeping an eye on your place. Officer Mills drives by every day." Sean jumped from the branch.

Luke lowered himself to the ground. "Yeah, we just heard on the news that you didn't do all that stuff. We knew that the whole the time."

"Thanks, guys. I owe you one." He pulled the pocket knife and lighter from his pocket and handed them to the boys. "These came in handy."

"Aw," Sean kicked at the dirt. "It was nothing."

Trevor put his arms around the two boys. "Come on in. We have some cookies."

"I never turn down food." Luke patted his stomach.

Trevor brought the boys inside, and once again, everyone congregated in front of the fireplace.

Trevor raised his hand. "Hey everyone, I have something to say." He stood behind Dani and placed his hands on her shoulders. "Dani and I would like to invite all of you back here in three weeks—for our wedding reception."

Ady squealed and ran to Dani. "I knew you were gonna get married. I knew it!"

Trevor made his way through the crowd, returning with some chilled sparkling cider. He poured the cider and passed the cups around. I have a toast. "To finding love," he winked at Dani. "And friends. To safety and . . . no more one-more-time jobs!"

$$\S$$

Dani stood on the balcony of Walt Disney's apartment above Pirates of the Caribbean in Disneyland. Holding onto the railing, she leaned her head back and soaked in the warmth of the sun. She jumped when Trevor came behind her and wrapped his arms around her waist.

"Good morning, Mrs. Willis."

Dani turned to face her new husband. "When I mentioned coming to Disneyland, I never imagined we'd be staying at the park."

"Only the best for you." The sound of his cell phone interrupted their kiss. "It's Don. Something must be wrong. He'd never call on our honeymoon unless it was an emergency."

Dani stood close to hear the conversation.

"What's wrong?" Trevor asked. "Are Traci and the kids okay?

"Yes, they're fine," Don assured him.

"Has Morales escaped?

"No, he's still at a secret maximum-security facility."

Trevor grumbled. "Then why are you calling me on my honeymoon?"

"You know how you're going on an Alaskan Cruise?"

"Yeah."

"And one of your stops is Juneau?"

"Why is my itinerary is any of your business?" Trevor said after kissing Dani for good measure.

"We need someone to pick up a package over there."

"No, Don."

"It's just a simple pickup. No danger at all."

"Nope. I'm not doing it." Trevor's thumb hovered over the disconnect button.

"Wait, let me talk to him." Dani reached for the phone.

Trevor kissed her again and relinquished it. "He's going to be sorry he called after talking to you."

"Don, what are you trying to convince Trevor to do?" Dani asked, smiling at her husband.

"Well, you see, there is a contact and he's in Alaska."

"And . . ." She rolled her free hand.

"And I'd like to have Trevor pick up a package. You know, with government cutbacks, to send someone out there would be over budget. And—"

Trevor leaned into the phone. "You'll never convince her."

Dani rubbed her ear where her husband's breath tickled her.. "Go on, Don."

"Well, since you're going there already—"

A smile played on her lips. "What are you asking us to do on our honeymoon?"

"I thought you could pick up the package."

Dani chuckled. "Will it be dangerous, Don?"

"Not at all."

Several seconds ticked by before Dani said, "Okay, we'll do it. Text us the instructions."

Trevor grabbed his phone. "No, Don, the answer is no." He disconnected the call and slid the phone into his back pocket.

"Aw, Trevor." Dani looked up at him with shimmering eyes. "It'll be fun, and Don said there's no danger involved."

"Yeah, knowing him, it will be no more dangerous than the spider-filled passageway we faced in Morales's compound."

Dani stood on her tiptoes and whispered in Trevor's ear, "It's just a package. What harm could there be? Please?"

He sighed. "When am I going to learn to say no to you?"

She threw her arms around his neck. "Never, I hope."

About the Author

Born in Illinois, Donna Fuller has lived in a variety of places and currently resides in Butler, Pennsylvania. At times she feels like a Ping-Pong ball—bouncing from coast to coast and back again. Her grandchildren bring her the greatest joy. Donna has always been involved in writing, from journals to plays for Cub Scouts, to short stories for her children and as a reporter for a small newspaper. She has won awards for her writing and has taught at writing workshops and retreats. Donna is the co-founder of the annual OHPA Writer's Retreat in Western Pennsylvania. *Code Name Scorpion* is her second published novel. Her first was *A Strand of Doubt* (Walnut Springs Press, 2014).

Learn more about Donna and her books at DonnaGustainis Fuller.com, or like her on Facebook (Facebook.com/donna -gustainis-fuller).

Author photograph by Mandy Myers

Jana Clawson has a propensity for Chinese food, M&M's, and chocolate-chip cookies, and she deals with opposition with a wry sense of humor. She is caught up in a whirlwind known as Trevor Willis, the most eligible non-Mormon bachelor in Portland. He is perfect in every way, but will his secrets be too much for their relationship?

While Jana escapes to the Oregon Coast to make a decision about Trevor, a car accident stirs Jared Carpenter—a physical therapist with kind brown eyes who never turns down a homemade meal—into the mix. Unknown to Jana, events set in motion six years ago threaten everything she holds dear, and her life depends on one or both of these men. Combining suspense, intrigue, action, and understated humor, this book will keep you turning pages until the exciting conclusion.